HOLD 'EM HOSTAGE

This Large Print Book carries the
Seal of Approval of N.A.V.H.

HOLD 'EM HOSTAGE

JACKIE CHANCE

THORNDIKE PRESS
A part of Gale, Cengage Learning

Detroit • New York • San Francisco • New Haven, Conn • Waterville, Maine • London

LIBRARY OF CONGRESS CATALOGING-IN-PUBLICATION DATA

Chance, Jackie.
  Hold 'em hostage / by Jackie Chance.
    p. cm. — (Thorndike Press large print mystery)
  "A poker mystery" — T.p. verso.
  ISBN-13: 978-1-4104-0733-7 (alk. paper)
  ISBN-10: 1-4104-0733-0 (alk. paper)
    1. Women poker players — Fiction. 2. Kidnapping — Fiction.
  3. Las Vegas (Nev.) — Fiction. 4. Large type books. I. Title.
  PS3603.H3559H65 2008
  813'.6—dc22   2008004219

Published in 2008 by arrangement with The Berkley Publishing Group,
a member of Penguin Group (USA) Inc.

This is for everyone who ever believed in me . . . and especially those who didn't disown me when I was at my craziest and those who offered a word of encouragement when they had no idea what they were doing!

Katie Day (she's the long-suffering editor — applause, please!), Jake, Cristina, Katy, Kelly, Betty, Ann, Bob, Donna, Jake, Nancy, Ben, Frances, John, Donna, Deb, Pam, Pam, Evelyn, Martha, Alison, Merrily, Annie, Steve, and Wanda

"Poker is a microcosm of all we admire and disdain about capitalism and democracy. It can be roughhewn or polished, warm or cold, charitable and caring or hard and impersonal, fickle and elusive, but ultimately it is fair, and right, and just."

— Lou Krieger

PROLOGUE

"Bee-Bee, you're a total luck vampire."

A serious game of Texas Hold 'Em with friends and family at the table is a recipe for disaster. But as my entire existence since I turned forty seemed to have been a recipe for disaster, I supposed this was just an ingredient in a five-course gourmet meal called Belinda Cooley's Life.

Don't think I'm negative. I was in the grocery store line and picked up my horoscope booklet. The first line read: You have more drama in your life in one week than everybody else has in a lifetime.

So there.

My twin brother, Ben, owner of the aforementioned luck vampire comment, sat across from me, glaring and down to his last ten-dollar chip, having just lost almost everything to me heads-up. My best friend, Shana, wiggled around in her chair, two to my right, giggling and drunk on a half dozen

Midori daiquiris. We'd entered a sit and go $100 tournament at the Image casino on a lark as we arrived in Vegas. I want to point out that I was the one to sit down first. The two boneheads paid their way into my table instead of waiting for another game to start. *Duh.* The way I look at it, with sit and gos, in which only the top two players are in the money, it's best to play against strangers, definitely not with people you have to sleep next to later. As it was now, even if the best scenario occurred — two of us won the thousand dollars at stake — one of us still would be losing a C-note. Someone would be cranky, which I wouldn't consider if we weren't sharing a comped suite at the swanky Mellagio hotel and casino down the road.

Shana went all in when a two/seven off-suit hit the board on Fourth and Fifth Streets after a Royal Flop. I shook my head. I flipped over my ten/Ace for a straight. She threw her cards in with a particularly color-ful Spanish invective (which I find ironic since she is half-Filipino/half-Irish and zero Hispanic but heck, we are from Texas, where everyone swears in Tex-Mex), pushed back her chair and knocked into a man working his way between her and the table behind us. The force of her water-bra-enhanced chest catapulted a ten-inch serrated, bloodstained knife out of his jacket pocket. It bounced across our table, finally coming to rest, point buried in the felt, pointed straight at me.

The knife wielder fled. Shana screamed and fainted into the arms of the Matthew McConaughey look-alike at the neighboring table with whom she'd been flirting mercilessly. Hmm.

Ben rose and headed for the door, only to be stopped by a phalanx of casino security.

We'd officially boarded the roller coaster that is Las Vegas.

And that was just the beginning.

ONE

"Honey Bee," Frank Gilbert purred into the phone. Most people would think this an endearing tone. I knew better. My quasi boyfriend was striving for patience. "I leave you for twelve hours and you get into trouble."

"I didn't *get* into trouble. Trouble found me," I argued. Out loud, that statement really didn't sound as good as I hoped it might.

"Uh-huh," Frank answered, patience unraveling. "You managed to be still long enough for it to catch up with you."

"I'm offended."

"You should be." I could hear the smile in his voice.

"So, when are you going to get here so I don't have to spend my entire vacation at the Clark County lockup?" I glanced over at the door. The cops had with amazing speed sequestered us in separate rooms, ostensibly so we wouldn't compare notes on what happened in the poker room. As I sat in the only chair in the room, I couldn't help glancing at what was on the desk in front of me, and I decided that I was in the office of the head of housekeeping.

"Surely you don't need me? If you're innocent, then you should be able to walk out of there anytime you want."

"First of all," I said carefully, now the one striving for patience, "you know better."

"About your innocence?" The laughter in his voice was undisguised.

"No! About the cops letting me go anytime I want. Come on. The knife was bloody. It was pointed at me. My überadroit traveling companion was the one who crashed into him."

"Who's the perp? What kind of blood was on the knife?"

"Well, the cops are so chummy with me that we're going out to the Black Bear Diner for breakfast later. I'm sure I'll find out over a cup of joe and some oatmeal hotcakes." I couldn't help the sarcasm — food deprivation made me cranky. And anything involving syrup sounded so good right now. My mouth watered. My stomach rumbled. "They've already asked me who I work for, meaning, of course, which pimp. Men!"

14

"Honey Bee." Frank sighed. The pause stretched on long enough to talk. Another sigh preceded his question. "Honey Bee, *what* are you wearing?"

I looked down at my clingy silver lamé hip-length sheath, Lucky jeans and Swarovski-crystal-covered strappy stilettos designed by up-and-comer Angel Rodriguez, who'd just hired my fledgling advertising agency to run his first campaign. I smiled at my sexy shoes. "Um, jeans?"

"And?"

I glanced down again. Okay, maybe the toenail polish in Hottie Mamma was slightly over the top. "I, um, have some new shoes. I know you'll like them."

I could feel him shaking his head through the phone line, although he reserved comment. He might have a future after all. "Have you asked about Captain Patterson? He'd remember you."

"I did. He's busy getting a tan — snapped up by Dade County, Florida, because he handled the media so well during our last fiasco here. He moved to Miami two weeks ago. Poor guy. I think I'd rather be in Vegas."

I heard Frank swear under his breath. "Without his help it might get a bit sticky, especially if someone connects you to the Steely Stan case, but don't worry. It'll all

15

work out. I'll be there as soon as I can. My flight leaves in an hour."

"That is, unless one of your famous mystery missions pops up between now and then."

"Don't start with that," Frank warned. Our last big trip, which was supposed to have been our first big trip together, was a poker cruise and had turned out to be a lot more and a lot less than we'd bargained for — more adventure, less romance. Suffice it to say, Frank wasn't by my side when we'd set sail, but he was when we docked back in Galveston. As for why and how that happened, well, that's another story.

What Frank did for a living was another story too, one I couldn't tell. He owned a company called FBG Enterprises and carried a business card that read "Security" but don't be envisioning a rent-a-cop on a donut diet. Frank was built like a human panther, carried a concealed Glock and handcuffs, knew how to use both, had an assistant named Joe who looked like the Marlboro Man and acted like Rambo, a part-time PR woman who could be a supermodel and, oh yeah, Frank kept the director of the CIA on speed dial on his phone. Don't you dare tell him I know that last detail, which I garnered through less than

16

honest methods. A breach in privacy that Mr. Security would no doubt disapprove of.

Thinking about those methods made me feel a little guilty, and besides, I was freaked out. I'd seen the county jail on my way to the morgue my last trip to Sin City, and it scared me. Heck, half the folks on the streets in Vegas scared me, so I shuddered to think of what the ones behind bars would do to my fear factor. I sucked in a deep breath and steeled myself to beg. "I'm sorry, Frank. I . . . I just *need* you right now."

Ouch, that cost my pride a notch or two.

But it worked.

"Aw, Honey Bee," he purred. I heard the door click open behind me, but I couldn't hang up. Not until I heard the rest. "Don't worry. Nothing's gonna keep me away from you. Let me tell you what I have in mind when I see you. . . ."

A hard finger poked my shoulder. I tried to sneaky-slide my RAZR phone into my cleavage as Frank kept talking. I heard "whipped cream" and "massage" as it disappeared.

"Miss Cooley!"

I smiled apologetically at the mammoth towering over me who had a Clark County badge conspicuously hanging off the pocket of his pearl-snap plaid shirt. A cowboy cop.

Being from Houston, you'd think I'd be used to those types but to tell the truth, my only brushes with the law had been when I was out of my hometown and on vacation. I really should learn that all work and no play was a healthier condition for me. Badge Man cleared his throat. I shrank in my chair. He glowered, unmoved by my charmingly submissive behavior, then spat a wad of chewing tobacco into the garbage can at my knee. Suddenly I was more afraid for my Luckys than my freedom. "Hey, watch it."

"You're the one who'd better watch it." He looked at my cleavage without an ounce of interest in anything nonelectronic. Thank goodness. Not that I haven't been known to use my feminine wiles to get me out of scrapes before, but using them with a snuff dipper was above and beyond. Although, throwing him a sidelong glance, I realized he kind of reminded me of Bruce Willis in the last *Die Hard,* ironic mouth and all. Then I remembered Bruce was really good at killing people. He glared. I quivered, just a little. "You were warned. No talking on cell phones. Hand yours over."

"Even if I *promise* not to do it again, Officer?"

Shaking his head, he opened up his hand

and waited. Impatiently.

I retrieved the phone and tried to put it to my ear to see if I could catch the tail end of what Frank had to say but the spoiler snatched it away before I could, severing the connection as he did so.

"Stay here and don't think about using that landline." He nodded at the receiver on the desk. "We've temporarily disconnected it."

I couldn't help frowning back at him. For some reason he brought out the second grader in me.

He narrowed his eyes and jutted his lower jaw like the playground bully. Guess I did the same to him. "Someone will be here shortly to take you to be interviewed. I'm Detective Sergeant Dale Trankosky and you'd better wish it won't be me."

The next time the door opened, about five minutes later, I could see that my friend had sent his alter ego. This cop had spent more on regular facials and manicures than Trankosky spent on a year's worth of chewing tobacco. His smile oozed a studied charm it took salesmen years to perfect. His well-cut spring suit could've made the cover of *GQ*. I was immediately relieved, not because I liked him — quite the contrary —

but because this was the kind of man I could work. Salesmen sometimes were the easiest sells. Cops not running for office rarely came with this mentality so I counted myself lucky this time.

"Miss Cooley?" he asked, smiling and extending his hand. I accepted it, along with the strong, quick shake. A clunk in the hallway called his attention and I noticed the tattoo on his neck, peeking out from the collar of his yellow dress shirt — a snake's fanged open mouth, a clawed hand holding a serrated scythe, a shark's tail. The creature's body was hidden beneath the suit. I was going to comment on it, but before I could open my mouth, he'd spun around, looking at me with eyes a bit cold for my taste. I reminded myself I wasn't marrying him. And cold was preferable to Trankosky's heavy distaste.

"I apologize for this terrible inconvenience. I'm here to make sure you won't be detained much longer. Follow me please."

I returned his smile and sighed. "How kind. Thank you."

Before I could work on him for a dinner from my favorite Egyptian restaurant on The Strip (I was still starving!) while I was being interviewed, his phone rang as we walked down the narrow office hallway that spilled into the Image's exotic gardens of amazingly real-looking fake greenery. "With me," he answered after holding the phone to his ear for a moment. He paused again, then lowered his voice, "I had to get her away from the five-ohs."

I assumed I was the "her," but I wondered what a "five-oh" was. Was that copspeak for the media? I made a mental note to ask Frank, or perhaps I could ask my *GQ* escort once he got off the phone. Hmm. He was currently doing a lot of rather unhappy listening to his cell phone. I tapped his shoulder. What was his name again? Um. I don't think I'd asked. I don't think he'd offered. Uh-oh.

I was following a stranger. I'd presumed he was a cop but he could be many other things. He could be hotel security trying to look like an undercover cop; he could be an undercover cop trying to look like hotel security; he could be a crime boss executioner trying to look like either of the above.

"Excuse me." I tapped his arm. "I have to go to the ladies' room."

He hid his irritation by smiling. Practiced and perfect. I halfway relaxed again. "Of course, we'll find you one," he lied to me, still listening to his caller and choosing a path deeper into the gardens instead of toward the reception desk and possible rest-rooms.

Hmm. I really didn't want to put him on guard by asking if he was really a cop. As much as I didn't like spending time with the cops, I probably would like spending time with someone pretending to be a cop less. The caller was apparently upsetting him, because he picked up his pace and forgot to keep me in front of him. It was perhaps my only chance.

I ducked behind the next palm tree. Why hadn't I thought to ask for any credentials? *Because, you stupid girl, you were so convinced you could manipulate him you didn't consider he was already doing that exact same thing to you.* Dumb, dumb, dumb. Considering I'd found myself caught with the wrong person in the wrong place a few times too many on my last trip to Vegas, I should've been more careful. Of course, if he was a cop, I was in bigger trouble than I was before. If he wasn't one, however, I was in even worse trouble, of an undefined variety. Why would a non-cop want to spirit me away anyway? My heart raced.

What was I going to do? I didn't know to which interrogation room the authorities had taken Ben after he'd chosen the exact wrong time to visit the potty (or so he said).

22

Shana was still rolling around semiconscious in the arms of the hottie in the poker room. Frank was still in another state. I was on my own. I slid into the depths of a gardenia bush as my escort came marching back down the path, pocketing his phone and muttering obscenities under his breath while maintaining a poker face I'd kill for. Oops, I'd better not even be thinking that. The security at these casinos was so high tech I wouldn't be half-surprised if they'd installed mind reading devices under the leaves. If my friend here had connections with the hidden cameras, he would soon know where I was hiding.

I sucked in a deep breath and did an inventory of what I knew before I was discovered. My escort wasn't wearing a badge but the Image wouldn't have stood for any uniformed rent-a-cops running around under their tony roof anyway. Each casino had a culture, I reminded myself, and my ability to properly play security would hinge on my understanding of those cultures. For instance, there was a certain casino on the south end of The Strip where they could back a paddy wagon next to the craps tables and none of the patrons would bat an eye. Now, a serial killer could be playing twenty-one in the middle of the

Mellagio and they would still send in an undercover security dude in a three-piece suit to lure him into the basement before they cuffed him so as to not offend the sensibilities of the high-priced clientele there.

Suddenly I knew how to out my escort — I'd approach the concierge desk as a semi-hysterical woman and claim I was being stalked. He'd have to identify himself if he were on the level or disappear if he were up to something nefarious. I crept through the garden toward the opposite side that dumped out near the hotel's reception desk. The only problem was the lagoon between here and there, with only the very public bridge as the connection. I tiptoed through the leaves and plastic rocks to the edge of the water, which, unfortunately for me, was the only thing real about the Image lobby. Damn.

I glanced up and saw the bridge did have a handy if rather flimsy-looking catwalk underneath, I suppose for the maintenance department's benefit. I'm not one for heights, and although this would mean dangling only about fifteen feet above the water, dangling was dangling. I considered scurrying across the bridge until I saw my escort, anger beginning to tighten his poker face, marching back, looking now into the gardens right where I'd been huddled. I steeled myself, grabbed the metal bar and heaved myself up onto the catwalk.

And nearly broke my ankle.

Unfortunately, Angel's stilettos weren't the best choice for cat walking. One heel was firmly wedged in between two slivers of metal, bending my ankle at an incredibly uncomfortable angle. Reluctantly, I slid my foot out and left the shoe, unbuckling and slipping the other off too. I placed it next to its pair, which I freed with a yank, in the hopes I would be able to come recover them soon. I guesstimated the distance from the top of the bridge to the stilettos and thought I might be able to reach them later on if I lay on the bridge and really stretched. Maybe if I got a hanger I could snag them by the straps. I backed up and fastened both buckles, trying not to let the sudden lurches in the catwalk make me too nauseous.

I'd gotten about a fourth of the way across when I heard: "I'll make sure she's sorry when I find her."

My heart pounded. Since I doubted the security staff considered the catwalk a big hangout for their patrons, I thought I was probably relatively safe from video surveillance where I was. As long as I kept quiet.

Famous last thoughts. I heard a metallic wheeze then a crack as the catwalk tilted dangerously south on the far end. I know I must have cried out when my shoes slid into the drink. But it really didn't matter because a moment later came another crack and the cable holding the whole farside of the walk gave way, and I suddenly knew what dangling really was. My toes brushed the water of the lagoon as my hands gripped the edge of the metal ramp. Since I am woefully behind on my bicep curls, like forty-one years behind, I knew I couldn't hang on for long. I heard a commotion above me and heads popped over the side of the bridge, pointing and shouting, all except my escort, who smiled slowly and coldly.

Just then I let go.

The water was colder than I thought water should be in the tropics. After all, wasn't this supposed to be a desert mirage where temperatures averaged around 120 degrees? I was in danger of dying of hypothermia. I made a mental note to mark that on my guest satisfaction survey. The water was a lot deeper than it should be in a fake oasis too, by the way — a big waste of the wet stuff in Vegas where every drop of water was prized. I nearly ran out of air by the time my feet hit the bottom and I could catapult

myself back to the surface. My hand hit
something above me. I felt flesh and cloth
under my fingertips and for a moment I
thought someone had dived in to rescue me.
Until I came even with unblinking eyes and
an eerie grin that upon closer inspection
was actually a bloody gash that opened the
stranger's throat to his backbone.

I screamed underwater and still don't
know how I made it to the surface without
drowning. Proof that God has a sometimes
cruel sense of humor, I guess, because if I'd
had to be resuscitated and hospitalized, I
might not have been subjected to the next
crazy week.

More screams met me as I gasped for air.
"He's bleeding!"

I didn't recognize any of the faces of those
leaning over the bridge. Where was my
mysterious escort?

"Murderer!"

"Is she okay?"

"Somebody call an ambulance!" A senior
citizen with slightly pink hair shrieked.

"It's too late for that, lady," Trankosky
deadpanned through the wad in his right
cheek. "I think all we need is a body bag for
him and a pair of handcuffs for her."

I slid sideways as Trankosky unloaded his
tobacco wad into the water just inches away

from my head and caught sight of my Angel
heels sinking out of sight.

TWO

"So how long have you known Keith Tasser?"

"I don't know anyone by that name," I insisted, shivering under the paper-thin towel the good men of the Clark County Sheriff's Department were kind enough to find me after I'd been paraded through the bullpen on the way — the long way, I later found out — to an interrogation room, accompanied by several suggestions that wet T-shirt contests be officially changed to wet silver lamé contests.

"Come on, Miss Cooley, we know better."

"Detective Trankosky, I am certain you know most things better than I do, but this is the one case I have one over on you. I don't know any Keiths, much less one named Tasser."

"He *was* a pro poker player who's followed the World Series of Poker circuit this year."

"Along with about ten thousand other people."

"An exaggeration, Miss Cooley. Not many are of your league. Keith was. We know."

"Good for Keith."

"We'll find out the connection, you know."

"When you do, clue me in."

"Interesting you'd use the word 'clue,' isn't it? Freudian, I'd say."

I rolled my eyes. He glared and deposited a wet wad of tobacco in the garbage can, that somehow was again near my left knee.

I'd known a really good member of the CCSD, who was now gone, and a really bad one, who was now dead. This guy seemed to land somewhere in the middle, which might have been okay except he seemed like the type who didn't like to hear anything but what he wanted to hear. And, nothing I said was what he wanted to hear.

"We don't like it when you lie, Miz Cooley," Trankosky's partner, Amanda Krane, put in, flipping her ponytail around her finger.

"I'm not lying. Why would I lie?"

"So you wouldn't have to go to jail?" Trankosky offered.

"I don't want to go to jail."

They shared a look. "What do you know. She *can* be honest."

"Maybe," Trankosky tempered.

"Why did you try to duck out before your interview if you have nothing to hide?" Krane drilled me with a practiced hard look. I thought these guys played good cop, bad cop. Someone was forgetting to play the good cop part.

I took a breath, "I didn't duck out, I —"

"Lieutenant." A uniformed officer popped his head in the door. "You want to take a look at this."

Trankosky disappeared with a warning look at his partner. She asked me why I was in Las Vegas.

"I'm playing in the World Series of Poker. It starts tomorrow. I mean, today."

"So you're a pro."

The disgusted look on her face when she asked made me wonder for a moment what profession she thought I was in. "I am a professional advertising agency owner."

"No, I asked about being a poker pro."

"No, I'm not a pro. I just started playing a year ago."

"So, lots of people who started playing last week call themselves pros."

"Well, I'm not one of them. I'd never rely on making a living playing poker. It's a sometimes lucrative hobby that I wouldn't want to count on."

"But you have a website," she said accusingly.

"So do numismatists, mannequinists and alien hunters who do it for fun more than profit."

"You're ranked as a pro on the Internet," she pointed out. "Number forty-one in 2008."

News to me, but I'd been lucky enough to be in the money at a couple of semimajor tournaments when Frank and I had taken a weekend here and there. I'd qualified for the WSOP by winning a circuit event in Tunica. "You probably could find yourself ranked on the Internet as one of the best-dressed police officers in America too." I pointed out. She slid me a hard but uncertain glance, not sure whether to take my comment as a compliment or a criticism. It was both, actually. Backhanded, to be exact. She wore an off-the-rack pantsuit that fit well but was as unoriginal as wallpaper in a doctor's office. "The Internet has as much misinformation as good information," I added.

She opened her mouth to speak and shut it as the door behind me opened.

"That video from the Image just answered my question," Trankosky said as he returned to the room. "You scooted out because you and the perp were trying to escape."

"What perp?"

"The guy you were hightailing it through the gardens with."

"I thought that guy was a cop."

Trankosky belly laughed so hard it almost made him appealing. "Wearing a thousand-dollar Italian suit. You thought he was a *cop?* Even cops on the take wouldn't dress that nice. You watch too much TV."

I tried hard to swallow but couldn't. "Who was he then?"

"That's what I'm supposed to ask you."

I shrugged. "I really thought he was a cop taking me to be interviewed. You told me someone would be coming to get me. I was hoping it wouldn't be you and it wasn't. Polar opposite, in fact."

Trankosky glowered, but more at the implications than my snide aside. I thought he might know the guy and was just fishing to see what I knew. "Did this man *claim* to be a cop?"

"Not exactly. It didn't dawn on me at first. We were already on our way when I realized he didn't identify himself at all. That's why I hid in the gardens." They looked at me with raised eyebrows. "Okay, why would I hide from him if I was making my escape with him?"

Trankosky looked at me like I was the village idiot. I might begin to believe him. "To hide the body."

"What body?" My voice rose an octave.

"The body you were found floating around with."

"That —" I sucked in a deep breath. "That was just an accident."

"Now we are getting somewhere." He nodded, his sharp dark blue eyes narrowing. "What happened — did poor old Keith just slip into the knife?"

"Was he coming at you — attacking you — and you were forced to protect yourself?" Detective Krane encouraged.

"What?" It took me a moment to realize what they were saying. Or rather, what they were trying to *make* me say. "No! I didn't kill the guy. I'd never seen him before I saw him dead in the lagoon. I never saw the knife before either. Who was the guy who dropped the knife on my poker table anyway? Isn't it your job to catch him?"

"We thought you could help us with that one. Was that an *accident* too?" Eyebrow jog by Die Hard, sidelong look at partner.

I forced myself to modulate my tone. "I have no idea what that was. You'll have to ask the guy you obviously haven't caught yet. What I meant to begin with was — the

34

reason I was floating around in the water was an *accident*. I was climbing on the catwalk under the bridge when it broke and I fell in." I paused, looking at their faces, seeing a lost cause. Hunger, fear, frustration and sleep deprivation morphed together into pure exhaustion. I shook my head. "Never mind, just throw me in jail."

They shared a knowing look punctuated by Krane's smug grin. "No way. We know jail is exactly where you need to be to finish this out."

"What?"

"When you're ready to confess, give us a call," she said, handing me two business cards. "Otherwise don't leave town until we give you clearance and know we'll be watching you every minute of every day."

"And good luck in the Main Event," Trankosky added. "If *you're* lucky, you'll win. If *we're* lucky, we'll get to take all your money away and shut you down for good."

"Shut me down?"

Another uniformed officer stuck his head in the door. "Detective, we just found out Belinda Cooley's been in trouble here before."

"The good news is, I have a free armed bodyguard while in Vegas," I told Frank brightly, handing him a wineglass of Perrier and brushing a kiss on his lips. He deepened the kiss for a moment but he couldn't delay asking the next question for any longer.

"That doesn't necessarily mean they're assigning you a tail. They're just trying to scare you. And the bad news is?" He breathed onto my neck as he caressed my earlobe with his tongue.

"The bad news is, the Clark County cops think I participated in a conspiracy to off someone, I lost my cell phone to the cops, and my stay in Vegas has been extended indefinitely," I answered quickly, turning away from him to glance out the window of our suite at the dancing lights and water of the fountains below and bracing for an onslaught of his protective fury.

"Depending on your luck at cards, the latter might not be all bad," Frank murmured, sliding his hands around my waist, surprising me as he ran the cold wineglass along my abdomen. "Depending on how long I can stay, the latter might have to move into the good news category."

I moved against him. "You're not mad?"

"Of course I'm mad, but I don't want to ruin the first time I've seen you in forty-one days, three hours and twelve minutes by yelling."

"Frank! You can't think about sex at a time like this!"

"Who said anything about thinking?"

"You are such a man!"

"Honey Bee." Frank sighed and set down his glass. "Have I ever told you that you are the woman who most makes me want to take a drink and the same woman for whom I want to *avoid* taking a drink? You are a living dichotomy. In the same moment, no less!"

Sometimes my undoing was what Frank said so introspectively and so revealingly. Sometimes it was the way he looked at me with those deep brown eyes. Sometimes it was both. Like tonight.

I know I would have fallen victim to my weak will and raging libido if Ben and Shana hadn't chosen that moment to walk through the door, Ben brandishing his key card at me. "I see you escaped, leaving us to fend for ourselves with the crime-fighting carrion."

I rolled my eyes to the ceiling and met Frank's disappointed but resigned gaze. My melodramatic brother was, as usual, thinking only about himself. Or was he? He took Shana's suitcase and walked it into the bedroom to the right. I drew my eyebrows together as I watched him return and put his hand on the small of Shana's back to guide her to the couch. Hmm. What was up with this? It wasn't unusual for Ben to have his hands on a sexy woman. It *was* unusual for him *not* to have plastered said hand onto a rounded body part, such as a breast or buttock. Shana was my best friend, and I had worked hard over the years to keep them away from each other, but, trust me, my feelings would have never entered into Ben's equation of behavior if he wanted to have her. I knew Shana had the on-and-off hots for Ben depending on who she was dating at the time, but fortunately, they'd never been the same times Ben had been without a woman. Ben, currently, was without a woman — having ticked off his girlfriend of two weeks by sleeping with one of the flight attendants on their flight back from the Bahamas. Literally, on the flight. With the girlfriend on the same flight. They got kicked off after an emergency landing in Birmingham because the girlfriend drew blood. He'd gotten the flight attendant's number. She was meeting him for drinks when we got back to Houston.

That was my brother in a nutshell. This hovering, fawning man was not.

"Don't ask about me, and about the strip search I had to endure while you guys just had to gab," I threw in.

Ben's eyebrows waggled. "Was it a man or a woman who searched you? How long did it take?"

Frank bit back a smile. I snorted in disgust. Shana didn't respond and I noticed for the first time the circles under her eyes. I shot her a questioning look which she shrugged off. Ben had gone to the bar, poured a glass of Perrier and handed it to Shana as he raised his eyebrows at me. "Why do you look like a drowned rat? Or do I not want to know because I'll have to clock Frank to restore your honor?" He winked.

"Ben," I admonished. "Not everything in life is about sex."

"You're right. The other parts are about money." He glanced at his Rolex. "Which reminds me, you have three hours to sleep before we head over to the poker room at the Flynn casino to warm up for the Main Event."

I shook my head. "Don't worry about my game, Ben. I've kept it pretty sharp over the last couple of weeks."

"I'm not worried about your game," he admitted. "I want you treating us to another cruise. They are having a WSOP warm-up — a sit and go with four cruise tickets as first prize."

"Why? The last cruise wasn't that much fun." I shared a quick look with Frank, feeling a sudden warmth building within my Luckys. "Well, the end was okay, I guess. Besides, what's wrong with *you* buying us a vacation on the seas?"

"Because you're more successful at Hold 'Em than I am. And, besides, I *am* treating this time."

"Thanks for the frequent flier miles, Mr. Generous, but in case you forgot, the Mellagio gave me the suite for a blurb on the website and if we are keeping track, you are about four vacations in the hole."

"You can't count it if I was broke at the time when you decided we ought to go to Bermuda, Grand Cayman and —"

"Whoa." Frank held up his hand to stop us.

I sighed, shot him an apologetic look and remembered my strangely silent friend. The friend who was now staring at her cell phone in her lap as if it were about to come to life. "Shana, what's wrong?"

Flamboyant and fearless, Shana would not normally be shaken by an interview with some cops, no matter how verbally rough they could get. Likewise, she wouldn't have been depressed if she'd been rebuffed by the object of her desire — the stud muffin in the poker room in whose arms I'd last seen her. Reluctant to look away from her phone, Shana's brown eyes met mine, full of worry. "It's Aphrodite."

Our problems with the police immediately faded to the deep background in the face of trouble with her daughter. I ran to Shana, sitting down next to her and putting my arm around her shoulders. "Is she okay? Is she sick? Has she been in an accident?"

Shana shook her head. "I can't get her on the phone. She hasn't returned the call I made when we landed. I've called a dozen times since then. Her phone is turned off. Or, went dead."

That hung heavy in the silence, broken finally by Frank. "Remember, ladies, it *is* the middle of the night."

"You don't know teenage girls," I interjected, resisting the impulse to tell him he would have to get to know teenagers one day soon, as he had a daughter and son tucked away somewhere in California — children I'd resolved to learn more about on this trip. Or else. "Teenagers answer their phones at all hours. You never know when your crush will call. Or your best friend will have a crisis with her boyfriend."

Shana shook her head. "Besides, we had

an agreement that she would keep her phone on at all times, so I could give her our room number at the hotel in case she needs me and I don't answer my cell. This is just unlike her."

My goddaughter was an atypical sixteen-year-old American girl, as thoughtful, careful and reliable as her mother had not been at that age, so for her to be out of touch for this long was indeed cause for serious concern.

"Is she staying home alone while you're here?" Frank asked, again revealing how little he knew about teenagers.

Shana looked a little more like herself when she threw him her you're-out-of-your-mind glare. "No. Really, Frank. She's staying with the Cooleys."

"Elva and Howard," Frank confirmed, acquainted with my parents to the point of over acquaintance as far as I was concerned. Mom routinely asked Frank when he was going to marry me in irritatingly indirect ways. Dad routinely asked Frank for advice on how to "off" people. Couldn't I have parents who politely just asked about the weather over dinner? "Have you called them?" Frank inquired.

Ben, Shana and I all shared a panicked moment where we all imagined what Mom and Dad would do when awoken by a middle-of-the-night Vegas call. "Not yet," Ben finally said. "We kept hoping Affie would call back, and we wouldn't have to."

"I guess Shana has to decide whether she is tired enough of waiting to disturb the Cooleys."

We were all quiet a moment while that sunk in. Shana blew out a breath, shook out her wavy dark hair and slowly rose to her feet. Ben rushed to hover next to her. Weird. I'd never seen him try so hard with any woman. Mostly they flocked to him, and he barely deigned to speak to them unless it regarded the next sexual position. He never chased, coddled or offered any kind of emotional or intellectual support. Hmm. I was going to have to nip this infatuation in the bud or else I was going to be caught in the middle when the relationship went south, which it undoubtedly would considering these were the two most promiscuous people on the planet. Finally, Shana tapped her clear-plastic-heeled Jimmy Choos a couple of times, then said: "Okay, let's call them."

Clearly Ben and I were the "us" in "let's," since Shana didn't move to use the cell that she held in her hand. I looked at Ben, who looked at me. He cocked his head. I guess his proprietary streak did not extend to calling Ma for Shana. I cocked my head right back. I had to deal with our parents more than he did, considering he was always "on the road" as a pharmaceutical sales rep and always busy going out every night. Of course, Mom still did his laundry, so he found enough time to go by and drop that off, didn't he? Frank tucked a hank of my unruly chestnut hair behind my left ear, leaned down and asked quietly, "Do you want me to phone them?"

Aw. It was love. It had to be. Nothing else would make a man brave enough to offer to deal with Elva at three a.m. I was tempted to jump his darling bones right then and there, but instead I shook my head. "No, Frank, I'll do it, but you know I owe you for offering."

His crow's feet crinkled. His eyes warmed to liquid chocolate. Dark, rich chocolate. I had to look away as he said quietly but not softly, "I can't wait to collect."

I walked over to the coffee table and dug around in my purse for my cell phone, forgetting that it was under arrest. I growled, made a mental note to switch service to a new phone, and grabbed Ben's from out of his pants pocket. "Hey!" he argued.

I held it out to him with a questioning

look. He evaded eye contact and leaned down to give Shana a shoulder squeeze. Jerk.

I dialed and waited, braced for Dad, who would certainly answer this time of night, but who would have the phone snatched from his hands as soon as Mom could knock him over for it. After six rings, however, it went to their voice mail. Not expecting this, I paused in the dead air, not sure what to say. "Mom, Dad, we all made it to Vegas fine. We wanted to give you our room number at the Mellagio, 1717. Oops, I just realized what time it is. Duh! So sorry! Y'know this place designs it so you never know what time it is. Call us as soon as possible and let us know Aph is behaving herself. We can't seem to get ahold of her on her cell phone."

"Why wouldn't they answer?" Shana asked, chewing on her lower lip.

Ben and I shrugged, holding each other's gaze. There wasn't a good reason. Our parents had never failed to pick up the phone next to their bed on the second ring for every crisis that involved an overnight phone call, and, believe me, there had been many when Bad Boy Ben was a teenager. "Maybe Dad needs a hearing aid," Ben offered.

Of course that didn't explain Mom, who still could hear a whisper through walls three houses down the street. I sighed and threw Shana a brave smile. Bowing her head, she looked away, knowing me well enough not to buy it.

"I say you three get a couple hours of sleep, giving Affie a chance to call back after the sun comes up in Houston, then we can proceed with some other venues."

"Us three?" I looked at Frank. "What about you?"

"I'm going to find my friend on the force here and see what he can tell me about where you really stand with the cops in this case."

I remembered Abel from our last fiasco in Vegas, nice guy, took bribes for inside information. I reached for my purse. Frank grabbed it first and slapped my hand away. "This one's on me."

"But I'll owe you even more," I argued.

"That's what I'm counting on." He dropped his voice to a dangerous level. I squirmed in my Luckys. He cleared his throat. "And when I get back from visiting with my friend, I'll check into our room."

"*Your* room?" Ben interjected, waving his hand around the suite that was two bedrooms and at least 2500 square feet.

"There's plenty of room for us all in here."

"Trust me, Benjamin, this suite is not big enough for the vacation I have in mind," Frank said smoothly. I squirmed harder and tried to contain the blush running up my neck by going to put a protective arm around Shana to guide her to the bedroom doorway.

The phone in our room rang. We all stopped and looked at the phone, then each other. I held my breath. Shana relaxed with relief, then tensed, then went weak against me. Ben looked frozen. Frank was the first to recover, as usual. He strolled to the end table and picked up the receiver. "Yes?"

I could see the tension around his eyes dissipate and knew he recognized the caller. "She's right here," he answered, holding the receiver out to me.

"Hello?" I tried not to let my voice catch on the lump in my throat.

"Bee, you're in d-danger. You g-gotta get outta Vegas and get out q-quick."

THREE

"Jack! I thought you were meeting us at the airport?"

"I'm sorry, Bee, I got caught under a game and had to wait it out, but that's where I heard something that scared me."

Jack Smack was currently the hottest journalist covering the poker world, thanks to a stint on *Good Morning America* after our rather deadly Texas Hold 'Em cruise last autumn. More importantly, he was my friend and did me the highly underpaid favor of writing a gossip column on my fledgling website called "Hold 'Em Hearsay." I was pretty sure his column was the only reason why anyone would log on. Well, maybe some came for Ringo's poker shades update. Anyhow, Jack had SAD. Yes, you got that right, he suffered from social anxiety disorder — a pathological aversion to social situations, which caused excessive sweating, heart palpitations and occasional stuttering, which ironically never struck him when on camera.

"Where were you and what did you hear?"

"I don't want to t-tell you over the phone. You know Vegas, b-baby. I'll come to your room."

"See you soon. It's 1717," I said in tacit agreement on the possibility of a bug. It had happened before. I hung up.

"What did he say?"

I considered telling Frank what Jack had said, but I didn't want him to overreact and order me to don a flak jacket, close the drapes and hide under furniture, so I just smiled. "He apologized for not meeting us at the airport, and is on his way up."

Frank searched my face, apparently seeing the lie by omission there. Truly I don't know how I get away with winning bluffs because I can't lie very well. It must be the sunglasses. Frank continued to wait for me to spill it. I resisted. Sometimes he challenged my independence and sometimes he didn't. Tonight, he didn't want to miss his date with Abel, so he didn't push it.

"Okay, Honey Bee, but don't open the door to anyone else." Frank raised his eyebrows, waiting for a promise. I nodded. He snatched the key card Ben had left on the bar and pocketed it on his way out the door.

"Bee Bee, you still haven't told me what the cops asked you," Ben said, pouring himself a Johnnie Walker Red. I was impressed at yet another sign that my brother might be growing a sensitive side at the ripe old age of forty-one; he'd waited until Frank left to open the alcohol. Not that Frank would have cared, but I would have. Frank's infrequent, temporary denials of his alcoholism had been serious obstacles in our relationship. (The dead bodies that seemed to crop up when we were together might be counted as others. Although Frank, I'm certain, would argue that it wasn't the murders, but my involvement in trying to solve them that was the problem.)

But that's another story.

Or was it?

"And, you never told me why you look like you took a shower fully clothed," Ben persisted.

I sighed, accepted the proffered glass of chardonnay and eased onto the couch to tell the short version of what happened after we'd been separated. "You lost your Angels?" Shana asked, distracted out of her worry by my fashion horror.

I stopped in mid nod. "I know where they

are, just retrieving them may be a bit difficult."

Shana wagged a finger at me. "Those are one of a kind originals. And besides, they are the sexiest shoes I've ever seen and I want to borrow them. We're going after those silver suckers."

Ben looked from Shana to me and back again, but apparently wanted to stay in her good graces badly enough to withhold comment. "So, the cops think you sliced the guy's throat, slipped him into the lagoon, passed off the knife, sat down to play a small time sit and go, got caught, then tried to ditch them by swimming around with the corpse?"

I shrugged. "I don't know what they think, but that scenario alone is ridiculous. I suppose that's why they had to let me go."

"Who was the guy who tried to sneak off with you?"

"I wish I knew."

"Or maybe you better wish you don't ever find out," Ben said.

"You're probably right," I admitted, suppressing a shiver at the memory of the cold fury in his eyes when he realized he'd lost me. "He had a really weird tattoo that looked like a combination of a dragon, snake and shark on his neck."

"A dragsnashark — sure, you see those everywhere."

My head snapped up. "Really?"

"No, Bee Bee, I'm joking. It sounds like some kind of gangland mark."

"I don't know what a gang would want with hassling me. Plus, the guy didn't look much like a gangbanger, more like he belonged on Wall Street." I paused, deep in thought for a moment as I watched the neon-lit pedestrians on The Strip below, then I turned back to them. "You haven't told me what the cops asked you two."

"Oh, they just tried to get me to admit I knew the knife guy, some Keith character. Then they wanted me to confess to killing the mystery person, because I guess you hadn't gone swimming with the body yet. Wanted to know what a badass you were and how many card games we'd ripped off."

"They think we're card sharks?" I asked, confused.

Ben shrugged. "Maybe they were fishing and just wanted to get lucky."

I turned to Shana, who sipped the orange-flavored Absolut on the rocks Ben had served her before answering. "They wanted to know what my relationship was to you, Ben and the mystery man with the knife. What we were doing in Vegas, that kind of thing. They wanted to make sure I knew to call them if I noticed anything 'untoward' in your behavior here at the casinos."

"Did they mention what untoward things they expect you to witness?"

"No, but when I said you were here to play in the Main Event, the room went electric."

"I wonder what that means. There are ten thousand people in Vegas playing at the Main Event," I mused. "And what could the WSOP possibly have to do with some guy with a knife in a poker room and a body at a casino across The Strip?"

We silently pondered that for a moment, then Ben said, "Remember, they may be isolated events. We are assuming your swimming partner was killed by the knife that fell on our table and by the man who was carrying the knife. We might be the only common denominators."

"Humph. Which is why we are suspects," I murmured.

"We?!" Shana and Ben exclaimed.

I put up my hands. "Okay, why I am a suspect." I bumped Shana with my shoulder. "What happened to Matthew McConaughey?"

I was surprised to see the dark look on Ben's face when she answered distractedly,

53

"Who? Oh, Kent? We have a date for lunch tomorrow. I mean, today."

"I thought you were playing in the first event? It starts at noon, you know," Ben put in quickly.

Shana frowned and glanced again at her cell phone display.

"Hey, none of us know what's going to happen by morning, Ben." I pointed out gently.

"Well, you're playing," he sulked.

"I don't know yet." I hadn't told them what Jack had said on the phone. I didn't know what it meant so I just decided to wait. They could hear the whole story from him.

Ben slid another dark look at Shana as he downed a swig of JW.

Hmm. Ben was acting jealous. That he was showing any emotion at all toward a woman was amazing. Where had this come from? Ben considered women his playground, running from the monkey bars to the swings to the sandbox. After years of keeping them apart, I'd finally acquiesced to going to the nine-day WSOP circuit tournament together because I thought Shana had finally seen and heard enough about Ben's antics to be forewarned against involving herself with him. Now in the time it took me to drop into the Image lagoon, they seemed to have developed some sort of relationship. At least, as far as he was concerned.

Uh-oh.

I jumped at the knock on the door.

Ben unfolded his legs and rose to let Jack in. "My man." Ben shook his hand. Jack did a little dance with his orange-lizard-skin-boot-clad feet. "My hero," he shouted, winking at me, "has finally landed in Vegas! My world is right again."

"I love your boots," I told him as I kissed his cheek.

"The Lucchese dudes were so c-cool to offer to make me a custom pair," he said as he plopped down on the couch and admired his toes.

"Not everybody can wear that color," Ben observed.

I introduced him to Shana. He kissed her hand. She blushed. Jack had a way with women he never would recognize.

"How's Ingrid?" I asked.

"She's s-so totally hot." He blushed. "But I guess you'd know that from Frank, right?"

I smiled noncommittally. Ingrid, the potential übermodel who worked with Frank, had hooked up with Jack on our cruise. However, I wouldn't know anything about the current state of her love life from

Frank as he was an antigossip to an extreme. I always thought he didn't talk about other people's relationships so as to not open the door for questions about his own. Admirable ethics, if irritating for his girlfriend (i.e., me) who had to ferret out his secrets by nefarious means.

"So tell me why you warned me on the phone," I said to Jack.

"What warning?" Shana asked, instantly tense again.

"Jack told me to catch the next plane out because I'm in danger."

"Huh," Ben grunted. "Maybe he saw you swimming around the Image lagoon with a guy with two smiles."

Jack sat bolt straight. "W-what?"

I waved off his question. "You go first."

Jack threw me a cautioning look but began his story.

"I'm working on an article on the secrets of poker millionaires for *On the Felt* magazine. I'm undercover at the Mellagio high-stakes poker room."

"Hold on, Jack," Ben said. "How did you get under a table in the high-stakes room? It's a raised room behind panels in the middle of the casino's main poker room that's completely open sided to passersby. Anyone could see you coming and going down the two ramps that lead to either side."

"That's the beauty of it," Jack said. "I hung out with the railbirds along the ramps and waited until we got a half-million-dollar stake in front of us and dropped a piece of paper, bent to retrieve it and slipped under the table next to the rail. If they noticed me missing, it wasn't mentioned and I knew it wouldn't be. In this age of political correctness, nobody wants to pipe up and say, 'Hey, where did the sweaty guy with the bad stutter and dumbo ears go?'"

Smiling, Shana and I shook our heads.

"So, I'd recognized this one dude, called Golden Hammer because he won last month's circuit bracelet at Rincon by dropping the hammer on the last hand. He's sitting there, winning with a lot of backdoor hands in a row, ticking off the table with his arrogance."

"Whoa, dropping the hammer?" Shana asked.

"When you win with seven/two in the hole."

"Huh, you can expect to win with that pocket?"

Ben threw her an arch, teasing look. "I thought you just tried that at the Image, you Maniac."

Shana stuck her tongue out at him as I marveled he'd noticed. Jack continued, "And Hammer's heads-up with a guy in high society who's sat in the luckbox all night."

Shana lifted her eyebrows at me.

"A luckbox is a novice who's won repeatedly, due more to fortune than skill. High society meaning with at least a hundred grand in front of him in the game."

"And I c-can't see the c-cards, but I can see sweaty palms wiped on thighs under the t-table, knees bouncing ninety miles an hour, so I know who's got c-cards, and who doesn't." Jack paused and I could tell he was moving into his reporter mode, because once he warmed to a story, his stutter stopped. "High Society and the guy sitting next to him, a real ABC player who doesn't belong at this table, start talking under their breath about the boss planning some moneymaking partnership with another group having a poker agenda. They need a fall guy. The groundwork had already been laid and more was going down tonight."

"So why is this dangerous for me?"

"Because when ABC asked High Society who was the duck, he laughed and said someone who will have a hard time showing off toe cleavage in paper shoes and an orange jumpsuit."

"It could be Clonie Gowen," Ben offered with a knowing grin.

I swallowed hard, unable to speak. My signature was my preference for dressing up instead of down for the game, especially in what I put on my feet. Clonie was beautiful and often dressed up but I wore beautiful shoes. Always. The phone rang. I assumed it was Frank. Shana assumed it was Aphrodite. We both reached for it but I withdrew my hand and let her answer. Shana's olive complexion whitewashed as she listened, handing the phone to me without a word, obviously stricken.

"Hello?" I said tentatively as I kept my gaze glued onto Shana.

"Bee Cool, welcome to Vegas. We have your goddaughter. We also have you framed for murder. You are going to do some things for us if you want to keep her alive and yourself out of jail."

FOUR

At first I couldn't speak. Honestly, at first I couldn't breathe. Closing my eyes against the panic creeping into Shana's big dark eyes, I broke things down into parts. Suck in some air. Let it out. Swallow. Suck in more air. Ignore Ben's hand gripping my left elbow. Listen to the background sounds on the phone for identification. Frank would ask me for details. Swallow again.

The line was still open, but the caller was cool enough not to check to see if I was still there. A bad sign. I vowed to be as cool as he was. He had someone who was as close as family to me. A good girl who was scared. This was war.

I waited a moment more. A torturously long moment. Then, I spoke: "What do you want me to do?"

"We find that if we intimidate before asking a question, we always get the right answer. Saves time and drama. You know how brutal we can be. We've already proven it."

"What do you mean?"

"We're sure, Bee Cool, you do not routinely encounter bloody knives and slashed corpses every day. We understand you have witnessed more than a normal WASP woman's share of murders but still, these should be strong selling points."

I willed myself to think. This was not Dragsnashark who had the hint of a European accent. This guy sounded as educated and as much a WASP as I was. What could they want from me that would make them kidnap my goddaughter? I opened my eyes and felt the pain Shana was carrying in her body, on her face. "Just tell me how much money you want."

He laughed then, honestly humored. It sent chills down my spine more than a cold chuckle would. "We want money, but not what you have in your money market, Bee Cool. We have bigger plans and that's what you will help us with."

"Where is Aphrodite?" Shana grabbed my free hand in hers and crushed it with her grip.

"That is the beauty of this. I don't have to answer you. You have to do what we say or she will die. If you don't care if she dies,

61

then we have access to your parents. If you don't care about them, we have already framed you for Keith Tasser's murder. You are missing some shoes from your suitcase that will be found in his apartment once they identify him, and then there is a video professionally doctored to show you two were having an affair. We own you. Best to accept it."

I wondered if Trankosky already had the shoes. I felt like I was suffocating. "Why would you get me in trouble with the cops if you want to use me? Won't that be hard to do behind bars?"

"They won't arrest you. We can arrange to stop what we start as well."

The looks on the faces of my brother and friends did not help me concentrate. I closed my eyes again and broke things down into parts, realizing I had to focus on Affie — first and only. For now. "What is it I am expected to do?"

Exhaustion had claimed me. After I confirmed that a pair of black patten Manolo pumps were missing from my luggage, we'd woken my parents' next-door neighbor. He'd promised to check on Elva and Howard, and after a few minutes, they called. The ringer had been turned off their phone,

certainly the act of the kidnapper, a supposition I kept to myself. We stayed on the
line while they discovered Aphrodite was
gone. Because we were prevented from
involving the police, Shana had come up
with the excuse that Affie had run off to
Galveston with friends in a bout of teenage
rebellion and our parents ought not to
worry. Mom was incensed, although this
fairy tale was nothing compared to what
Ben had put her through in his teen years. I
ached for Shana that she had to withstand
an undeserved parenting lecture from Elva
in the midst of worrying about the safety of
her child.

I'd fallen asleep in the bed opposite
Shana, but only after I'd warded off Ben
four times. He claimed he was only checking on Shana, but that was so out of character for him I knew he was just covering up
what he was really after. Nothing else made
sense.

"Honey Bee." I heard Frank's voice but
knew I had to be dreaming. I'd been imagining what Ben had on his mind and now it
was on mine. "Get up."

His voice was quiet and urgent, but not
quite the tone I wanted to hear from my
lover in action. "Get up or I'll drag you out
of bed."

"Urgh, isn't it supposed to be the other way around?" I croaked, eyes still closed, half hoping this was the beginning of a nightmare I could turn around.

"Later," Frank whispered, pulling the covers off my head and easing me to a sitting position. "Maybe. If you're a good girl and do as I say."

"I'm not very good at that." I pointed out with a yawn.

Frank bit back a grin that would've softened the worry lines around his eyes. Uh-oh. Sparing a glance at Shana, who seemed asleep, with her back to us, I threw the covers off and tiptoed to the door. Frank followed me, lifting my short nightie for a peek. I slapped his hand away lightly, and he pushed me through the door and closed it with a quiet click.

"What time is it?" I asked as I blinked against the bright sky out the picture windows. I stifled another yawn.

"Nine," Frank said, reaching for one of two coffee shop cups on the foyer table and bringing it to me as I plopped onto the couch.

Folding my fingers around it, I savored the aroma of the rich Columbian for a moment. "I think I love you," I breathed.

"Me or the coffee?"

64

"The coffee, but you by extension," I murmured into the cup.

"Remind me to never come empty-handed."

"Good advice."

I took two luxurious sips and, though I was tempted to, couldn't delay any longer. I'd have liked to, especially since Frank hadn't spoken yet, and that meant it was bad. Frank was frank by nature, and, when he wasn't, it was a sign of trouble.

"Okay, what did you find out from Abel and how much do I owe you for his grand-mother's next gallbladder operation?"

Frank had to smile. Abel, his friend with the Clark County cops, liked to think of himself as an honest guy, trying to provide for his family's emergencies through shar-ing bits of gossip.

"Word on the street, according to Abel, is that there is a major crime planned for this year's Main Event. Vice has been tracking down leads for a month."

I shrugged, sipping my coffee, looking out the window at the group of hookers solicit-ing in a way that most people walking by on the street wouldn't catch. Illegalities oc-curred in the most holy events and Texas Hold 'Em was far from holy. In fact, gam-bling on the game was against the law in most states so the fact that someone was polluting it with a shady deal or two didn't surprise me. I hadn't knowingly seen anything underhanded going on besides a murder here and there, but I was no Pollyanna and the fact it existed didn't scare me.

"And," Frank continued, "your name keeps cropping up in the tips."

"What!?" I sloshed coffee on my robe as I spun to face him.

He was wearing his cop face, which softened for a moment as his gaze drifted to where the coffee and cream had landed in my décolletage. "Would you like me to clean that up?"

Raising my eyebrows, I shook my head and reached for a napkin on the bar. "Considering you're going to use something other than a towel to do it and we are sharing a suite with others, you might be starting something you can't finish right now."

"Oh, I promise I can finish it." He flashed a grin. "Remember, we have a suite to ourselves just floors away. We can be there in minutes."

"Frank . . ." I sobered. "I can't. I have to stay with Shana right now. She's an emotional basket case."

Frank frowned. "Ben's here with her."

I blew out a breath. "And you think my

brother is going to help her *emotionally?*"

His frown deepened. "Dammit, Bee, can't you put *us* first for once?"

I cocked my head at him and let his question hang in the silence. All the times he'd had to cancel weekends together because of his mystery missions that I couldn't know about or he chose not to elaborate on popped up like silent sentries. Over the last year and a half, we might have evolved into an "us" but definitely not one with a capital *U.* "Come on, Frank. You can't be serious. It's not 'us first' once in a while. The 'us' needs to be first always. Your life is so severely compartmentalized that you wake up each day and prioritize your compartments and sometimes the 'us' is first and sometimes it's last. Sometimes it's not even on the list."

He spun on his heel and turned away from me to stand at the window, looking down at The Strip. "That's not true."

"And," I continued, "it's okay if the 'us' is last if you let me into the other compartments every now and then. Because then what you have to do is what we have to do."

"You know I can't do that," Frank told the window.

"Yes, I'm clear on the fact that you can't. I just don't know why."

I could see Frank wrestling with himself. Nothing about him was easy, except maybe the sexuality he exuded. Whether it was the secrets he kept, the life he led or the hurt he'd endured, he found it difficult to trust. The muscles along his jaw rippled. The knuckles whitened on his coffee cup. He sighed, still looking down at Las Vegas Boulevard. "You know I love you."

"I do." And I did. But it might not be enough.

Finally Frank turned away from the window. "Right now, I just want to find a way to keep you safe."

He was prioritizing those life compartments again, but I let it go. A part of me realized I might never know Frank, not completely. I'd pushed as hard as I could right now.

"I might remind you that I asked you to quit playing Hold 'Em. As much as you love your independence, taking my advice might be for the best, at least for right now. Forgo the Main Event and just hang out in Vegas until the Clark County boys clear you to return to Houston. Have a real vacation for once."

"I have to play," I murmured, closing my eyes.

"Yeah." Frank kissed the top of my head.

"With me."

"No, Frank, I really have to go through with the tournament," I said softly, still avoiding opening my eyes to the intensity I knew was coming.

"Honey Bee, you're not losing anything if —"

"Except maybe Affie."

"What?" He put his hands on my shoulders and turned me to face him.

Opening my eyes, I took a deep breath, trying to ignore Frank's deepening frown and the strength of his fingers as they unconsciously squeezed my shoulders tighter. "I don't know if it was the Drag-snashark guy or his boss but one of them called after you left. He told me he'd kidnapped Affie, and that if I wanted to save her, I would have to take my seat at the Main Event."

"And do what?"

I shrugged. "I think they want me to make them money. He said to make sure I was still in at the end of the day, which I suppose I can do by just posting my blinds and playing only the nuts. Of course, this kind of exaggerated conservative play will compromise my stack and what I can accomplish later on, but maybe that won't matter. Maybe this is all they want from me. Maybe tomorrow they will set Affie free." Saying it out loud seemed like a good idea, but instead made the option sound ludicrous. I sighed and sat back down on the couch.

"What are they after? Why blackmail you into doing something you were planning to do anyway?" Frank mused, sliding his hands down my arms before dropping them to his sides as he strode to the window, looking out, his eyes obviously seeing nothing in the scene before him.

"I asked, but he wouldn't say. He just reminded me he knows where my parents live, that he knows Shana and Ben are here with me, that Affie is scared." I paused, trying to swallow the sudden lump in my throat. "He was cold, matter of fact, which was actually more frightening than an overt threat. His voice didn't sound like the guy who'd tried to run off with me at the Image."

Frank had paced over to the bar, and now with his forearms braced against it, he closed his hands into fists, opening them again, studying them with an intensity. "Ingrid should be flying in about now, to keep an eye on Shana. I considered having Shana go home, but our routines at home are much easier for a kidnapper or stalker to predict and follow. Here, they can lose a tail. Joe is already here, searching out a couple of leads for me. I have a man on your parents. We can keep him as a silent shadow, or tell Elva and Howard about him."

I shook my head. "No, I think if she knew, Mom would manage to dilute his protective capabilities."

Frank allowed a quick smile as we both imagined Elva chatting with a Joe look-alike, aka the Marlboro Man, nonstop, trying to set him up with all the single daughters of friends within two decades of his age and telling half of coastal Texas she had a bodyguard. "You're right."

"Frank, this is very kind of you, but I hate to interfere with whatever jobs all your people are supposed to be working on."

"Bee! Stop worrying about everyone else and worry about yourself and your god-daughter. My people don't work without me. Now we are all working on this. End of story."

I opened my mouth to ask more, wanting as I always did to know more about what Frank did and for whom. He would say for himself because he ran FBG Enterprises but it was his client list I wanted a peek at. I suppose I was on it now. I closed my mouth and figured a way to be sneaky. "I don't think I can afford you or Ingrid, for that matter, she told me she doesn't work for you, just *with* you."

Frank rolled his eyes. "Just like a woman."

"Hey!" I warned to hide my "ah-ha!" "So what will I owe you?"

Frank raised his eyebrows. "Probably more than you are willing to deliver, but I'm willing to work something out in trade."

"Be serious, Frank."

"I am."

I sighed. Enough playing footsies. Fun as it was. I had to know what he wasn't telling me. "So how did my name keep cropping up at the cop shop?"

Frank's face tensed, and he turned away. I wasn't going to get the whole story. "You are the highest-profile player being bandied about as being dirty, therefore making you prime game for any publicity-seeking investigator or prosecutor. Unfortunately, there is one of each in Clark County right now, salivating over the possibility you are corrupt."

"The cop wouldn't be Trankosky, would it?"

Frank shook his head, and stalked off, pacing the room behind me. "That's not the name I was given."

"Great, then I have two enemies in blue now."

Sighing, Frank came up behind me, wrapping his arms around my torso. "I wish we could go home."

Since our homes were in two different states, I didn't quite know how to take that so I kept quiet, as uncertain of my safety as I was of my relationship with the man whose chin rested on my shoulder.

FIVE

"You look like the wrath of God," Ben croaked, stumbling out of the bedroom, rubbing his hands across his face and up through his hair, leaving a disheveled mess that on me would look like hell and on him looked like sex-god heaven.

"You're not the only one who thinks so," I murmured, motioning at the television screen where the morning news was showing a scene outside the Fortune casino that was hosting this year's World Series of Poker. About a hundred protestors carrying signs decrying gambling, most specifically poker, as the devil's work, paced the sidewalk. I turned up the volume to hear the reporter. "So according to the Church of the Believers, the longtime poker greats, here to begin the tournament today, like Danny Negreau, the Phils, Jennifer Harman, Annie Duke are committing a sin." The camera cut to a well-dressed middle-

74

aged man with a thick head of slicked-back silver hair and a self-righteous air. "It is not only their participation in this vile game that we are here to protest, but also their use of their celebrity. They promote this sin against humanity, gambling, making it not only a seemingly sanctioned recreation for our young people to pursue, but also a glorified one. We must save not only America's youth, but the youth of the world from this dark road into debt and destruction." The camera cut back to the reporter, who stood before the waving signs. "The Reverend Phineas Paul says his 'Believers' are embarking on a religious campaign to push poker from the forefront of international gambling to the backrooms again."

The camera zoomed in on a sign that I'd seen in the pan shot at the beginning of the story: "DEALING DESTRUCTION — THE RISE IN POKER SIGNALS THE RISE OF THE DEVIL AND THE IMPENDING END OF THE WORLD."

"Friendly." Ben reached over, grabbed my coffee and swigged it. "Welcome to Vegas."

"I'm glad Frank took off before he could see this," I murmured, feeling suddenly queasy.

"Look." Ben pointed at the screen, grinning. A bleach blonde, poured into a silver spandex minidress, pranced across the street in five-inch electric Plexiglas platforms, right through the middle of the picketers and into the front door of the Fortune casino. No one even turned to look.

I had to smile. Only in Vegas would you see a hooker wander through a group of religious protestors, unaccosted as they protested card playing.

"They certainly are one-track-mind protestors," Ben observed drily.

"I saw them at the airport too," Shana's unusually small voice said from the other bedroom doorway. We all turned to look at her. She always bounced out of bed, looking pert and perfect. I'd never ever seen bags under her eyes before. My heart ached for her.

I moved to go to her, but Ben had already hurried over and led her to the couch. I cocked my head, still trying to figure out what was going on as they murmured in low tones.

Frustrated and overwhelmed, I snapped, "Ben, this is all your fault. If you hadn't gotten me into the stupid game in the first place, we could all be vacationing in Cancún and Affie would be home. Safe."

In the middle of my tirade, the door had opened to Frank, with Ingrid and Jack in tow. They paused in the foyer as Ben's eyes narrowed at me in an anger I hadn't seen from him. Not ever. "Don't you lay this on me, Bee Bee. Don't you dare. You're the one who continues to play the game with no gun to your head."

"Right, except now the gun is against Affie's head," I snapped, then immediately regretted my flash of temper as Shana sucked in a breath. I couldn't miss Frank's raised eyebrows. Okay, so now I was the bad guy? Suddenly I was sick and tired of all the men in my life. Save the one shooting me an empathetic look with his big puppy dog eyes.

"L-listen, everybody," Jack piped up, letting his arm slide off Ingrid's waist as he walked toward me. "Blame is overrated. G-guilt is a waste of t-time and energy. Neither will f-find Aphrodite."

"Well spoken, Jack," Frank said, shooting me a warning look then looking pointedly at Ben. Obviously he expected me to apologize. *Ha, dream on, dude.* "You and I should go try to hunt down the two guys who mentioned Bee at the high-stakes room last night. Ingrid is here to keep an eye on Shana, so —"

"I'm going home," she announced. Ben patted her hand.

Frank shook his head, repeating his theory about the dangers of being at home when under surveillance. "You need to stay close. But I understand your need to do something. Why don't you register for one of the major satellites, throw Bee's name around a bit, and eavesdrop hard. The more ears and eyes we have out in Vegas, the better. Affie's abduction obviously has something to do with the game in town. If we all have something to do with the Main Event, the higher the odds we'll luck into some information that will lead us to our girl."

Shana bowed her head, sighed heavily, then raised it again. "I just don't know what's right."

Frank brushed his fingertips over the top of her head. "We'll just have to play that by ear."

Sparing me a vicious glare, Ben whispered something in Shana's ear then disappeared into his bedroom. "He's going to get changed for the tournament," Shana explained.

Frank looked at me, wearing his cop face. "Good, you two can get over there together. Take your car but it's best if you valet park from now on too — there are too many dark corners in parking garages."

Jack and Ingrid had wandered over to the

alcove behind the bar, fawning over each other. It was cute in a sickening kind of way. I don't think they'd ever had a disagreement since they'd hooked up on the cruise last fall. I don't think Frank and I went a day *without* a disagreement since we'd hooked up the winter before that. Should I take that as a sign, or was I just hard to get along with?

As if reading my mind, Frank cupped my elbows in his palms and brushed his lips along my cheek. Then he ruined the gentle gesture by speaking. "You need to make up with Ben, Honey Bee. You hit him with a low blow."

"Yeah, but what I want to know is why is he taking it so hard," I narrowed my eyes at Ben's bedroom door, deep in thought. "Usually he doesn't feel the impact of those through his overinflated ego."

Frank shrugged. "I don't know why. And it doesn't matter. We are stronger working together as a team, and you're dividing us."

Grr.

Sometimes cascading warm water and perfumed soap change everything. Today, however, a shower didn't make me feel anything but clean. I supposed it was still an improvement, although not as big a one as I'd hoped for. At least the Church of the Believers couldn't fault me for my hygiene. Pulling my sash on my robe tight, I stepped out of the bathroom to find my wardrobe laid out on the bed. My sometimes fashionista had obviously been busy, apparently rifling through my Burberry bag with her eyes closed.

That motley collection of pieces was what I was supposed to wear to a nationally televised event? Well, that was going to change or I'd have Believers Against Fashion Disasters marching on me at my next tournament. I left the bedroom to fortify myself with a mineral water from the wet bar. As I poured, I was struck by how quiet the suite was. "Ben?"

No answer. I strode over to his bedroom door, which stood open. I jammed my hands on my hips and talked to the molding. "Ben, I know you're mad at me. Quit being juvenile."

No answer. I walked into the room, finding only a waft of Balenciaga Cristobal left behind. Ben had ditched me.

Angrily, I stomped back to my room and finished slapping on my MAC. I was halfway through the bronzer when another possibility occurred to me — Ben might have been kidnapped. It wouldn't be the first time. I called his cell phone. It transferred immediately to voice mail. "Where are you?" I demanded. I raced back into his room, but could see no sign of anything but sloppiness. I returned to my room, and, after smoothing on lip liner and gloss, began to paw through the clothes in my suitcase. It was no use. I couldn't concentrate now that Ben might have joined Affie in the great unknown. I turned to Ingrid's fashion disaster on the bed and blew out a breath. It would have to do.

"Hubbahubba."

Suppressing a wince, I handed the taxi driver my cash before he started drooling, then turned toward the Fortune. Of course Ben had taken the car, or at least the car keys, leaving me to fend for myself. The insensitivity actually comforted me because it was so in character and, unless the kidnappers came to snatch him without transportation, Ben was probably okay.

Unless, that is, they took the keys so I couldn't follow. I hated having such a fertile imagination. It was mostly a pain in the ass.

Since Frank had produced one of his "company phones" for me to use until I could get a new one of my own, I'd considered calling him, but didn't — partly because I was still put out with him and partly because I didn't want to distract him from the "team" work just to worry about me getting to the WSOP. That would definitely be my excuse for not calling him if Ben really was AWOL. Turning his advice around that way would make Frank furious. I smiled to myself. I'm a bit perverse that way.

My reflection in the building's mirrored glass turned my smile into a grimace. The hot pink satin blouson shorts didn't at all match the long-sleeved, tailored white Ann Taylor button-down shirt. The charcoal gray velveteen vest was part of a three-piece Donna Karan, although it did admittedly have a barely visible strip of hot pink thread that ran along the seam, its saving grace in this ensemble. The dark silver pumps were meant for my somber Prada suit. The gypsy beads around my neck Shana picked up from a seer at the Renaissance festival and the sea glass dangling from my ears said "Kokomo" not "raise you two mil."

I was aiming to avoid the picket line by ducking into the side door of the casino, but unfortunately, as I turned the corner, I saw they'd staked out that door as well. Sliding my Gargoyles from the top of my head to my nose, I realized I should've worn my church lady suit, because sneaking by in hot pink is hard to do.

"There she is," I heard ripple through the protestors.

I sped up. They rallied around as a reporter from KLVS weaved her way to me. "I'm sorry, you must be looking for Clonie Gowan. She'll be along in the next taxi." I waved my hand toward the street and dove for the door.

"No, Miss Cooley, I'm looking for a comment from you," the reporter said, grabbing my forearm in such an intense vise grip that I wondered if they didn't send reporters to ambush boot camp.

"I can't imagine why." I smiled tightly. "There are so many other players more worthy of your attention than I am."

"I don't think so," the reporter answered, gleefully pointing at a sign held by a teenager that read: *Bee Cool, BURN YOUR CARDS OR BURN IN HELL.* "What do you say about that?"

"This country is built on free speech, although that right is restricted to not injuring another with that freedom. An inflammatory statement such as that would certainly be considered injurious and thus not protected by the first amendment, wouldn't you say?"

"And what would you say, Miss Cooley,"

a booming voice spoke from the back of the crowd, resonating so deeply I wondered for a moment if he didn't have a megaphone. I could see the coiffed snow white hair move through the protestors who suddenly parted like the Red Sea. "If I told you that you are injuring millions of people, young and old, throughout this God-given world of ours by your sinful decision to play poker and flaunt your body in such a way as this?"

The Reverend Phineas Paul. I had to admit he was impressively charismatic, although I had to say his tan looked more artifical in person. Fighting him head-on would only play into his hand so I hit where he didn't expect it. After all, we hadn't been introduced, had we? "I would ask who it is accusing me."

He blinked, temporarily speechless, but recovering quickly, extended his hand. I took it as he said, "I am the Reverend Phineas Paul, supremely blessed to lead the Church of the Believers."

The camera was taking it all in. I dropped his hand as soon as I politely could, resisting the urge to wipe it on my shorts. Although it hadn't been sweaty, his shake had left me feeling somehow soiled. He smiled knowingly at me. "And your answer to my question? What would you tell these impressionable young girls here today about the devil's work you do?" In a grand sweeping motion, he indicated the teenage girls holding signs around us.

"I would tell all of you to choose what you want to do in life and do it lawfully, honestly and to the best of your abilities."

"You are saying, Miss Cooley, that anything sanctioned by secular law is right?" Paul demanded. "How about alcohol? It isn't against the law to drink an entire gallon of whiskey at once but is that *right?*"

He'd hit me where it hurt. Frank's alcoholism continued to be one of the heartaches of my life. I looked at Paul, wondering if he'd just gotten lucky in his barb. Of course, he had. He was a professional verbal attacker. He used scare tactics for a living. I shrugged off the paranoia and dredged up a polite smile. "I suppose you are right. I shouldn't be telling people what is right and wrong, that is your job. I'll just live my life and stay out of everyone else's."

"Ah, but it isn't that easy, Miss Cooley, with fame and fortune comes responsibility and you must face the fact that your private life is now public. What you do affects millions of others. Choose the path of righteousness before it is too late!"

Shaking my head, I pushed away, through

the crowd and to the front door of the Fortune where a phalanx of deputies and casino security surrounded me and escorted me through the lobby to the registration table for the 2008 World Series of Poker.

As I was giving my name to the brush, I looked to my right and saw Dragsnashark standing amid the railbirds. He shot me a weighty glance, ducked his head and disappeared down the hallway.

SIX

According to the registration desk, Ben hadn't checked into the tournament yet.

I had flirted with the idea of calling Shana looking for Ben, but hadn't wanted to worry her. I decided to call Ingrid instead.

"You look so *bad*," Ingrid exclaimed.

"I know," I snapped. "Only, how do you know?"

"They have the TV turned on in the poker room here. I see you're popular with the religious right."

"They are more like the religious wrong if you ask me, but I suppose they are well-meaning." I sighed. As stressed as I was over Affie's disappearance, the last thing I wanted and needed right now was the pressure of media attention. I wasn't sure how I would focus on the tournament. "If you thought I would look so bad, why did you choose this getup?"

"I meant baaaaad, like hot, like awesome,

rad, cool."

"Enough. I get it. I just don't agree," I muttered. Ingrid was a runaway train when she got started with something. The more I'd argue, the more it would stoke her engines. I changed the subject. "How is Shana?"

"She's okay. She started off very distracted but since the game got going, she's down to checking her phone only every thirty seconds instead of every five. She told me at the last break that the guy sitting next to her was unduly interested in your encounter with the good reverend. She wants to get him to open up about why. I've seen her chatting him up."

"Have either of you heard from Ben?"

"Ben? I thought he was with you!"

Uh-oh. I hoped Ingrid wouldn't squeal to Frank. "Well, I don't see him right now, and I'm curious about he and Shana being in each other's back pockets. It disturbs me on many levels."

"Stop trying to control your brother's life, Bee," Ingrid advised.

"Actually I'm trying to control my own since I know I will be caught in the middle of whatever debacle my brother creates here. There's no winning if these two get involved."

"You don't think your brother is so low he'd take advantage of Shana when she is this vulnerable, do you?"

The silence spoke volumes. We both knew Ben was capable of that, even if not in a malicious way. "Forget I asked that," she added quickly.

The tap on my shoulder made me jump. I'd stepped into a dark alcove to dial Ingrid and now felt trapped. Spinning around I looked down at a twentysomething guy with longish brown hair that looked like it hadn't been washed in days, wearing a wrinkled and coffee-stained button-down and jeans, holding an open tablet and a voice recorder. Perhaps worse than Dragsnashark, it was a reporter. Print if his appearance was any indication.

"Gotta go," I told Ingrid, hanging up on her protest.

"I'm sorry to bother you, Bee Cool," the pip-squeak said, flapping the press credential around his neck at me that claimed he was from the *Las Vegas Tribune*. "But I'm looking for your reaction."

"America is the cornerstone of religious freedom in the world. Aren't we fortunate to host a forum for everyone's beliefs?"

He drew his eyebrows together. "But what does that have to do with murder?"

"Murder?" I parroted. Oops, I'd almost forgotten my poor swimming companion.

"Clark County brought you in for questioning in the overnight murder of a man found floating in the Image lagoon."

Stupid cops leaked it. Probably Trankosky. Probably on purpose. I wanted to wrap my fingers around the reporter's pencil neck and get him to confess who ratted me out, but I decided that might reflect some guilt on my part. Best to play ignorant. I flashed my incisors and hoped it passed for a smile. "I happened to be in the vicinity of the man's unfortunate demise and was questioned as a matter of routine, I'm sure."

"That's not what I hear."

"From whom?"

"Oh no." Mulish set to jaw. "I'm not telling you. I protect my sources."

Of course. "You ambush a poor, helpless woman in a dark corner and protect a big, burly gun-toting cop. How chivalrous."

"I work for the American public and the First Amendment, not for the Knights of the Round Table."

Okay, a shrimp *and* a smart-ass. Just my luck. Grr. Time to change tactics. "Look, do you know Jack Smack?"

"Sure, the Smack is my hero! He's been

on network TV and everything. With Diane."

"Then run along and give him a ring. He's my publicist. He'll give you a comment."

Pip-squeak shook his head, throwing a hank of greasy hair into his eye. He brushed it away. "He can't be. That's an ethical violation. It would undermine his ability to remain neutral in his reporting if he was on someone's payroll as a flack."

Damn this little news-hunting bulldog. The bells outside the WSOP room tolled to mark five minutes to the start of the tournament. Finally, my karma was turning. I squinted at his credentials. "Sorry, Aaron, but I have to find my table."

He shrugged and stepped back so I could pass, giving up so easily it made me nervous. "Good luck."

I frowned at him as I passed. "Thank you."

"You're welcome, although luck might not do you any good since the cops expect to have enough evidence against you to put you behind bars by nightfall."

I spun around to see him wave and scoot off down the hall. *Goody.* Painful as it was, I scanned my appearance in the glass along the gift shop, flecked a piece of lint off the right cuff of the shorts, smoothed a smear off the left pump, tucked a bit of my chestnut hair back into its braid and strode toward the ballroom, fighting a sick feeling in the pit of my stomach. Before I reached the door I was set upon by a couple dozen fans and autograph seekers. I signed playing cards, markers, T-shirts, programs but drew the line at one man's bare, hairy exposed shoulder. Fame was highly overrated. A railbird named Thelma whom I'd met at the tournament in Tunica walked with me to the door, talking fast and low. "My cash flow has a clog currently, Bee Cool. I was hoping you could float me a loan so I could go rake it in at one of the big cash games going down at Neptune's."

Flush from my first win, I'd once given money to a railbird with a sad story and a promise of payback only to be chastised by Frank as being a fool. A fact proven at my next tournament when I found myself surrounded by sad stories, and needless to say never saw that loaner 2K again. Yet, as I shook my head at Thelma, I was struck with an inspiration. "I might be able to help with a couple hundred, but only if you can do something for me in return."

Thelma nodded eagerly. She was whip thin, so ageless she could be anywhere from twenty to sixty and of indeterminate ethnicity. Sometimes she looked decidedly Asian, other times I saw some Indian in her and other times she looked as Caucasian as a Midwestern farm wife. Her colorless Dollar Store cotton shift and canvas slip-on shoes made her even more invisible. A human chameleon might be worth putting on the payroll. "Keep your ears open for any mentions of me. Something wrong is going down here this week, and I want to know what it is. I want to know why my name is associated with it. Can you do that?"

Again she nodded and stuck her hand out. I knew I'd never see the George Washingtons again, but I knew if she wanted more she would have to produce what I asked for. I was going codependent for her gambling and begging addiction but I was desperate.

As I entered the room, I heard the commentators from *Poker Live.*

"And now here is the other half of the Twin Terrifics — Belinda 'Bee Cool' Cooley."

"Now, Phil, you know that the moniker for these Houstonians is case specific. Those who play against them — Bee Cool and Ben Hot — call them the Twin Terrors."

"The other half" made me think Ben was already in the room. I scanned it and was relieved to see him sitting down at table 114, with an uncharacteristically serious set to his face. He didn't even spare a wink at the pair of triple Ds sitting next to him. This was really bad. Perhaps he was coming down with a terminal illness.

"Of course, it's Belinda, not Ben, who looks *hot* today, Trixie."

"That's a matter of opinion, Phil."

"Or maybe it's a matter of gender." Ha-haha.

Fortunately I was out of earshot before the commentary descended any further. I found my table, introduced myself around, sat in my free seat and thanked the dealer for being there. The 2008 World Series of Poker was about to begin, and I couldn't be dreading it more.

I'd been dealt three combination hands in a row and it was giving me a headache. Players like Ben relished combo hands as energetically as I despised them. They just presented so many opportunities for self-made failure. You couldn't get by without counting cards at each street and even when you did, played tight, played smart, you still got stung in the end. It was the close-but-no-cigar hand that tempted you with the possibilities only to leave you wanting.

I peeked at my pocket of 9 of clubs, 7 of clubs once more. A fish move, I knew, but since I was the big blind and the dealer was letting the table nap in between bets and I had been watching Ben, I'd needed a refresher as the dealer burned a card. Since no one raised Preflop, I didn't have a decision until the first three cards went faceup.

Since I was well on my way to my fourth combo in a row, I sucked in a breath, praying for a clean trio of nines to fall on The Flop. Wasn't my life difficult enough? Fate must not have thought so, because 8 of clubs, 7 of hearts and 10 of clubs flopped. So now I had a flush draw for a golf bag (club flush), a straight draw and a pair of sevens. Wow, this could go to my head. Except for all the outs for the others — including the real possibility that I would end up drawing dead twice and a pair of tens would beat me.

Ack. In first position, I couldn't even wait to see some bets. I checked. The chair to my right was empty — a Saudi Arabian oil prince without a head for numbers and without a lick of sense had busted out in the second hand after going all in on a 2-Ace-7 off-suit Flop with sailboats (pair of 4s). The next six were a racehorse jockey from Ecuador who was an emotive jackal, a staid banker who had done nothing but check so far, a couple of lotto player (play any hand) college kids, an off-duty dealer from the Flynn who played like he shouldn't give up his day job and a stay-at-home mother of five who'd won her seat in an Internet tourney. To my left was a woman who was so wrapped up and covered up it was amazing she could breathe. She wore butter-plate-size black Diors, her hair wound up under a turban and a feather-plumed hat á la Dorothy Lamour, a black dress that went from floor to chin and shockingly white satin gloves. She hadn't spoken — to anyone — and I, frankly, was kind of scared to talk to her. I didn't think anyone had anything, even the jockey was being conservative. Then ole Blackie, as I'd come to call her, pushed in a raise of a thousand. Of course.

She was impossible to read with only a four-inch strip of skin showing on her whole body and absolutely still countenance. Then I saw her lower lip twitch. Just barely. I called.

The jockey did too. I think just for the hell of it. "Jou remind me of my fav-o-rite chestnut 'orse. Fire on outside, ice on inside. Sizz . . ." he said as he pushed his chips across the felt.

The Turn came an Ace of hearts, a blank for me. Could be a homerun for her, a pair of Aces, trips, a possible heart flush draw.

But if she'd had less than a heart flush draw a card ago why would she have raised then? On a bluff? Blackie's lip twitched again as she pushed in another raise.

She'd won two hands so far and I hadn't noticed the twitch. I had to go with my gut. I raised her. Everyone else fell off the board, even the lotto players. But Blackie reraised, no twitch, dammit.

I called. A 7 of spades fell on The River, wiping out the heart flush draw, turning my candy canes into trips. If she had Ace trips or trips with any other card on the board, I was sunk. Her lip wasn't twitching anymore. Shoot. I ought to fold. My gut told me to quit even though I was pot committed.

I didn't.

She turned over her pocket rockets and still didn't smile.

I'd lost all but three thousand dollars in chips. My cell phone vibrated with a text message. As the dealer let the machine in front of him shuffle the cards, I read: *Frank called us with your new number. No word from Affie. Good luck at the Main Event. Love, Mom and Dad.* I'd just slipped it back into my pocket when it vibrated again. The dealer spent the burn card and began passing out our pockets. I glanced down at the screen on my phone: *Remember: If you bust out, so does she.*

Gasping, I looked around frantically — for what? An answer? Help? Someone to tell me how these guys had found my new phone number so quickly?

"Are you okay, Miss Cooley?" the dealer asked.

Then I saw him, over the hundreds of tables, behind the tape. Dragsnashark drilled me with a look, then turned around and disappeared behind a tall, leggy woman who was waving. Her face came into focus and I smiled, waving back. Carey, my old pal who'd literally saved my life at my last Vegas tournament. She cocked her head and looked at Dragsnashark's back as he disappeared. She raised her palms in question. I nodded. She took off after him.

"Miss Cooley?" The dealer interrupted sharply. "It's a good thing that didn't take place in the middle of a hand or you'd be called out."

"What?"

"Security has been tightened this year. No talking on phones at the table, no motioning to railbirds behind the tape except on break. I noticed you checking your text messages."

Thank goodness I had an overpair. I bid conservatively and hoped I could afford to protect the nuts. I saw the jockey flirting with the idea of scaring me off the hand, but he must have learned from being burned the few times he'd tried to do that. He folded. Blackie folded with a twitch. Damn, what did that mean?

In the end, I won barely more than the blinds. At least I was moving in the right direction. The bell rang for our first break. Two hours down, only dozens more to go to the final table. I hoped I could keep it together to make it that far. Or as far as it took to bring Affie home.

I sensed Ben would prefer to avoid me, but too bad. I made my way to his table, which was still in play, having been dealt the last hand just before the bell, apparently. A couple dozen other players stopped to watch too. Ben looked like he was playing as distractedly as I had been, although with much more success. Eyeballing the table, he looked to be the chip leader. It's where I'd fancied myself to be at this point, instead of barely hanging on.

On The Turn of a 4 of diamonds (joining the Ace of spades, Jack of hearts, 6 of clubs Flop), Ben placed what looked to me like a post oak bluff, raising the couple-thousand-dollar pot by a hundred dollars. He could have a Jordan (two/three) in his pocket hoping for a straight draw or sailboats (four/four) to give him trips but then why not raise more aggressively? Sure enough, all the players who had muck folded. Ben won. The dealer flipped over what would've been The River — a Jack of diamonds — and the guy to Ben's right groaned. Normally, this would have made Ben giddy. Instead he didn't even smile as he raked the chips his way.

The table cleared out for the remainder of the break. Ben stacked his chips. A minute later, he still hadn't looked at me when we were the only two left at the table.

"Ben," I said softly, ready to apologize.

He finally looked at me, the tension lines around his eyes making him appear older but also more mature while still a traffic-stopping ringer for Colin Farrell. His kismet. Mine was to look like Aunt Hilda. The woman walking by behind me sighed. Instead of winking at her, Ben looked back down at his chips. *Whoa.*

"What is the matter with you?" I demanded in my surprise. Shouldn't I be thrilled? I'd always wanted my brother to grow up. Here it looked like he had, and I was irritated. I suppose I hadn't expected it to happen in twelve hours' time.

"You know what's wrong," he snapped, fiddling with his chips. "This is all my fault."

"You know I really didn't mean that," I pushed out through a tight jaw. I sort of had meant it but took Frank's teamwork message to heart. "Yes, it was your idea to get involved with it, but I play poker because I want to, now. It's my loved one, not yours, these creeps are after. You don't have anything to do with it."

Ben dropped his head and muttered what sounded like, "That's what you think." I opened my mouth to ask him to elaborate when one of the television commentators approached, dragging a cameraman behind him. "It's the Terrific Twins together! What are you two doing, concocting a winning strategy?"

"Yeah, a winning dinner strategy." Ben blew him off. I shook my head. I'd never in my life seen Ben shun the chance to be on camera.

Phil cocked his pointer finger and fired at me. "We've got our eyes on you two. Nothing would be more fun than a Twin Terror showdown on the final table. Talk about ratings!"

I smiled as they zeroed in on another victim. Ben bowed his head and fiddled with his chips again.

"Have you heard from Shana?" he asked.

"No, but Mom and Dad texted to report they haven't heard from Affie. And . . ." I handed him my phone. "I got this."

He read the last message, his jaw bunching as he ground his teeth. His narrowing eyes slowly rose to meet mine. Focus mode. I didn't know what to make of this state of being I recognized my brother adopting, which was typically only in relation to attaining things he wanted — winning the state baseball championship, stealing the biggest pharmaceutical client in the Southwest, discrediting the guy who gave Texas Hold 'Em a bad name on our last trip to Vegas, which incidentally almost got him killed.

For Ben, focus mode meant winning something for himself. What did he hope to win now? What would getting Affie back get him?

Maybe he truly had picked a really weird time to grow up.

The bell rang the tournament back into play before I could make up my mind. I rose from the seat next to Ben and headed back toward my seat. "Bee Bee," he called. "Take care of yourself."

I mulled that tender warning over in my head as I scanned the railbirds for Carey.

She was nowhere to be found. Carey had proven she could take care of herself but Dragsnashark was scary. I hoped now I hadn't sent her off into some serious trouble. I had enough to worry about without adding my transvestite pal onto the list.

Being scared to death for my goddaughter had a positive effect on my play. I won the first three hands after the break with marginal cards. I'd finished stacking my last chip when I noticed Ben standing up. Bathroom trip, no doubt, since I hadn't given him the chance during the break. It wasn't until the final round of betting on The River at my table that I saw a figure sitting down in Ben's chair. The three-hundred-pound woman in the muumuu sure wasn't Ben. He'd busted out and they'd filled his seat with a player from a short table.

Chip leader to a bust out in three hands? No way. Ben was too good a tournament player for that. Something bad was definitely up.

SEVEN

As if life wasn't complicated enough, I got The Trucker in my pocket in the next deal and half the table folded, tempting me to stay in to see The Flop. The Trucker is probably the worst starting hand in Texas Hold 'Em — a ten/four unsuited. Not much you can make out of that, unless three tens fell on The Flop. I stared at Blackie and saw the lip twitch as she raised the big blind in an early position. Ack.

My phone vibrated just then and I would have to remember to thank Frank later. I folded and walked away from the table to take the call.

"Have you found Affie?" I demanded.

"Wow, you must think I'm Batman. I'm honored," Frank said, just like a man, because if he'd asked me that I would've assumed guilt for my failure to produce, not assumed success. I sighed. "Where are you, Not-Even-Robin?"

"Ouch, that hurt. We're just pulling into the Fortune, although it looks like there might not be any parking. We might have to park down The Strip and hoof it back over here."

"Any luck?"

"Nothing to get excited about. How are things going for you?"

"I'm having a hard time concentrating." I paused, unsure of whether to tell him about the text message warning. Sometimes death threats distracted Frank. I was afraid this latest would derail his attempts to run down the freshest leads. And although I was worried for Carey, there wasn't anything Frank could do to find her right now other than put out an APB. Although I was worried for myself, I'd rather he get a line on Aph. I decided to wait to tell him in person, after I heard what he'd learned.

"It's understandable. You're still in it, though."

"Yep," I answered neutrally. "Ben isn't."

"Really? Surprising. So, he's just hanging out around there?"

"Uh, no, he left."

"What?!" Frank hollered into the phone. I held mine away from my ear in case there was more. "He's supposed to be keeping an eye on you."

I heard him yell at Joe to pull over, then I heard street noise, the slamming of the car door and running feet. "Sit tight. I'll be right there."

"Frank, don't kill yourself. I'm in the middle of the game in a ballroom filled with thousands of people."

"Yeah? And that's the same kind of place someone tried to kill you the first time!"

Oops, forgot that little detail. "Okay, see you soon."

I pocketed my phone and headed back to my table. I'd missed another hand, in which one of the college big mouths had been eliminated. Darn, hated to miss that fun. It looked like Blackie had done the deed. I'd probably been dealt a Big Slick on a Royal Flop, with my luck. Oh well, no use crying over cards already in the shuffle box.

My next pocket was a spade-suited Baskin Robbins (Ace/three, get it?). Not something I would usually stick around for, but since I was in the late position and everybody folded but the blinds, I decided to check to see The Flop. Staying was worth it for a deuce of spades, 4 of spades and 7 of hearts. If it didn't get too expensive, I could hang around for The River. Blackie and the jockey checked. I noticed no twitch. Maybe I should go for it. I'd sure like to lower her

106

stack. A seven of spades fell on Fourth Street. Blackie raised half her pot, which was all in for me. Damn and double damn. The jockey folded. No twitch. What had she gotten, trips? Flush like me? Straight? I counted cards, and decided to go with my gut and push. "All in."

I saw her fingers go tense and suppressed a thrill. The *lack* of twitch meant she was bluffing!

Fifth Street brought a 5 of spades. Of course, overkill when I had no chips left to force her to fold. Despite the dealer's warning glare, I slow rolled my cards in the hopes she would show hers, but she just shook her head, and hid behind her Diors. Frank showed up at the rail and located me like I was wearing a homing beacon. Hmm. I checked my purse quickly. I wouldn't put it past him.

I maintained pretty well for the next three hands. The fourth was a killer, though. I lost about a quarter of what I'd earned from Blackie. One of the railbirds hollered, "That's not like you, Bee Cool. You'd better play better than that for a happy ending."

What I'd have usually taken as harmless jibe took on a whole new meaning under my current circumstances. I spun in my seat to look behind me and to the left, and saw

107

a clean-cut twentysomething man in a pressed plaid button-down shirt and starched khakis retreating through the crowd. Frank was making a beeline to him from the opposite side of the rail. The dealer called my attention back to the next hand. I peeked at the two cards on the felt in front of me: a beer hand (two/seven off-suit). I folded.

At the next break, Frank pulled me into the hallway where Carey stood with Joe aka the Marlboro Man. Joe was Frank's assistant in his mystery job and I desperately wanted to fall in love with him. He was drop-dead gorgeous in a rugged "I can carry you across the desert with one hand tied behind my back" kinda way, really nice, humble and, although I didn't know him well, seemed to come with a lot less baggage than Frank. Love's a bitch, though. My heart just couldn't do it. I sighed.

"Honey Bee," Frank whispered in my ear as we approached the pair. Patience strained his tone. "I wish you'd told me you sent Carey off after the bad guy."

"I didn't want to worry you."

"Wouldn't you rather me be worried than angry?"

"Hmm . . ." I paused to think about that. Frank's glare deepened the longer the seconds ticked by. "No, not really," I finally decided.

"Girlfrien'!" Carey grabbed me in a bear hug, putting an end to what was warming up to be a bit of a lover's spat.

I'd met Carey Beckwith on my first trip to Vegas. We had shared a brush with death and been fast friends ever since. We text messaged all the time, but I hadn't seen her in a long time. She was a star of Wall Street Women, one of the most popular transvestite shows on The Strip. Carey was a he but thought of herself as a she and, therefore, so did I.

"You look fabulous," I told her, waggling my eyebrows at her silver spandex minidress and some Christine LoPresti open-toed boots I'd die for. It was seriously wrong that a man could have legs better than mine, by the way.

"You know, girlfrien', I just get so sick of wearing that suit for the show that I go a little overboard when I'm out of costume."

"Not all your costume is a suit," Joe blurted out. We all stopped to look at him. He shrugged. "I've seen the show. It was good."

"Thanks, Big Boy." Carey winked at Joe, who nodded and shrugged at Frank. "Well, it was. You should see it."

Their interaction was cute, but I thought Frank was going to be sick. Have I mentioned, he is rather macho and very old-fashioned?

"What did you find out?" I asked, putting my pointer finger over Frank's lips as he opened his mouth to say something likely to be inappropriate.

"I was just telling Big Boy here that I followed the dude just south of the Aladdin where he met a woman and traded off an envelope for another. Then he went on to an office building on West Crandall, the only twenty story on the street. I got into the elevator with him —"

"Carey!" I interrupted. "That guy is scary. I didn't want you to get hurt."

"I didn't." She did a little pirouette. "Thing is, dressed like this I can act like a whore and get away with it." She giggled.

"He knew I'd been following him, obviously, and the best thing to do was to confirm who he thought I was, or he might have gotten suspicious."

Frank nodded, impressed despite himself. "You've got a knack for surveillance, Carey."

"Anyhow, I told him he looked like the best money on The Strip, so I was after him. That part definitely flattered him, but he said he was working and maybe we could get together later."

"What would you have done if he'd taken you up on it?"

"That's the best part, girlfrien', when they really think you are a whore and you turn out to be a man, you're off the hook immediately — in more ways than one!"

"Ingenious," Joe murmured.

"That's not the best part," Carey continued. "He got off on the fifteenth floor and gave me his card."

"What?" Frank blurted out.

"Wow," Joe said, looking suddenly insecure about his job. I couldn't suppress the smile at the image of Carey as Frank's right-hand wo-man.

"What are you smiling about?" Frank muttered in my ear as he snatched the card out of Carey's hand. It was fancy — gold with black lettering — but didn't say much. J. Nunez. A toll-free phone number. No address. No profession.

"Colleague of yours?" I asked snidely of Frank. His card was almost as cryptic, with only the word "security" to narrow things down for the ignorant.

"Very funny," he snapped. Frank seemed a little out of sorts. "Can I keep this?" he asked Carey.

"And what am I going to do with it? I

111

don't think this dude was my type."

"What are you going to do?" I asked.

Frank opened his wallet and slipped the card inside. "I'm not sure yet. I don't want to put him on the defensive so maybe Joe and I will head over to Crandall and see if we can find out more about where he was going. The only problem with that plan is . . . I don't want to leave you alone now that Ben took a powder." Frank told his phone to dial Ben.

The bell rang to bring us back to the tournament. "Don't worry about me."

Frank shook his head ruefully. "Sometimes I really wish I could do that."

Humph.

I could hear Ben's message from Frank's phone. "Ben Hot Cooley here, chill and I will get back to you." Frank ordered him to call asap. Ha, Ben only did by accident what he was told to do. Usually he did the opposite. Frank walked over to one of the casino security stiffs and apparently asked him to keep an eye on me, because the suit edged over our way and stared at me through his Ray-Bans.

"For your information, you have a stalker."

"I see that."

"Not him," Frank snorted. "He's our protection."

"I already have protection, remember? I am being followed by an undercover cop."

"That's no protection, even if they did follow through. He's probably following you to frame you anyway. I can trust the casino cop to try to prevent any crime from occurring in his property — that's part of his job description — minimize bad PR. So, FYI, he is watching you because you are receiving some threats from a stalker."

"What did you find out that makes you think the cops want to frame me?" I asked, suddenly dry mouthed as I inched my way toward the ballroom door. By my estimate, I had about a minute to make it for the next deal.

"I'll tell you later, when I take you to dinner."

"Oh?" I asked archly. "What if I have plans?"

"Change them. You're going with me." With that, he spun on the heel of his black lizard Luccheses pushed Joe in front of him, and they disappeared into the sea of people in the hallway.

Carey sighed. "That's one stud man."

"Hmm, the 'rough around the edges' is a little sharp this evening."

"Stop talking like that, you're turning me on and I don't have anyone to spend it on.

113

Unless I can convert that Joe. He's got some nice pecs."

Laughing, I shook my head and gave her a hug. "Thanks, Carey, for the detective work. If you ever want a part-time job, you might want to look Frank up."

"I think I'll just keep my amateur status. Less pressure. You call me, girlfrien', if you need any more help with your stalker. And I'm taking you to dinner on my night off."

"Deal." I waved and hurried back to the table.

The first hand was a killer — the other college smart-ass and the man sitting next to me were eliminated on the royal flush draw on the board that got two too many excited. I hung around with a straight draw, hit it and won. The rest of the cards weren't fabulous but they were decent enough to play for the next couple of hours. It wasn't long before I'd tripled my stack.

The dinner break came. Frank didn't. My phone vibrated with a text message. *Meet me at the Neptune Show at Poseidon's.*

A bit out of the way, but there was a good restaurant in the hotel that I wouldn't mind trying. A couple dozen people milled in the circle around where the animated statue of King Neptune rose from the rock formation and the show began. I looked around for

Frank, but only found Dragsnashark linger-ing in the shadows.

It suddenly, and obviously belatedly, oc-curred to me that Frank had not signed his text message to me and that in fact it may not have been Frank after all. Damn and double damn. Dragsnashark was approach-ing through the throng that was so en-tranced with the high-wattage spectacle before us that no one noticed I was sud-denly panicked. I wove through a family of five to make it to the front row of onlookers so I could skirt the stage and get out the other side. "Hey!" the red-faced mother yelled above King Neptune, who was now stomping his triton on the fake rock to a thundering boom out of the speakers. "You pushy bitch! My kids want to see and you're in their way. We were here first!" Whoops. She might be more dangerous than Drag-snashark. I threw her an apologetic grin but still headed for the stage. I felt someone grab my arm and I turned to plead with Mommy Dearest and saw the hand instead attached to the man who told me I wasn't going to have a happy ending.

Instinct told me this was not good.

"Help me!" I yelled to Mommy Dearest.

That Dragsnashark yelled "Get her" was *especially* not good.

"Right," she mouthed as she reached for her hairy husband in muscle shirt and pointed at me accusingly.

Seeing no other option, I jumped onstage. The collective gasp that arose from the crowd was that of awe unfortunately, not surprise, which meant they thought I was part of the show. Only in Vegas. King Neptune's daughter then arose from behind another fake rock and began waving her arms around and bellowing at her dad. I dove behind her at the exact wrong time and nearly got backhanded off the stage by her swinging arm that I was forced to grab. She waved me around in the air, back and forth. Her computer-generated voice was screaming like a banshee and I was worried this might go on for longer than I could hang on. Not for the first time in Vegas I lamented the fact that I didn't frequent the gym. Weird, I know, but welcome to my life. The audience started clapping wildly. I was an accidental hit; I just hoped I lived through it. I saw Dragsnashark waiting with a creepy anticipation for me to fly off Despina's right arm. My good friend the king stamped his triton with a bang and put an end to her tantrum. Her arm whipped down to her side, flinging me onto the plastic that was harder than it looked.

The three automated figures continued their disagreement, including some distracting special effects that allowed me time to crawl around the stage and see it was circular. Dragsnashark's friend was following me and I had no avenue for escape. I could jump off now, break a bone or two and hope the audience would stop my stalkers from abducting me. Since the collective group thought I, in my magenta walking shorts and silver stilettos, was part of a legendary show, I didn't put much stock in that option. Then I remembered how the motorized beings arrived on the scene — they arose from holes in the fake scenery. Hmm. Suddenly, Despina screamed and dissolved in a mass of steam into the hole, way too quickly for me to reach her even if I had considered sustaining a whole body sauna to get free. I was closest to the king at this point, so edged over and grabbed him just as a bolt of fire came out of his triton and felt like it was singeing every hair on my body. The audience gasped and stepped back. Man, it was hot. I almost gave up and went for the broken-bone option but just then I felt the stage move. The king and I sank into the hole under the stage, where it was dark, and blessedly cool.

My phone rang. "Hello?" I whispered. "Where the hell are you, Honey Bee?"

EIGHT

Getting out from under the stage at Poseidon's might have been a bit tricky if Frank hadn't shown up. Apparently it was controlled by a remote computer. Humans only ventured under the stage for routine maintenance, conducted by my savior — Eminem's mini-me.

"Wow, like, people were talking about how totally rad the Neptune show was there in the casino and we were like, what? It's totally lame, except for the fire at the end that feels like it's burning your face it's so hot."

"Hmm, try being in Neptune's lap," I muttered.

"Anyhow, then somebody asked one of the dealers how they came up with the idea to put a real person with the, like, fake figures and then, whoa, we were totally, like, blown. I'm sure we would've come to check on the place in a couple of days to see what everybody was talking about."

"Great, how comforting," I said.

Frank, who'd come with Junior Pranksta to set me free, wasn't talking. Not a good sign.

Fortunately, Frank had somehow fixed it with the casino so I wasn't in big trouble for messing with their stuff. He passed the kid a fifty-dollar bill. Damn. I hated owing anyone, especially Frank when he was mad at me.

We paused in the walkway. Frank grabbed a tendril of hair off my cheek and examined it. "Hmm. You might want to consider getting a trim."

"Why?" I stepped just out of his reach.

Frank leaned in to examine my face. "And maybe some fake eyelashes."

"What?" I trotted over to the Prada store, ducked in and looked in the first mirror I encountered. Ack. It hadn't just felt like I was getting singed. I had been! Super.

"The good news is, though, you won't have to pluck your eyebrows for a while."

I glared at him. "It's not *that* bad." He raised his eyebrows. "Is it?" I demanded, looking back at the mirror and leaning in for a closer inspection.

Putting his arm around my shoulders, he led us out of the store. "What's bad is your behavior. Why did you ditch me at the tournament and decide to come ride on King Neptune's lap for fun? You knew I was coming to get you for dinner."

I explained about the text message and the misunderstanding, about seeing Dragsnashark and his colleague in the audience. Frank's mouth narrowed to a thin line. "Bee, this is serious. We don't know what these guys want. We don't know what they'll do. We have to be more careful. Maybe I should get you out of Vegas right now."

"Frank, I can't! What about Affie?"

"All you can do might not make a difference for Affie."

My imagination spelled out what that meant in the silence. I swallowed hard. "Well, I can't live with myself if I don't at least try. I refuse to run away and hide."

Frank shook his head. "Let's come up with a code word no one else can figure out, but if it's not used in a message, it isn't me, it isn't you. Okay?"

I nodded.

"Rediwhip," he said.

"Why that?"

"Remember that first long weekend we shared after the Big Kahuna . . ."

Aw. Maybe the man was a romantic after all. Either that or he was a sex fiend.

Frank glanced at his Rolex, grabbed my elbow and led me down the Forum. "We barely have time to grab a bite."

Las Vegas, once the prince of cheap all-you-can-eat buffets (keep them full, keep their wallets full for the casinos) now boasts some of the finest restaurants with the most sought-after chefs in the world. In fact, I could easily eat my way across The Strip without stopping. The last trip I gained five pounds even *with* all the running from bad guys I'd had to do. Odds were, grabbing a bite here would be a culinary sensation.

I wasn't wrong. Frank led me to Spago. I'd never been to Wolfgang Puck's famous eatery but heard it was fabulous. It sat right on the Forum promenade, great for people watching.

"I wanted to take you to a quiet dinner, but I think we'd better keep our eyes open for Dragsnashark and his friend. Just in case."

It was probably a good thing Spago's was a crowded, electric atmosphere instead of a candlelit, romantic one, because over a bottle of Chianti, his legendary meat loaf and my seafood fettucine, Frank insisted on lecturing me on changing my life.

"Honey Bee," Frank began. "I just want you to consider a new hobby. Trouble follows you when you hold cards."

"Does that include you?"

"What?"

"I met you because of Texas Hold 'Em."

Frowning, Frank shook his head. "You know that's not what I meant."

"Life is trouble, Frank. If I weren't having it playing poker, I'd be having it somewhere else."

"Not necessarily."

"Come on."

"What was your hobby before you started playing Hold 'Em?"

I thought for a moment. "My job and my fiancé."

Frank raised his eyebrows.

"I didn't realize it at the time but I did the laundry list of things Toby asked me to do. I kept myself up the way Toby wanted me to, and all that took a lot of time. Beauty maintenance, what a drain. There was no time for anything else. I don't want that hobby again. Ever."

"Should I be insulted?"

"Are you my fiancé?"

"No." Frank shook his head to punctuate his answer.

"Well, then, I guess you shouldn't be insulted." I tried not to look at the emotions playing through his dark eyes. I'd never be able to figure them out and even when I thought I had, I'd be wrong. There were too many of his ghosts I knew nothing about. "Look, Frank, I have a hard time 'playing' for the sake of fun. I always have. Everything I've done for 'fun,' I've turned into work. When I was in Brownies, I pressured myself to get all the badges so I was working so hard, none of it was fun. When I was in a sorority in college, I had to organize *this* fundraiser and *that* membership drive. When I joined a country club for a while, I had to be number one golfer every week or I was unhappy."

"And how is Hold 'Em different? You are ranked as a pro. You have a website. A fan club. It's a second job to you."

"Hey, now, you can't blame me for the website. You sicced Ingrid on me and that was her idea. And, if you will notice, I delegated all the work away except the little intro I write every month and the e-mails I answer."

He shrugged, conceding the point. I continued, "Despite all that you mentioned, I don't think about working at playing poker — except when I am forced to play to save my goddaughter's life. I just play and have fun. Probably because I think luck plays such an incredible role that hard work and talent don't matter all that much. I can relax when I sit down at the table and try to read the players, hope for some decent cards, get a charge when I win, chalk it up to entertainment when I lose."

"I just don't like the way *I* feel when you're in danger," Frank finally admitted, obviously grudgingly.

A sudden flash of intuition struck me with no warning. Perhaps my psyche had finally read what lurked in a shadow behind those sexy dark eyes. "Frank, did something happen to your ex-wife?"

The color drained from his face for only an instant. He slipped his aviators down over his eyes and stood abruptly, throwing some bills on the table. "We have to go, to get you back to the tournament in time if you are so dead set on playing."

His body was wracked with tension, although he still put his fingertips on the small of my back as was his protective habit. Even through them I could feel anger, hurt and defensiveness.

And guilt.

The picket line was in full force as we arrived back at the Fortune. Phineas Paul was at the other end preaching to a group of onlookers about the evils of gambling, most especially that of poker. "It is as seductive as sex. Texas Hold 'Em requires no skill, no brains and is driven by greed and temptation. If you want to break every commandment our Lord God has sent down, then sit down at a felt table."

"Amen!" chorused the picket line, rather desultorily, I thought.

"Do you notice something about the picketers?" I asked.

Frank looked them over carefully as he held the door for me to enter. I was immediately flanked by a phalanx of security. Frank elbowed his way back next to me and spoke in my ear. "They are predominantly teenage white girls."

"Isn't that weird?" I asked. "How many teenagers do you know are born-again Christians? Maybe young, idealistic twenty-somethings, but not many teens. It's against their hormonal religion."

"Every now and then I'm struck with the fact that you would be a good investigator, and then you pull a stunt like the King Neptune thing and I know I'm wrong."

Ever the master of the backhanded compliment, Frank left me feeling simultaneously deflated and uplifted. Go figure.

The chimes rang us back to the tables. Frank whipped out his trusty notepad and jotted down my description of Drag-snashark's possible partner. "Maybe I can get a look at the security tape," he mused. That's how he'd kept me out of jail after the Poseidon's incident. He knew someone on the inside. Sometimes Frank's life was so labyrinthine it gave me a headache, and I was sure I only knew a tenth of it, if that.

He brushed a kiss on my cheek. I resisted the urge to move my mouth into it. "Remember our code. I'll contact you or you contact me if they close the tournament down sooner than expected. The security here is watching you, but only when you are near the Main Event action, understand?" I nodded as he continued, "So you make sure you stay here until I get back or I send Joe or Ben or Ingrid to take you back to the room. Under no circumstances do you leave alone — got it?"

I smiled and waved as I made my way to my table, trying to ignore his dark gaze boring into me. Another player from a short table was moved to ours. Without introducing himself, the short, dark man who reminded me a bit of Joe Pesci shook my hand with a quick smile. He paused halfway into his seat, his eyes hung on something on the felt in front of me.

"Excuse me, ma'am, but where did you

get that marker?" he asked with a studied calmness as he eased into the chair.

I fingered the worn wooden piece Frank had given me as a lucky charm before my first tournament. Made of rare Hawaiian koa wood, it had some faded marks on it that neither I, nor anyone I asked, could discern. Frank wouldn't tell me the story behind it. Maybe this guy had stayed at the same casino and remembered what it had looked like when new. Maybe it had been won in a underground tournament in some shady bar in Casablanca. Believe me, I'd spun those stories and more.

I tried to contain my excitement when I answered: "Why do you ask?"

"Because the man I lost that marker to ten years ago is the coldest killing son of a bitch our department has ever known."

NINE

"How do you know it's the same marker?" I asked when I finally found my voice. Many questions had rolled through my mind along with my version of the answers, including deciding that the guy's department was with the SPCA — after all, Frank did have a hunting license. I'd found it when I pilfered his wallet one early morning. But, if it weren't the same marker, then all the questions and answers didn't matter because we weren't talking about the same guy, right?

The dealer had demanded we post blinds so conversation was suspended for the bets. With my mind reeling, I couldn't remember now what my pocket cards were so I just checked, while waiting for my neighbor's response. It didn't come immediately. He seemed terribly intent on the hand. Come on, guy, my boyfriend might be an infamous murderer. Who cared about poker at a time like this? I cleared my throat. He glared and slow played a little longer, until finally the dealer nudged him into a bet.

When two Aces fell on The Flop I remembered what was facedown in front of me — bullets. I had four of a kind and I couldn't even get excited about it. Normally, I would stay cool, draw everybody in to staying until The River, but I so wanted the hand to be over that after a check-raise, I went all in. A chorus of groans went up around the table. Blackie shook her head, her first show of any sort of normal communication, and I was almost distracted out of my intensity toward Marker Man. I don't know what skin it was off her nose, anyway. After all, I'd saved her several bets' worth of chips by being stupidly impatient. The whole table folded to me.

As I quickly raked the chips toward me, I accidentally flipped over a card. Two of diamonds? Huh? The table howled. "She bluffed us!"

I guess I did. Had I been so upset by Marker Man that I'd mistaken what was in my pocket? Sheesh. Good thing I hadn't known or my blood pressure would've been dangerously high. I really don't bluff, especially not in the first day of a tournament.

"Of course it's the same marker," my

neighbor answered in an undertone as one of the WSOP officials came to see what the ruckus was about. She leaned down to whisper in the dealer's ear as Marker Man continued, "Look on the other side and find the tiny Y-shaped crack. It's filled with crimson paint."

I found it. Damn.

"I suppose you topped the man in a game to get it," he said. "That's the only way he'd give it up, unless of course, you killed him. And if you did, I won't tell."

I suppressed a shiver at his matter-of-fact tone. Still, I knew he had to be mistaken. Markers were a dime a dozen, thousands out there alike. Surely all old markers like this one wore in a similar pattern.

"So are you going to tell me his name?" I asked finally, three hands later, after I'd lost nearly two thousand in chips in my distraction.

"You tell me where you got it."

I shook my head. "No."

"He favors white T-shirts, Levi's and Luccheses."

The liquor made me swallow a gasp as I shrugged coolly. "That could be half the cowboys where I come from."

"You from L.A.?"

Uh-oh.

"Guess it's the same guy." My Italian seat-mate nodded knowingly. "You sure got talkative eyes."

Averting the offenders, I dropped my Gargoyles back over them and spent the rest of the next hour just playing my hands, slowly regaining what I'd lost on the table, if not in my heart.

"Can I buy you a drink?" I asked my seat-mate when the chimes indicated our next break.

As we meandered our way to the nearest bar in the Fortune, I found out his name was Rudy Serrano. He didn't drink anything but Mountain Dew by the truckload, he said, when he was playing cards. He'd lost two hundred thousand dollars, his entire life savings, one night two years ago in a cash game in a dark corner of San Luis Obispo drinking ouzo. From then on, he didn't swear off alcohol, just alcohol when he was playing Texas Hold 'Em, which was his great white hope for earning back a retirement fund.

"What do you do for a living?"

"I'm retired from the Los Angeles Police Department, detective, first grade, but have to work as a rent-a-cop for an apartment complex to supplement my pension until I win enough playing poker."

I wanted to tell him not to give up the day job but concentrated on information instead of self help. "You said some pretty strong things about Frank. I want to know the story."

"I guess you didn't beat Gilbert at a game of poker to get that marker, then, huh? And I'd say from the look on your face when you say his name, you didn't off him to get it either."

"No. I'm, uh, a friend of his. He taught me how to play."

"You were taught by one of the best, I have to say that. To play Hold 'Em, that is."

I ignored his implication, and he finally continued when I didn't elaborate on our relationship. "I'd say Gilbert was one of the most successful Texas Hold 'Em cash players there ever was — before the game was a household name, that is."

"Why did he quit?"

He shrugged. "He quit playing when he quit his marriage and started drinking. Who knows why. Maybe he was just turning his back on everything in his life except the job. Most men have to have a job to breathe. He's no exception."

"Turned his back. Even on his kids?"

"No." He took a swallow of his Mountain

Dew. "He sees them on a regular basis."

"His wife, he sees her too?"

"No. Not at all, except by accident."

That would be tough. See young kids, not wife. Hmm. Weird. How did he manage that? Maybe they were transferred by nanny. And how did this guy know so much? I sucked in a deep breath as my companion watched a couple arguing in the corner of the bar. I knew I had to be careful. This guy was smart and just telling me as much as he wanted to. His motivation concerned me, but not as much as my desire to know answers to all my questions. I had to ask them in order of importance before he decided to clam up.

"So, who did he kill?"

"Sheesh. You finally got around to asking what a man would ask first. Gilbert was in the middle of an international investigation when his wife was tortured and almost killed on orders from the principal in the case. It was supposed to be a warning to Frank to back off. It was a death sentence for themselves instead. Ronald Trucek and two of his associates were tortured and killed not twelve hours later. An eye for an eye. Frank works for — or used to work for — a government law enforcement organiza-tion. I can't tell you if it's the CIA, or something deeper, something none of us has ever heard of. The murder was personal, I can promise you that, but whoever signed his paychecks made sure he got a free ride. We were told to look the other way. It pissed me off, because it plays hell with your stats, wrecks promotion possibilities. I got a helluva lot of grief from the media for not solving the case. I never really got my mojo back. My boss told me to lie, make up a story about the associates turning on Trucek and him killing them before he died himself. I couldn't do it. Couldn't ask the detectives working for me to do that. Instead, we still have an open case in the LAPD books, one of the most notorious killings in our history is unsolved."

"If the incidents were similar, nobody put two and two together?"

"The details of Monica Gilbert's attack were kept under wraps. The same with the Trucek murders. Most of what you think you know about some cases actually comes out at trial. Neither of these went there. So you, the public, will end up knowing little."

I almost didn't want to ask, but knew I had to. "What happened to Monica?"

"She was hospitalized for a month, touch and go for nearly three weeks, in rehab six months. Frank was a stay-at-home dad during that time — the kids being only two and five. It was easier than being home after she returned, though. From what I hear, she never blamed him, but he blamed himself every time he saw her limp, struggle to stand, every time her eyes filled with tears of frustration when she couldn't lift one of the kids up when they begged her, 'Mommy, carry me.' Gilbert couldn't see her every day and live with his own guilt."

This was worse than my wildest imaginings. "He left her because she was crippled?"

He shook his head. "He left because he was emotionally crippled. He couldn't see her and not blame himself 24/7 that his job had almost killed her and left her almost worse than that for the rest of her life."

I'd become accustomed to the image of a model-beautiful woman who wasted her days shopping Rodeo Drive, playing tennis at a Hollywood country club and toting mini-Frank and mini-her to overdone birthday parties where every child got a Chihuahua á la *Legally Blonde* as a party favor. Of course ex–Mrs. Gilbert was gorgeous but cold, a decent mother (because Frank let her have the kids), but never a decent wife. Perhaps she cheated on him in my mind once or twice. Perhaps she'd remarried the plastic surgeon who'd done her fifth needless cosmetic surgery in as many years. Perhaps she'd been a heartless workaholic who never had time for him.

But in my mind, she'd never been a good-hearted woman, crippled by a maniac set upon her by Frank himself, whom he'd loved, who loved him. Who'd been a hapless martyr. Never.

"You're retired now." I interrupted the negative direction my imagination was taking me. "Why don't you turn Frank in and solve the case?"

"Frank and I were friends once. Law enforcement compadres of a sort. He doesn't have much of a life left, but I can't take away what little is left — even if I can't ever look him in the eye again after seeing what he did to another human being."

I shivered at the stark reality in his voice. I couldn't ask the details of the murders. My mind's eye was doing more than his words could anyway. Instead, I asked something that would prove infinitely more painful.

"Do you think he still loves her — Monica?"

Rudy Serrano paused thoughtfully — considering more my feelings than the truth, I was certain. "Yes. Yes, I'm sure he does love Monica, in his own way."

"And she loves him?"

"Yes, I've talked to Monica. There's no doubt about that."

Great. I was in love with a vicious killer who still loved his wife.

Could it get any worse?

I knew better than to ask that question.

"Any idea where Gilbert is right now?" Serrano asked.

There were lots of answers to that one, but I decided that the most precise would be the safest. "No." I shook my head, took a sip of pinot grigio and shook my head again. "I sure don't."

TEN

Because Ben, morose and brooding, had arrived at the Main Event to escort me back to the Mellagio, I'd missed the opportunity to see Frank's reaction to his supposed old friend Rudy Serrano. I cursed fate or perhaps Frank's sixth sense that seemed to alert him to potential dangers. I'd needed that reaction to know how to proceed — whether to interrogate him, avoid him or to continue to trust him until I found out more. I loved him, but more importantly right now, I felt like I knew who he was, under his skin. Or I thought I had. The man in Frank's skin might well have killed someone to avenge a loved one, but wouldn't have tortured him on top of it. The man in Frank's skin wouldn't have left his crippled wife to raise two babies on her own.

Maybe who Frank was now wasn't who he used to be. And if that was true, how did

I feel about that?

My head was beginning to hurt with my self psychoanalysis. "What's your problem?" I snapped at Ben. Maybe I could analyze him instead. "Pouting because you're not going to win the Main Event this year?"

He slid me a slitty-eyed look. "No."

A pair of women walking past us paused in midstep to stare at Ben. One grabbed the other's arm and stage-whispered, "Do you really think it's Colin Farrell? I think he plays poker. No, he looks more like Ben Affleck. He played one time in a cash game with my best friend's sister's brother's niece's uncle's mother."

It was Ben's usual invitation to flirt with a wink and a grin. He didn't even look their way.

"How'd you do that anyway?" I continued to taunt him, hoping for anything, even an explosion. "It's hard to bust out of a tournament that early, especially one with ten thousand people playing."

With a grunt, Ben strode on ahead. His phone sang a strain from "Lord of the Thighs" by Aerosmith. I never had the stomach to ask him where he found that as a ring tone but now it reminded me Ben was still Ben. He hadn't yet changed his ring tone to the theme song of *The Wonder*

Years, so maybe I didn't have to worry. He answered, striding so fast he was almost running to keep me from hearing him. Stilettos or no, I still caught up with him. Ha! He ducked into a men's room. Damn, I was tempted. Sorely tempted . . .

"Excuse me, Bee Cool," a young female voice asked as a finger tapped me on the shoulder.

"Yes?" Ingrained politeness answered. I turned around, even as I realized I probably should be jumping away in case it was another Dragsnashark associate in drag. Before me stood two teenage girls, dressed in jeans and logo tees, one of them reminding me so much of Aphrodite that my heart ached.

"Can we have your autograph?" They shoved WSOP programs forward. They were both stuffed with some extra paper behind the page with my photo and I moved to slide it out of the way. One of the girls stopped me, tapping on my photo. "Sign here."

I did, a bit of an awkward signature because of the bulkiness underneath, but oh well. "We are big fans of yours, Bee Cool. It's awesome the way you dress so model, act so hot, play so cool and beat all those stuck-up ugly old pros who think they're so smart.

"We want to be like you one day. Like, wear Marc Jacobs and Derek Lam and Manolos and Choos, come to Vegas and play poker all day."

"Is that right? Let me tell you, first you need to have a real job too, you know. And go to college. I couldn't have money to put on the table if I didn't work as an ad executive."

"That's not true," the petite blonde said. "You won half a million dollars last year. The Internet said so."

"Don't believe everything you read, especially on the Internet." I warned. "Playing poker is entertainment, so when you're old enough you can set aside what you want to spend on that and only spend that much. No borrowing to win money, understand?"

Neither girl looked convinced. "Speaking of money," the brunette put in. "We caught the bus here from Oregon just to see you, our idol, but now we don't have enough to go home."

I sighed. I hated this. I didn't want to encourage this kind of behavior, but if Affie were somewhere now needing bus money home I hoped some kind soul would give it to her. I reached into my purse, found my wallet and extracted two hundred-dollar bills.

I dangled the money out to them but held fast as I ordered, "Now, your parents are missing you, I'm sure. Go straight to the bus station and —"

"So you see, my good people," a voice behind me boomed. "How your children are being corrupted by the evil poker players of the world. This gambling game, this Texas Hold 'Em, it is poison, and its players are akin to the devil. Plying our youth with money, money, money, addicting them to the game so young. It is to be scorned. It is to be STOPPED!"

The girls snatched the cash out of my hand and ran. I spun around to see Phineas Paul with a gawking bunch of tourists who were pointing at me and shaking their heads. Then I noticed the cameraman and reporter. I turned and looked at where the girls had disappeared, narrowing my eyes in thought. It couldn't have been staged, could it? They really had seemed inordinately thrilled with my fashion sense.

Ben emerged from the restroom just then, took in the scene in a split second, grabbed my arm and hauled me in the opposite direction and around the corner. "Wait. Wait! Miss Cooley. We'd like a comment," the reporter yelled.

"Do you think Paul's been following me around waiting for me to do something to play into his twisted, sick hand?"

Ben's mouth twisted into a tight grin, making him look a little more like himself than he had since last night. "Even you have to admit, Bee Bee, it wouldn't have been a bad bet. Considering all the messes you get yourself into on a regular basis."

We could hear feet running behind us. Ben dove into the next open doorway and we found ourselves in the Harley Davidson shop. Not pausing, he wound us through the clothes racks and shoved me headfirst into a dressing room. He followed and slammed the door.

"How long do you think this is going to take?" I asked after a minute.

Ben opened his mouth but before he could speak a knock at the door silenced him. "Hey! Hey! We don't allow that kind of thing in here," a heavily accented Eastern European female voice warned. I knew from my last visit to Vegas that those with a bossy foreign accent probably were in employ at the hotel or casino.

"What kind of thing is banned?" Ben asked. "Talking?"

"*Nein,*" she barked. "I mean, no. Hokay, if

you try on, then you can stay in there. Hokay?"

"Hokay," Ben answered. "Why don't you pass us something to try on, then, sugar?"

I could feel the poor woman melting on the other side of the louvered door. Ben's appeal surpassed his looks. It was truly disgusting.

A half second later a trio of shirts, a black leather skirt with lots of chain and a pair of black leather pants wafted over the top of the dressing-room door. Ben grabbed them, allowing, I noticed, his fingertips to brush Miss Nein's hand. She sighed. I coughed to hide my gag. Ben looked over the selections. The pants were his, the skirt was mine, two were men's shirts, the other was a women's shirt that he passed to me. It was a black Harley-emblazoned T-shirt that looked like it ended at a cap sleeve but really continued with a see-through fabric that was dyed to look like skin tattooed all the way to the wrist. Okay!

Ben surveyed my shirt, putting his fingers behind the tattoo fabric. "This is cool. You ought to try it on."

"Sure," I muttered. "It's just my style. High fashion meets low rider."

"It's exactly *not* your style, which is exactly the point." Ben nodded. "Look, Bee Bee, between the bad guys after you and that scary preacher, I was just thinking you could use a disguise. If this works, it might be it."

"I'll look like an Annie Duke wannabe," I argued.

"As long as you don't look like Bee Cool." Ben shrugged.

Just to shut him up, I turned my back and doffed my button-down, and squeezed myself into the skin-tight shirt. The transparent sleeves went down past my wrists in an impressive faux effect. Ben gasped and spun me around to face him.

"This is unbelievable, Bee Bee," he exclaimed. "They look real! Even from this close up."

"Hokay, you two," the store clerk whispered through the louvers, "if you don't take care of *things* not so loud, I got to call security."

Ben and I looked at each other in question.

I opened the door and stepped out. A small crowd had gathered outside the dressing room and, since I didn't notice Reverend Paul and his impromptu congregation, I just assumed the line meant there was a big midnight demand for Harley wear. That is, until one man nudged his buddy, pointed at my chest and said, "Yeah, I'd say those look pretty real even close up too! I win the bet." He held out his palm to his friend, who fished for his wallet as he peered at my breasts.

"Listen, dude," I sneered in an attempt to match my tattooed persona, "he was talking about the tattoos!"

"Sure, and what were you all doing in there, comparing artwork?" Yuk yuk yuk.

"He's my brother," I answered in full affront mode.

"You like it a little kinky? We could go for that," his companion chortled.

I spun around to see why my loser brother wasn't helping me, and saw him with a leather hat, the leather pants and the leather skirt. Abandoning my impromptu fan club, I hissed in his ear, "What are you doing?"

He reached into my purse and pulled out my wallet, handing over my credit card with a skilled aplomb. "We are buying your disguise."

"Oh." I arched an eyebrow. "I see I will be wearing men's size 32 leather pants also?"

"Those are my early birthday present," Ben said, winking at the store clerk whose name tag read "Helga." She wiggled and giggled.

Ben grabbed the hat with one hand and gathered my hair in the other, stuffing the

147

tendrils under the hat. I'm sure I looked just terrific. "Don't I need some black lipstick to go with this?" I asked.

"Actually, midnight blue is in right now," Helga told Ben, who reached for a tube off the display at the register.

I grabbed his forearm in a death grip. "Don't you dare!"

"Come on, Bee Bee, gotta be authentic if you are going biker chick." He clamped a metal chain-link bracelet that looked like an instrument of torture on my wrist. Horrified, I dropped his arm and he snatched up the lipstick and passed it to Helga, his very willing partner in crime. Nearly four hundred dollars later (he, armed now with Helga's phone number), we walked out of the Harley shop and down the corridor toward the parking garage. He'd made me change into the skirt. I held my ground on the lipstick and refused Helga's suggestion that I get some knee-high boots.

"I think it would've been cheaper to buy a real tattoo," I complained.

"Do you want one?" Ben asked, proud owner of a giraffe tattoo on his abdomen. A giraffe that incidentally tucked its head just inside the waistband of Ben's swim trunks. Sick. Don't ask me where his head ended up when Ben had his undies on. I don't want to know.

"No!" I said

"It might be good for your investigation." Ben pointed out. "After all, we could ask the tattoo artist about your bad guy's tattoo — what it means, who might have drawn it on him."

Evil. My brother was completely evil. Of course I was tempted to investigate. "Why don't you get another one?" I asked.

"Bee Bee, I already have three."

"Three? Where are the other two?"

Ben raised his eyebrows. "You wanna see?"

"No!" I blurted so loud that several groups of people in the parking garage turned around.

"Okay. Be that way."

We walked in silence for a while, me holding out as long as I could to ask the next question. "What are they, then?"

"What do you mean?"

"What kind of tattoos are they — in case I need to identify your body."

"That's uplifting, Bee Bee."

"Well, it's happened before," I reminded him.

"Okay, okay. They are a pair of lips with an eye in the middle and a tree frog."

I knew I shouldn't ask the next question. "Where?"

"Well, the tree frog is climbing up —"

I was saved by Aerosmith singing from Ben's phone. "Hello? Hi, Frank. We are going to get Bee Bee a tattoo."

I punched his shoulder. Part of me was relieved to see Ben seemed more himself since we'd done the Harley stop — the part of me that wasn't pissed off about me being transformed into a biker chick. I wondered what my police shadow thought of this.

"I'll tell her," Ben promised as he handed over the phone.

"Frank wants you to get a butterfly on your —"

I snatched the phone out of his hands. "Where are you? Any leads on Affie?"

"Joe and I are chasing down information on the tenants in the building where Carey last saw your stalker. I'll see you back at the hotel in a couple of hours."

"I ran into one of your old friends."

I could hear Joe in the background calling Frank's attention away. "Really? I want to hear all about it when I see you. Have fun getting your tattoo."

Typical man, so titillated by the image of me getting a tattoo in the mystery place he wanted it that it never occurred to him that we were going to be doing investigative work. Because if it had, Frank would've never let me go.

I handed the phone back to my brother and offered him my arm. "Lead on to the best tattoo parlor in Vegas!" There was no doubt that Ben would know exactly where that was.

ELEVEN

After spending my whole life imagining a tattoo parlor as a dark, dirty hole-in-the-wall, the Tattoo Palace was a revelation. Cleaner, more welcoming and more well-appointed than most spas I'd frequented, it was also the size of a department store. And, it was packed.

The clientele might be generally a little rougher than the spa, but not entirely. A fiftyish country-club wife walked by wearing Burberry and carrying Prada, and flashed the Chanel logo newly tattooed on her upper thigh. I almost swallowed my tongue.

"I want to be classy even with nothing on," she slurred, winking at Ben.

"I wonder what she's going to think about that once she sobers up and gets home to Cleveland?" Ben said in aside to me as he returned her wink.

I suppose there would be no better place to have a tattoo business than Vegas —

where people were more spontaneous due to the gambling windfalls, the flowing liquor and the sexual aura surrounding the city. Face it, whether you like them or not, want one or don't, tattoos are sexy.

While we awaited our turn, Ben wandered away and I saw him a few minutes later talking intensely on the phone. When he returned, he was frowning again. While it was gratifying to see that he was working on putting some character lines on that perfect face of his — it worried me.

"Who were you talking to?"

"You know, Bee Bee, some things are none of your business," he snapped.

Dr. Jekyll was back. But before I could delve deeper into his emotional state, a woman who was tattooed from fingertip to toenail appeared in a flimsy dress. We could see straight through it, although her voluptuous body was so artfully covered with ink that you couldn't tell where her private parts began and ended in the mass of serpents and flowers and leaves. I think it was a scene from the Garden of Eden. Wow.

I must have been staring with my mouth wide open. Ben was panting, I think. She let us look, paid no doubt more for her advertising abilities than her secretarial ones. After a few moments, she snapped her fingers in Ben's face. "Roll your tongue back in." She jabbed me in the shoulder with her index finger. "Get a move on, Joaquin is ready."

She led us down a hallway decorated with photo after photo of tattooed skin. Not just a catalog, this was real photographic art of subjects in poses that juxtaposed and confused, enlightened and engrossed the audience. Woman, man, human or animal, sometimes combinations of all of the above — it was often impossible to tell. I paused at one and studied it. "This is a litter of piglets."

I swallowed. Tattooing seriously smarted from what I understood. Poor little porkers. "Who would do that?"

A young Native American man poked his head out of the next private suite.

"Someone with vision. Cool, huh?"

Our escort left us without an introduction, and we were ushered into the suite. Full body, Joaquin was a human art form. He wore his hennaed hair in a modified Mohawk, with a ponytail cascading down his back. His skin told the story of warriors through history — not only various American Indians but Viking, samurai and even an Amazon. I strained to see the images stretched from his shoulder to his back.

154

"They made a helluva ear-shattering noise when we took the needle to them, though," he said, breaking into my fascinated examination.

"Who?" I asked, imagining the samurai brandishing the sword, mouth gaping in a scream, on his left pectoral.

"The piglets."

"Oh," I answered, nonplussed.

"So," Joaquin asked. "Who's becoming art today — the tattoo virgin, or you? Nice work on your tricep by the way."

Ben smiled, rolling up the sleeve of his golf shirt to expose his new tree frog (that was *not* where I'd guessed it would be). "Virgin." He chuckled in my direction. "I guess Bee's Harley shirt didn't fake you out, huh?"

Joaquin rolled his eyes. "It's like comparing a comic book to a Jackson Pollock."

Okay. "Ready for another Pollock?" I looked at Ben but he waved his palms at us.

"No more for me. Three is my lucky number."

No problem, I'd planned for this. If Ben had gone for it, I was going to interrogate Joaquin about Dragsnashark while he drew a picture in permanent ink on my brother. If Ben chickened out on me, then I was going to fake like I was going to get the needle, but slide my questions in before it made a mark.

"I guess I'm up then."

Joaquin's black eyes lit up with an excitement that was a bit disturbing. "Awesome. That alabaster skin, so smooth and perfect, will be a challenge. Heady." He started nodding to himself. I think he had a thing for tattoo virgins. I was close to losing my nerve.

"What do you want?" Joaquin asked. "And where?"

What did I care, I wasn't really going to do it. I shrugged and waved a hand in cavalier fashion. "What do you think?"

Ben smiled and leaned down to whisper in Joaquin's ear. He nodded. "We can do that."

"It's what her boyfriend wants," Ben elaborated.

Uh-oh, but I thought Joaquin would be less on guard for the interrogation if I played up the dumb bimbo routine. "What Frank wants, he gets." I giggled.

Ben raised his eyebrows, then narrowed his eyes, suspicious. I must have gone a little overboard. "That's not like you, Bee Bee."

"Love does funny things to a person," I responded glibly.

Ben looked pensive for a moment, shocking in and of itself, then walked to the door.

"I'll leave you to it then. Let me know when you're ready to head back to loverboy."

I held my breath, waiting for the word on where the tattoo was supposed to go and hoping that I wasn't going to have to disrobe too seriously for the tattoo artist. If I was dropping my pants, I might have to speed up the questioning.

"Lie down on the futon," Joaquin instructed as he moved to the table and began to examine a table full of tools, one of which looked extremely sharp. I swallowed hard as I stretched out on the pad.

"Now, turn over," he instructed.

Ack. I took my time arranging myself on the table, unable to swallow around the fear lodged in my throat. This was going way, way too fast.

I heard the door open and a woman old enough to get a double senior citizen discount at the movies entered, nodding to me. What was someone's grandmother doing at a tattoo parlor? "Milne is here to do the prep work, then I will draw your art."

Milne gently pushed up my Harley shirt and began swabbing the small of my back with a soothing cool liquid. Humph. This wasn't just Ben's bright idea, after all. Frank really had told him what his favorite place on my body was. It only made me more nervous. Yet, I had to get my mind back in gear. I hadn't expected much interrogation time and I'd better make the most of it.

"So Joaquin," I said, as he inspected his tools with a disconcertingly loving touch. "I hear most tattoos carry a hidden meaning. Is that really true?"

No eye rolling allowed. Remember, I'm supposed to be playing bimbo.

"Sure it is. There are volumes written and more legends told than we have time for today."

Joaquin's voice sounded like he'd been smoking some of the incense burning in a pot in the corner of the room. He pulled out a pad and started sketching with a charcoal pencil.

"Wow," I breathed. "I wish we had all night to talk about it."

"We do, baby, you got a lot of skin just waiting for my instrument."

Ook. I stifled my gag in a cough. Milne patted my back. "Do you want an arnica smoothie to soothe your throat, dear?"

"No, thanks. I'm going to be okay." I sucked in a breath to fortify myself to address Joaquin again. "What does a dragon/snake/shark creature mean?"

"Where is it?"

I told him.

"That's quite unusual. I have heard of it, but let me give you some background. The Western dragon is wicked, a destroyer, representative of greed, wealth. But in the East, it can represent great wisdom and power. The shark is the pure predator, vicious, often striking with no provocation and without mercy. The snake is the most difficult to discern. How was he represented?"

I paused to remember, then explained the head, the open mouth. "The snake is probably the most controversial of all tattoos — it can reflect a myriad of meanings. It can reflect the evil in the Bible, but even there, the snake was very smart as well, wasn't he? It can represent wisdom. Gangs can use them to show their ferocity. Or, convexly, it can reflect the positivity of nature. Even poisonous snakes rarely strike unless provoked, so what does that mean? It's a popular tattoo because it's difficult to interpret. Many don't want you to know why they wear on their skin what they do."

Wow. I was impressed with the deep meaning behind something I'd always considered a bit of a boneheaded, often drunken branding. "Thanks for your insight. You said this tattoo I mentioned was unusual, but you'd heard of it?"

The door clicked.

"I think I've found him." Ben said as he let himself back into the room.

Thank God. The suspense of whether I was going to finish asking the questions first or he was going to finish the sketch and move to the needle first was killing me. I relaxed only to feel a burning sensation on the small of my back.

"And I thought the pigs were bad." Joaquin shook his head as we walked down the hallway, following Ben.

"Very funny," I muttered. I'd screamed when the tattoo needle hit home. I would be the only woman in the world with a single dot of ink on the small of my back because I had news for everyone — I was never ever, ever doing that again. I hadn't had the guts to look, even though Joaquin had offered the mirror.

"No, it wasn't funny, actually. I think my eardrums are bruised," Joaquin groused.

"Oh?!" Milne appeared at his elbow. "Do you want an arnica salve?"

Joaquin sent her off with a polite refusal. I looked at him with raised eyebrows. He shrugged. "She thinks arnica is a cure-all, kind of like my grandmother thought of Phillips' Milk of Magnesia."

160

Ben and I both smiled. So even this new age hippie tattoo artist and I had something in common besides two legs and two arms. Huh. Go figure.

"Now, who do you think you know in our gallery?" Joaquin asked Ben.

Ben led the way in the opposite direction from the way we'd entered. Around a corner was a collection of portraits with particular themes. Stars, butterflies, flowers, frogs, moons, Celtic art, Chinese, it was a huge space full from floor to ceiling with photos. Ben walked over to the freestyle tattoo wall and pointed. There he was, Dragsnashark.

Joaquin pursed his lips then turned to us. "It's the tattoo of the Medula, a low-profile but powerful gang. I don't know what they want it to mean. They designed it and keep their own in-house tattoo artist. You take what I told you and I'm sure it's supposed to mean all that and more."

Ben refused to tell me how far Joaquin had gotten with the needle on my back or what Frank had asked for in the first place. My skin still burned where the needle seared it.

We made it to the seventeenth floor, and I let us into the room. Frank held his cell phone to his ear as he paced. He acknowledged us with a passing glance, then did a double take, especially at my arms. Oops. I'd forgotten about the Harley shirt. I heard the caller trying to get his attention, but Frank remained silent as he walked shell-shocked over to us, sparing a glance that bespoke both amazement and irritation at Ben.

Running his hands from my elbows to my wrist he found the seam and lifted it, still not convinced that I wasn't a hogette convert. He apologized to whomever was on the other end of the line and pulled at the fabric one last time. Finally satisfied, he spun me around and peeked under the shirt at the small of my back. He raised his eyebrows in question.

"It's a long story," I mouthed.

Frank looked like he probably didn't want to hear it. Then, he urged the caller to continue, kissed me on the top of the head and stalked back over to the window where he looked out at The Strip, not seeing anything but what the caller was saying, forgetting there was anyone else in the room. I sighed, envying that ability to compartmentalize at the same time as hating being the victim of it. Multitasking was way overrated, if you asked me. I think it's generally bad for my mental health and my physical beauty. Look at Frank, for instance.

Sure, he had wrinkles, but they were the sexy kind — not the worrywart, ugly kind like I had from trying to juggle too many things in my mind and my emotions at once.

Ben marched straight to the bedroom I was sharing with Shana and knocked at the door. When there was no answer, he let himself in. He'd become distracted again on our journey back to the Mellagio. Fleetingly, during our foray into tattoo land, he'd seemed himself. Now he was back to Brooding Ben, a brother I didn't know and didn't know how to deal with. I realized I constantly complained about having a narcissistic twin but I have to admit, I have learned to manage him in a way I've become accustomed to. This mute time bomb was scaring me.

"Where is Shana?" he demanded, bursting from the room.

"Last I heard she was playing in a small tournament at the Egyptian. Don't worry, although I don't know why you should. Ingrid is with her. If Ingrid could say no to sleeping with you, I feel confident she could effectively repel the worst kind of terrorist and keep Shana safe."

Ben responded with a glare as he punched a number into his phone.

"Who are you calling?"

"None of your business."

I'm sure that wasn't true, but I was tired of that game. I helped myself to a Perrier as Ben snuck into the bathroom to make the call. It gave me the opportunity to watch Frank and wonder why I wasn't wary about the man I thought I loved. Yes, I admitted as I watched him grind his jaw at something the caller said, watched his biceps flex and his mouth harden into a thin line, the fact that Frank Gilbert could kill wouldn't surprise me. The way it had been described did. That Frank Gilbert could leave a wife didn't surprise me. That it was because she was a cripple did. I had to remind myself I'd been stupid before about men, most especially about silly, shallow Toby whom I'd come dangerously close to marrying, so perhaps trusting my instincts wasn't the best option.

Frank turned to me, his face softening, as he slid the cell phone into the back pocket of his snug-in-the-right-places Levi's.

It would have been comfortable to share my evening with him. It would have been fair (and probably smart) to give him a chance to share his evening with me and ease into my meeting with his old nemesis.

"Frank, do you know a man named Rudy Serrano?"

He didn't have to answer. The look on his face said it all.

TWELVE

"This was here when I got back," Frank said, motioning to a paper on the coffee table as he turned his back on me. I studied him for a moment, great stone man (was he breathing?), then looked at what he'd pointed to.

"Don't touch it," Frank said. "I'm sending it to one of my techs after you see it."

"Aren't you going to answer my question?" I demanded as I looked down and gasped.

Aunt Bee,
Do what they tell you to do, please. I want to see you again. Sorry.

Love,
Aph

The note had been written on regular copy paper in alternating red and yellow ink. The "o" in love was shaped like a heart.

"Isn't that kind of immature for a teenager — to write in colors like that?"

"It would be for Affie," I answered, thinking.

"It's probably a fake then."

"What is that supposed to mean?" I snapped.

"You have to be realistic, Honey Bee." Frank's voice softened. "Affie may be gone. We have to accept that possibility and not put you in danger for nothing. Part of any effective investigation is realizing all options. That is the only way to find the truth."

"But, that *is* her handwriting. The colors, because they are out of character, have to mean something. She is sending me a clue, I just need to figure out what it is." I paused, then added, "Don't kill my goddaughter yet, Frank."

Frank paled, glared and said: "Bee, that's not fair."

"None of this is fair, Frank," I said, suddenly tired. "Especially the fact that you won't answer my question."

Frank turned, met my gaze, and I felt the pain in his face burn through me like a blowtorch. I steeled myself against it as he said quietly, "I know Serrano. I don't know what you know about him or why."

"I know the story of you and Monica."

Frank's jaw tightened. He broke eye contact and I felt suddenly bereft, as he stated flatly, "You know his side of the story. In time, you'll know mine."

"If I still have time to hear it by the time it gets told," I answered, willing myself to stay strong, turn around and not find those hypnotic coffee-colored eyes again.

The knock at the door surprised both of us. Frank looked through the peephole, threw the deadbolt and let Joe in. He looked at me and Frank and back again. "Is everything okay?"

I waited to let Frank answer and wondered how much history Joe and Frank shared. Did Joe know Serrano? Did Joe know Monica and the kids? Not that Joe would tell me. He was, as far as I could tell, dead loyal to Frank. He'd do anything for me but rat out the boss, I'd guess. Still, I'd try, later. I'm hardheaded that way.

"Bee just saw the note," Frank explained, although, of course, that only accounted for half the discord in the room. Joe accepted that with a nod, although I think he would have treated a nonsensical response like "Billy goats eat rainbows" equally if Frank had said it.

The two of them donned some surgical gloves that Joe plucked from his back pocket and loaded the note into a plastic lab bag. Frank filled out some paperwork as some synapse in my brain made sense of Affie's color scheme. "Red and yellow — catch a fellow," I murmured, remembering all the times we'd chanted it from first grade to last week.

Joe and Frank shared a quizzical glance then looked at me. "And that means?"

"That's what Affie and I used to say when she would like a boy. I would tease her to catch a guy you have to wear red and yellow."

"It may just be a coincidence," Frank cautioned.

"But what kind of guy would she be catching while she's kidnapped? Or is it who I should be catching?"

"I'd think you already have your guy," Frank put in, sticking out his lower lip.

I wasn't going to justify his pout. "She must mean it a different way. Police catch criminals. Maybe it's the criminal I'm looking to catch."

"Big clue since eighty percent of criminals are men."

"There's got to be more to it. I'll figure it out."

"Or maybe it's coincidence, she's bored and that's all she had to write with."

"Maybe," I allowed, just to keep Frank quiet.

Ben emerged from the bathroom, brooding again. Joe used his reappearance as an opening to retreat and take the note to the lab. He and Frank huddled at the door for a moment before Joe waved and departed.

"Has anyone heard from Jack?" I asked.

"Jack is undercover, under something," Frank said, shooting me a non sequitur questioning glance I wasn't about to answer. "We'll hear from him when he can communicate."

I knew he was right, but I still worried. I could be the poster child for Guilt-R-Me. The door opened again and in walked Shana and Ingrid. Frank leaned in to me, sliding a loose tendril of my hair behind my right ear. "The revolving-door atmosphere of this suite is wearing on my nerves."

"Go stay in your own suite then," I advised.

He raised his eyebrows, then jogged them up and down.

I shook my head.

Frank sighed and turned to the women. "How did your tournament go?"

Ingrid yawned. She didn't play poker. She shopped and shot people and created websites and looked unrealistically gorgeous.

Shana shrugged. "I won about twenty-seven hundred. I used it to hire a medium to find Affie."

"What?" Ben and Frank and I blurted simultaneously.

Shana looked at all of us. "You all are wearing out the evidence angle. I can't add any expertise there. You send me off — out of sight — so I can't get in your way with all my tears and emotion. So, I thought I would cover an angle none of you would think of, so I took my winnings and hired Moon to feel what she can of Affie."

We all turned to Ingrid. She was on the couch, perfect knee (an oxymoron for every woman in the world but Ingrid, trust me) crossed over perfect knee, flipping through the latest *Time.* Finally, she realized all eyes were on her. She looked up, blinked, cocked her head and shrugged. "She seems to know her stuff."

"What?" Ben yelled. "What? The medium knows her *what?* Alignment of the stars, ghost talk and crystals? How is that going to help Aphrodite?"

Shana stuck out her lower lip. Bad sign of a Filipino meltdown. I cringed.

"I am helping *my* daughter the only way I can, right now," she raged, flipping her sheet of dark hair around a petite doll-like face

171

twisted in frustration, talking with her neon pink fingernails, stomping with her size five and a half stacked heels. "And anyone who doesn't like it can just give up, because I'm willing to do whatever it takes to find Aph. I'll sell my soul to the devil to do it, if I could find his cell number. I'd sell my body to the highest bidder if it got my baby back."

"Shana! You can't mean that," Ben cautioned sharply. His handsome face was twisted and red. What? That was more shocking than the psychic hiring.

When did he become such a prude?!

Shana stuck a fist on her hip. "You wanna bet?" They began a staring contest.

"You know," Frank cut in when the silence became uncomfortable. "Cops use psychics. I've heard claims that they have actually aided an investigation. But I have to warn you, Shana, it can be a big waste of time, money, energy and hope as well."

"When is hope ever wasted?" I argued.

"When it is placed on a lost cause," Frank answered.

"This is a lost cause?"

"No, on the contrary. I just want everyone to stay realistic. Use the psychic's information to support the evidence. Follow what she suggests only if it makes sense."

"Sense to whom? Who's playing God in

all of this?" I demanded.

"I guess we'll all just have to walk hand in hand with our hearts and minds," Frank finally said, piercing me with a hot look. "And make our decisions with influence from both."

I knew that cost him. He was a total mind man. He was compromising — willing to use his heart on Affie if I'd use mine on him? Or maybe he was just hoping I would use more mind on him than I normally would since heart usually wasn't in question with me. Hmm. Affie was worth the bargain.

"I guess we will, then," I said softly, wrapping my arms around Shana and leading her to the bedroom. "Hearts and minds and the supernatural. Maybe it will combine to find a scared little teenager."

Get to the next round. Talk to as many reporters as you can. Dress up!

You know, if it weren't made up of letters cut out of a newspaper and slipped under our door, I'd have thought the note was written by she who dubbed herself my fashionista/imagista — Ingrid — trying to give me some PR pointers. Instead I realized it was Aph's captors, giving me my orders.

173

Your goddaughter is counting on you.

I'd put on some coffee before the paper on the floor caught my gaze. Now the smell of java brewing made my knees weak. Pouring a cup, I studied the note, remembering belatedly only to handle it at the corners so Frank's lab could get any possible fingerprints. It sounded like a pep talk not a kidnapper's demand. I just didn't get it. Why would they be forcing me to do something I had intended to do all along — except maybe talk to reporters?

I turned on CNN, kept the volume low since I seemed to be the only one awake and sipped my coffee. I needed to think about Affie and ways to find her, but heaven help me, all I could think about was Frank, and his ex-wife, and the men he killed. I couldn't wait to get back to the WSOP to quiz Serrano with all the things I'd been too brain-frozen to ask the night before. As I paced behind the wet bar, I glanced at the TV. The news anchor had a WSOP emblem graphic by her head as she introduced the next news story. I hurried over to the set.

". . . a bit of controversy was stirred up at the largest poker tournament in history — the World Series of Poker 2008, being held in Las Vegas this week." The camera

174

switched to video of the protestors outside the Fortune. "A band of religious followers of the Church of the Believers picketed in front of the hotel hosting the event that has attracted more than eleven thousand entrants to the most popular card game in the world — Texas Hold 'Em." Up popped Phineas Paul. "Sins and devils who promote them will steal our children away to darkness!"

Ack. That scared even me, and I was the evildoer he was talking about! Then, as if conjured, up I popped on the screen. "I certainly respect Mr. Paul's right to free speech."

Hmm. Not a bad sound bite but my voice sounded a bit twangy and the fuschia shorts had to go.

The landline on the coffee table rang. I jumped, then plucked it up quickly. "Keep it up," the androgynous voice said through the receiver, followed by a dial tone.

I swallowed hard and slowly replaced the receiver. I changed the channel and saw Fox was showing the same story. I switched again to local news and they were just finishing playing the same sound bite.

I suddenly felt so alone and vulnerable, I considered waking Frank.

The anchorwoman had moved on to the

next story and I only half listened as I stood, walking toward the opposite bedroom door. ". . . a middle-aged man found dead in an alley behind the Fortune."

I knocked on the door and waited and the anchorwoman chattered on, ". . . thought to have died of a knife wound or wounds . . ."

Ben yanked the door open, glaring. "What?"

"Wake Frank," I glared back, savoring a sip of coffee just to irritate him.

"Frank's not here," Ben snapped back. He slammed the door and added behind it, "He never went to bed."

Annie Anchor sounded way too chipper as she explained, ". . . not yet releasing his name, they say that he is a resident of Los Angeles, California, and a former police detective."

My heart seized. I gasped.

A click sounded outside the front door. A second later, in walked Frank. I ran to him and gathered him in a hug. He kissed the top of my head. "Wow, I should go out all night more often."

Then I got mad. "Where have you been?"

Thirteen

"I knew that had to be coming," Frank muttered jokingly. He grabbed my coffee cup, nabbed a sip and pulled a face. "Too strong."

I always used double the grounds recommended to brew a pot — the more caffeine the better. "Don't change the subject. I want to know where you were. I thought you were dead."

I waved toward the TV, which was showing the sheet-draped corpse being loaded into the medical examiner's van.

"Why did you think that was me?"

"It's a former LAPD detective."

Frank ground his jaw and turned away, pointing to the note on the bar. "What's this?"

"Love note."

"You didn't touch it, did you?" Frank demanded, fishing a plastic evidence bag out of his computer case and carefully slipping it in as he read it. "Weird," he murmured.

"No kidding." I said. "He called too, right after the news ran some coverage of Paul's protestors and me spouting off about the First Amendment. The creep told me to keep up the good work."

Frank frowned. The phone rang. I jumped and he grabbed the receiver, barking into it, "Yes?"

With a brief greeting to Jack, he passed it to me. "I was worried, Jack, when I didn't hear from you last night."

"Bee Cool, stay c-cool. It's hard to remain b-believably undercover if you're phoning home every other m-minute, issuing upd-dates."

"Okay, okay, point taken."

"This is the b-buzz: apparently there is some high-level c-collusion going on in the high-stakes ring games in the major p-poker rooms. Nobody I found knows any names, so I g-guess there aren't any faces involved — just d-day players. No one's been caught but everyone's talking about it. Two b-big-name guys I overheard said even if they found a c-colluder they were going to go protectionist."

"What does that mean?"

"They'll d-deal with it privately because

178

of that religious n-nut and his p-protestors. They don't want any bad press for the game right now, especially during the WSOP."

"Since when do gamblers care about press?"

"The m-main answer to that is — since Hold 'Em became the world's favorite g-game. That means more money but also more s-scrutiny, and possibly more regulations. Most of the pros who really make a l-living at this would just rather have the old days back, I think. P-poker's a different world than it was even five years ago, Bee."

"So I suppose the casinos have extra security in the poker rooms?"

"They d-did where I was, but that may j-just be because of the higher volume of players in t-town r-right now. Every p-poker room is expecting more offshoot action."

"Now, what do you think this means to me?"

"No clue, b-baby," Jack said. "Maybe n-nothing. We'll see. People bound to be talking about you today, what with your f-famous sound bite."

I grimaced. "Ugh."

"Hey, d-don't c-complain. Ingrid's already b-been on your website m-making the most of this. She's intent on f-finding a way for you to c-capitalize financially."

"I don't want to do that," I argued.

"Whatever. Ingrid usually g-gets what she w-wants."

Understatement of the year. Ingrid also got ten percent of my poker income but I doubted that was her motivation. Making my life complicated was her juice.

"S-speaking of which," Jack continued, "She wants b-brunch. You think you can h-hang with Shana until eleven or so?"

"No problem, she's intent on going back to this medium, and I want to be with her for that. Meet you outside the Fortune at eleven thirty, okay?"

"It's a p-plan."

As he rang off, Frank came in from the bedroom. "I don't like the way this feels, but I don't know why."

"Were you listening?" He cocked his head. Great investigator I was. I'd seen him disappear into the bedroom, but never listened for the click on the line. Humph.

"Are you going to tell me what you found out at the tattoo parlor or not?" Frank asked.

"Maybe not, unless you tell me about the murders in L.A. and your ex-wife."

Frank turned his back to me, striding to the window. "My story won't help Aphrodite and it will only distract us from the search."

"Damn you," I whispered because, of course, he was right. I gave him the low-down on the meaning of the gang's tattoo.

Frank turned around, his face transformed with tight intensity. "I have an informant who is in jail in Los Angeles. He'll know about this, but I'll have to fly to see him in person. I hate to leave you." I could see in his eyes that he wasn't going to be missing my company as much as he was afraid I was going to get whacked.

"I'll be okay. Ben's here. Ingrid's here. Joe's here. My invisible cop bodyguard is somewhere around."

Frank shook his head and pinned me with a hard look. "Remember, consider cops an enemy, although they will save you from bodily harm so they can prosecute you without public sympathy."

"Heartwarming, but we will use what we can," I chirped as I sipped my coffee. The caffeine was making me brave. "Besides, I'll ask Shana's psychic if I have anything to worry about."

"Don't you dare." Frank turned dead serious. "Her kind of vague predictions will only make you second-guess yourself, your judgment and the facts. Promise me you will not listen to anything she says about

181

you, okay?"

I sighed. "Go on to the airport. Hurry back. I'll try to be alive when you get here."

Frank shot me a warning glance, grabbed his computer and strode out the door.

Brooding Ben accompanied Shana and me to the psychic, despite my protestations. I hated to say it, but this earnest brother business was getting on my nerves. I wanted my narcissistic twin back. Moon the Medium operated out of an arch-shaped tent in a trailer park. It was already ninety-eight degrees in the shade at ten thirty in the morning and Moon's office was not air-conditioned.

We ducked under the edges of the tent, open sided and about the size of a tennis court. The interior — to use the term loosely — reflected a celestial theme, the night sky, planets, stars, moons (duh) painted on the underside of the tent that soared to at least twenty feet in the center.

"How did you find this goon?" Ben stage-whispered in Shana's ear.

She glared and batted him away.

"It's Moon, dear, not Goon," corrected the woman sitting cross-legged on a pillow dead center under Mars.

Shana threw him a triumphant look. Ben refused to look abashed.

Moon continued to address only Ben, with a singular focus from her pale blue, almost tintless gray, eyes. It was entirely disconcerting, even for someone on the outside of the range. "It's good to open your mind to things metaphysical, especially when you have been entirely *too* physical your whole life."

I snorted. I couldn't help it, because her meaning was clear. Ben was promiscuous. "I like to stay in shape," Ben said, a little uncertainly.

I looked at him askance. He was naturally muscle tight with absolutely no effort and no regular exercise. Just another example of me being gypped at birth. "You know very well, Benjamin, Scorpio, that it is not what I was referring to. Your aura is one of a . . . tomcat."

A giggle escaped. Shana almost smiled. Frowning, Ben leaned in to Shana. "Why did you tell her all this stuff about me?"

Shana shook her head in denial. "Maybe it was a good guess."

"Maybe one of your conquests has already been here, those odds are better," I put in.

Ben narrowed his eyes at me as Moon said, "Yes, one has."

"Really? Who?" I asked.

Moon just smiled directly at me, serenely and very oddly, then looked up at the tent and closed her eyes.

"We brought something that was once Affie's. It was hers for a long time," Shana said to Moon. "Like you asked."

On the drive over, Shana had explained that Moon used psychometry — the use of solid objects — to try to feel her subjects. Impressions can't be erased over time, according to Moon. Something owned by someone will continue to radiate that person's aura. It made me think of a dime and how much aura it was exuding. Supposedly metal transmitted "impressions" the best. I considered handing over a dime — think of the headache that would give Moon — instead I passed Shana the talisman Affie had given me when I opened my own business — it was a copper disc that read: "Determination destroys all fear."

I held my breath while she fingered the copper.

"Belinda, you are in crisis," Moon informed me, still with her eyes closed, neck bent back. No duh. If stars didn't tell her that one, the line between my eyebrows that rivaled the Grand Canyon sure did.

"Blood, I see."

I gasped. "No! Not Affie?!"

She shook her head gravely. "No, I have to get through your impressions on the coin before I get to hers. Water. A man." She paused. I wasn't impressed. She probably saw the news, although none of the stations had connected me to the body in the Image lagoon that I knew of. Still, maybe she knew someone at the cop shop.

"No, three men and blood. Maybe even six now. I feel your love there — for which I don't know. Money? A wheelchair? A Bible?"

Her eyebrows were drawn together as she dropped her head and pinned me with a look through to my soul. I shivered. Whoa. Nobody around me knew this stuff but Frank himself and Serrano.

Who were the six men? Maybe the men Frank killed, the man in the lagoon, Frank — that left two unknowns.

I shook my head. I was buying into this, exactly what Frank warned me against. "I hope not. I hope there's no more death." Enough about me, it was freaking me out. "What about Affie?" I asked again.

Moon moved the copper disc to her forehead. After a minute or so, she spoke. "I see lots of teenage girls. Is she in camp?"

"No," Shana said, obviously disappointed.

"She's never been to camp. She's not the type."

"Dormitory atmosphere, the great outdoors. I see her playing volleyball, kayaking. I see a snake?"

Shana, Ben and I shared a look and shrugged. Frank had warned me not to get our hopes up but I had regardless. Damn.

"Is that all?" I asked finally when Moon didn't elaborate.

"She's missing you, but not hurting. And . . ."

We all leaned forward as if we could draw more out with our bodies. "That's all." Moon pivoted her head back forward and slowly opened her bizarre-colored eyes. Suddenly she started pouring with sweat, like a faucet had been opened. Now, I have to admit I'd been sweating too, after all it was a hundred blasted degrees, but while I might've felt like I'd just run a marathon, I don't think I looked like Moon. She held her arms out to her sides and the corners of her wrap dripped.

"Thank you," Shana breathed. Ben was watching the sweat pool on the tent floor like it was going to come to life. And then it did, in a way. It began to flow like a tiny river, to form a tiny lake in a divet in the rug-covered sand.

186

"Time to settle down, Benjamin." She smiled at my brother. "Time to become a penguin."

"I don't like tuxes much," he answered Moon. She smiled benignly and closed her eyes.

"Hey," Ben mused a second later as we walked away, "don't penguin males take care of their young while the females go out on the hunt?"

"She probably sensed you'd gotten one of your latest dates pregnant. Now you have to go home and figure out who it is. That alone could take nine months." I laughed and bumped Shana, who normally would enjoy digging Ben. Instead she looked away, tension wracking her body. Slightly suspicious, then immediately guilty for feeling suspicious, I wrapped my arm around her shoulders. This emotional roller coaster was taking a toll on my best friend. I was going to have to find her daughter soon or she was going to lose her mind.

FOURTEEN

Ringo waited inside the Fortune, in the hallway leading to the WSOP ballroom, holding a big white FedEx box and bouncing on the balls of his feet. Ringo was my sunglass savior, BeeCoolHoldEm.com columnist of Ringo's Shadey Report. He was an accountant in Nova Scotia when he wasn't wasting his time trying to keep me properly shaded at poker tournaments. I was forever forgetting my sunglasses and, according to those who knew me, I would never have won a hand at Hold 'Em without hiding my tell-all orbs.

Ben had dropped us off with Ingrid across the street from the casino. Jack had a hot lead and ran off to follow it before we'd arrived. Since Paul's protestors were still mobbing the Fortune's entrance, I made the duo take off from there for a satellite at Poseidon's, anticipating Shana's sadness at seeing all the girls near her daughter's age at the picket line. They were painful reminders of Affie, somewhere out there.

As I wove my way through to the front door of the casino, I'd asked one of the girls, "Does your mother know you're here?" I wondered if the church was a family affair.

"Hell no," the girl said, waving her sign that read: *Poker Sinners: REDEMPTION is the Only Holy Bet.* Cute. "And even if she did, she wouldn't care."

Huh, maybe Paul had a really strong youth program. I hoped he didn't hear her using profanity, though, because I ventured to guess he wouldn't be too keen on it. A casino security guard who apparently thought I was in trouble reached into the throng and grabbed me out before I could ask her any more questions. Probably good thing, because Paul came around the corner about then and seemed intent on me. I slipped into the casino before he could open his mouth.

"Ringo." I bent down to kiss him on the cheek. He blushed and fingered his four hairs over his bald spot. "You didn't have to come."

"What? Are you crazy? And miss Bee Cool winning the biggest poker tournament in the history of the world?"

"Don't get your hopes up," I put in. "The

odds of that are less than getting struck by lightning."

"Not quite. Richard says they are nine thousand one hundred and twenty-three to one. We just posted it on the website." Richard was the unusual but irresistible mathematician I met on the poker cruise. Ingrid had talked him into a column on the website, "Odds Are Odd."

Shaking my head, I sighed. I was really going to have to check the website more often. Apparently even more than I thought. I might not have wasted my time on the tournament if I thought my chances were that bad. "What are you wearing?" Ringo demanded.

I looked down at my Donna Karan black linen knee-length sheath. Ignoring Ingrid's selection and ensuing pleas, I chose to go low-key today. I thought the one shoulder added a bit of style, the clunky jewelry a bit of hip, the braided zebra heels a bit of vogue. I thought wrong, apparently.

"That's not on your list of WSOP outfits," he chided.

"What list?"

He opened his mouth and I put up a hand to stop him. I was going to kill Ingrid. No wonder she'd been so insistent about what she called the "fresh green" layered dress with pointy, open-toed half heels. That must have been on the list. "Don't tell me, 'it's on the website.' "

Ringo nodded apologetically and ducked his head. Oops, I'd pissed off the help. "Well, Ringo, it's too late for me to change, so I guess we'll have to just pick out shades that rock so my fans forgive me. Should I go with the classic Gargoyles, the new age Dark Hots . . ." I paused as I reached into my purse to pull out the choices I'd actually remembered to pack.

"Wait!" He patted his box. "You have a bigger job than that. Chanel saw your sound bite on CNN this morning and was so pleased you had theirs on, they same-dayed more over to the hotel!" He paused.

"Shades for a sinner, huh?" I flipped open the box top and began rifling through my choices.

"But, you have those to consider as well." Ringo motioned to the nearby bench that held no less than a half dozen boxes.

I shook my head. "Ringo, time to do your job. Pick a pair for me to wear tonight."

He fidgeted. He played with his four hairs again. "That's a lot of pressure, Bee."

"Some of the best decisions in the world were made under pressure, Ringo. Go for it," I said over my shoulder as I marched to the registration desk. It was amazing how quickly the numbers could dwindle . . . Ten thousand had become around a thousand players in just a day. Masses of WSOP hopefuls were on the loose in Vegas doing who knew what. If I'd gone into the game knowing this, I would have never played. I am a glass-half-empty person, to be sure. Backing into liking the cards, chips and felt, and then having life-and-death stakes on winning in my first experience were the only ways I ever would have kept on playing.

Fate was a strange force.

"Bee Cool." I felt a tug on my sleeve. I turned to see Thelma, wearing the same clothes she'd been wearing the day before. I wanted to get her a bath. I wanted to get her a hairbrush. Then I remembered I'd sent her on a mission. I'd forgotten because Richard might have given her a ten percent chance of showing up again with any information and I would have hoped for five. "I found out some stuff," she whispered, furtively glancing over her shoulder. Suddenly I felt like I was in an old Alfred Hitchcock movie.

"Okay," I said, nodding encouragingly, only realizing, after an awkward moment, that she was expecting me to show her the money. Frank would have throttled me for passing her the C-note before she started talking but I did it anyway. I was rather impatient. Something Frank was *occasionally* grateful for.

"That preacher man who's hassling you?"

I nodded again. This wasn't the tree I'd really wanted her to bark up, but maybe there was more.

"The girls he has out there holding those ugly signs?"

I nodded, feeling like a bobblehead doll. Perhaps this was all I was going to get out of her — a series of rhetorical questions.

"Those girls are off the street, a lot of them. They runaways. He pays them to hold the signs."

Interesting. I guess that was something I could throw at him if he irritated me again. "So he picks them up off Vegas street corners, gives them a twenty and tells them to walk around singing 'Swing Low, Sweet Chariot' all day?" I couldn't remember if I'd seen the same faces every day or if the faces changed.

"No, they not Vegas girls. They all say they live in the woods up northwest."

"The woods?" That was weird.

She nodded, certain of that.

I didn't know what any of this meant or how it was going to help me, besides perhaps a way to blackmail Paul to shut up if I had the time and energy.

"Thanks, Thelma," I said. "You hear anything else, let me know."

"You know I will," she said, shoving the cash into her bra and melting back into the crowd. Talk about the perfect surveillance operative. I doubted 90 percent of the public even noticed Thelma existed. I made a mental note to mention her to Frank. Maybe I could make an honest woman of her.

"So," a voice said to my right. "I finally get to meet the woman with the buzz."

It was one of the famous Phils, a real player, a true poker pro. Wow. I was a bit starstruck. He gathered my hand in his to give it a shake. Thank goodness because I wasn't sure I could function. "Nice to meet you," I began.

"I've never gotten the opportunity to thank you for edging Steely Stan out of the game. Thanks from all of us pros," he said. "He was scum."

Wasn't that a diplomatic way of putting it? "Well . . ."

"Now, you can learn to play the game so you don't embarrass the rest of us."

"I have an intuitive technique," I defended myself, finally finding my brain. "It might be different from yours, but still valid."

Laughing, he shook his head. "You are a PR queen for sure. Maybe you truly are the future of the game. Scary."

With that, Phil walked off. "Hey, what do you call your tantrums if not PR?" I hollered after him.

Ringo reappeared, proudly squiring a pair of Africa Golds. Giving him a thumbs up, I donned them and walked into the ballroom for day two. But truth be told, I was anticipating my interrogation of Serrano more than the cards leading me to a twelve-million-dollar jackpot.

Serrano didn't show. And once again Blackie was there well before I was, seated and composed. Organized, show-offy bitch.

With a bit of a fuss all around the table about me being late, the first hand was dealt and Serrano's seat remained empty. I leaned over to the man next to me. "What happened to the ex-cop?"

He shrugged. "Maybe he tied one on last night and couldn't get up this early."

Most people didn't consider noon early, but we were in Vegas, so I guess he had a point. No one else at the table seemed to know what happened to Serrano either. The disappointment I felt at losing the info train to Frank's past was surprisingly sharp.

The cards fell my way, though. The first deal gave me a pair of Kings with a Flop of a pair of Kings and a Queen, two of which were spades. That was good, because it might give someone with a queen in the hole enough gumption to stay in to see The River and those with a flush draw a glimmer of hope. A rope-a-dope strategy would earn me the most chips. I raised conservatively and promised myself not to show I had the nuts.

Sure enough everyone but Blackie and the small blind folded before Fourth Street. The third spade, an eight, fell on The Turn, which conveniently kept the small blind in the game, apparently having made his flush draw. I called, waiting to raise on Blackie's reraise. The pot had grown considerably. I was tempted to push, but thought I should scare them off less dramatically. I wouldn't play aggressively tonight, it was way too early in the tournament for that. I wanted to milk the funds out of the table gradually. Aph's captors just told me to stay in it — not to win.

I don't know what Blackie had in her pocket because she finally folded on The River reraise when I made the all in decision.

Two breaks later, a WSOP official came around and motioned across the room for a player to take Serrano's place.

"What?" the dealer asked. "The guy just didn't show?"

"You could say that. Rudolph Serrano is dead."

I gasped. "A heart attack? Stroke?"

"Nope, he was offed. Found in an alley this morning. Knifed overnight. Cops are working the room right now." He pointed to a couple of plainclothes detectives under close watch of a phalanx of plainclothes casino security. "Why? Anyone at this table have a special interest in the guy?"

The dealer paused in middeal. Everyone turned and looked at me.

Detective Trankosky wasn't happy to see me when the WSOP official dragged me over to their impromptu interrogation room at the next break. The tournament wanted the cops to go away and they apparently were willing to sacrifice me in order to accomplish that goal.

"You again," he growled, hitting himself on the forehead with the heel of his hand.

"What are the odds that of all the hundreds of detectives in this county, I would encounter you twice in forty-eight hours,

Detective?" I smiled sweetly.

"What are the odds that I would have two poker players slashed to death in two days and you were around both of them within hours of their deaths, Belinda?" he returned.

Mexican standoff. Though naturally impatient, I waited silently because I knew he'd hate it. I expected him to arrest me this time, and I wanted to make sure he had to work for it.

Finally, he said: "How long had you known Serrano?"

"About three hours. He sat down at my tournament table. We met."

Trankosky waited again. I bit my tongue again. "But I hear you chatted him up all night."

I shrugged my left shoulder. There was no way I was going to tell him about the Frank connection even though suspicion had sprung directly into my mind. Where had Frank been all night? I hated this operating half in the dark.

"Well, what about it?"

"It was no big deal; I like to make conversation."

"With everyone but me, apparently," Trankosky said out of the side of his mouth. I thought he might be ready to get rid of one of his wads of tobacco but there wasn't one there. "What did you talk about?"

"Nothing in particular . . . good shows, the best restaurants . . ."

"So you didn't know he was from the same hometown as your boyfriend?"

I blinked, taken aback by the fact that the cops knew I had a boyfriend. Did I have no secrets from either side of the law? "I think he mentioned it. It's a pretty big hometown."

"It's a pretty big coincidence that Serrano and Gilbert both were cops there too, huh?" Trankosky sounded like someone else I knew for which coincidence was a four-letter word.

"I guess so," I said, wishing I could ask Trankosky how much he know about Frank's past. Argh. How could a stranger who'd never met Frank know more than I did?

"Did Serrano mention he and Gilbert actually knew each other?"

"Not in so many words," I said, damning my mother for ingraining the inability to lie in me. A *little* ability to prevaricate might come in handy right now to keep me out of the slammer.

"Did Gilbert explain it all to you when he got home *after dawn* this morning?"

Show off. I guess the police tail had been

there all along. Either that or they were using the hotel cameras to view our room.
"Hey, Detective Dale, if you know so much,
then I imagine you know *I* didn't kill Serrano," I pointed out.

"Believe me, this is the one time I've
regretted setting up a surveillance on someone. If I hadn't, I would've had enough
circumstantial cause to lock you up —"

"But I didn't do anything, and you just
admitted you know that!"

"— just to get you out of the way!"

"Oh," I said, my anger suddenly deflated.

"I know you know *something* but I just
don't know if it's worth all this pain and
suffering and the time of my guy —"

"That's easy, pull him off, then."

"Are you kidding? He's having way too
much fun. He loved the Harley shirt and
miniskirt."

I glared.

"By the way, he wants to know where you
got your tattoo and if you could get his
horoscope the next time you visit your psychic."

Enough was enough. With that I stood,
and huffed off as Trankosky laughed at my
back. I decided being a joke was worse than
being a suspect. I was determined to lose
the police tail, no matter if I knew which

guy he was or not.

In the first deal back after my rendezvous with Trankosky, I held two off-suit midlevel cards. Crap.

I hated to play these. A 9 of diamonds and a 5 of clubs do not engender much confidence, especially early in a tournament at a table that had dropped all but me and Blackie of the original players. I'd been so distracted that I hadn't gotten much of a read on the other five currently sitting there. The only saving grace was I was the last seat on this hand and all but Blackie and a dolphin trainer from Florida folded.

Surely they had better odds than I did. Blackie was impossible to figure. She could have my hand or she could have the total nuts. The other girl looked like a fish (no pun intended), but a rock of one. If I bet on anything, it was that she had a crown or two in front of her. I called, hoping for luck.

The Flop came an Ace of diamonds, a 3 of diamonds and — a gift — 9 of clubs. Either one of them could have a flush draw now. Or a pair or trips. Calculating the outs, I put my win odds somewhere below 20 percent. Usually a place to fold. Blackie wasn't even breathing, I think. A good sign. She was probably bluffing. Flipper's friend, on the other hand, was eyeballing her chips. She had a pair of Aces. I was going to have to play aggressive near the end to scare her off or not play at all.

So I drew her out, limping in with soft calls through Fourth Street that was a 4 of diamonds. Darn it. Someone could have made the flush. Still, Blackie wasn't breathing, but was still calling. Good, it wasn't her — she was just after stealing the pot. When the 9 of hearts fell on The River, it made me be brave doing what I had decided to do no matter what card came — I pushed. Blackie was tempted. She had to have the flush. Dolphin Girl studied her chips, counted mine and hyperventilated for a few moments.

We must have looked dramatic, three women about to go heads-up, because the ESPN cameraman swooped in and stuck his lens in the middle of our table. The dealer gave the girl a little extra time, no doubt to let the commentators blab on, building the suspense if they chose this clip to run later.

Finally, she blew out her breath, shoved all her chips forward and waited. The dealer reached over and selected two stacks of my chips to return to me — so I wouldn't be eliminated no matter what was on the other side of her cards, just seriously handicapped. Then, with a flourish, he turned over our cards simultaneously. She had an Ace and King spade suited. She started crying as one of the commentators came over to interview her about her bad decision when it really hadn't been a bad decision at all. If I'd folded and Blackie had folded as we should have, she would have raked in the blinds. Instead we'd made it a game and luck fell my way. I smiled and gathered my chips. Richard wouldn't be proud of me — that was no way to play the odds — going from seventeen and a half percent to a hundred with pure luck, but I was proud of myself. Finally maybe I was learning to calculate odds, read the players and intuit the fall of the cards in proper measure.

Either that or I was just lucky today.

I slow played the next hand, just to keep everyone guessing. Most of them thought I had nothing as I had before, and figured I wouldn't get lucky twice. Truth was, I'd been dealt American Airlines (a pair of Aces) so I waited until four other players were deeply committed to the pot to raise when another Ace fell on The Turn. Now they all thought I had a mere pair when my Rockies were the nuts according to the mishmash on the board. I won a big pot and made everyone mad.

"How can she be so lucky!?" the banker from Nebraska whined.

"Something fishy is going on here, and I'm getting to the bottom of it," a pro from Council Bluffs threatened.

Blackie smiled and that's when I knew something was wrong.

FIFTEEN

I'd found Blackie's hands hovering near my chip stack when I returned from my cop shop session and hadn't thought much of it. I didn't think she was wholesale stealing my chips or anything. More likely, freaky as she was, she was putting a curse on my seat. I'd been in such a hurry when I'd sat down I'd knocked a couple of hundred-dollar discs that were on the edge of the felt off onto the floor; I figured I'd wait until an all in or a break to pick them up. It hadn't mattered, since I was chip leader and frankly, I'd forgotten about them.

Now, a couple of tournament officials marched over to see what the ruckus was all about. Of course, the TV cameras followed. Good thing, since I'd forgotten all about the kidnappers' demand that I talk to reporters. Maybe I could think of something stimulating to say that they would put on

TV tonight to keep the cretins happy.

Keeping only half on ear open to the whiner and the complainer, I checked my text messages. Just one from Mom, reporting no word from Affie and the impending botox injection of the lips of the president of the garden club. That's when all hell broke loose.

"What's this, then?" Whiner demanded, pointing under the table. Down dove Moaner, who hollered, "There're chips down here."

One of the WSOP officials ordered him back out and he crawled under the table, reemerging with two hundred-dollar chips. I looked up from my phone and opened my mouth just as he flipped them over and said, "Look, they're marked!"

The WSOP officials huddled, shooed away the TV cameras and called in reinforcements. Blackie's attention was on me through her black lenses. Creepy. The TV guys came over and hung out with me. We chatted awhile, then one of them was paged. "Mike says he overheard one of the WSOP dudes calling this collusion."

I raised my eyebrows. My heart pounded, guilty about something I hadn't even done. "Really?"

"Will you give us a sound bite on that,

Miss Cooley, before they run us out of here?"

"Sure."

One of them held the mic and both started up their cameras — CNN and a local news station. I remembered my shades and that I better slide them down over my eyes to give my sponsors a boost. "How do you feel about collusion?" one of the cameramen asked.

"First of all, I have so much trouble keeping track of pot odds and counting cards that I don't know how anyone would have room in their head for one more thing to keep straight. Secondly, why would you think you could cheat Lady Luck? It seems like one way or another she'll get even."

"That was awesome." They disappeared as the WSOP officials reappeared and asked Moaner if he'd touched the chips.

"No, they were there, right in the middle under the table."

"They could be anyone's. Who's going to claim them?" the official asked, obviously not expecting an answer.

A staff member walking by pointed at me and said, "They're hers."

Everyone looked at me again. I dug deep for two cells' worth of dishonest genes, remembering Grandpa bragging that one of our Confederate relatives was a bootlegger during the Civil War. I'd have to rely on that to give me confidence to get me through this. Thank goodness I was wearing my shades when I said, "I apologize, gentlemen, I can't enlighten you."

"Miss, you sit next to her," he addressed Blackie, who was wringing her hands under the oversize sleeves of her black swaddling clothes. "Perhaps you can tell us if you know these are Miss Cooley's chips?"

She went mute. The officials looked at the dealer, who shrugged. "I didn't notice anything and this gal lost a big pot to Bee Cool just a couple of hands ago. So if anyone would have a grudge it would be her."

Blackie spun on him and shot him her lens-shielded glare. It still hit home. He recoiled. I felt sorry for him.

About a half dozen more WSOP officials had descended on the table and were checking all the chips. "What I don't understand is why a marked chip would be a big deal anyway? A marked card, I get, not a chip," remarked the TV commentator.

"Any way that you can communicate with another player that can't be understood by the rest of the table is against the rules. It's cheating." With that they gathered for an official powwow. All us players at the table stood awkwardly, trying to ignore the curious stares of the rest of the players pushing chips across the felt. Blackie was back to sending bad vibes my way. I made a mental note to ask Moon how to deflect a witch's power.

The powwow broke up after a few minutes. "We'll be monitoring this table carefully," the head honcho said as he and all but two of his ducklings departed. They stationed themselves at opposite ends of the table.

"Good," I said, and meant it. Someone had to keep an eye on Blackie and I didn't want to be the only one.

Everyone was tight when the dealer resumed play. I tried to use this to my advantage and did on the first hand when all but two of us folded at the pocket peek. Unsuited King/ten usually isn't playable with a nine-player round, but heads-up it could go. I read body language relatively well one-on-one. I guessed by the flexing of the biceps through the too tight polo shirt and the cocked eyebrow that the small-town high school football coach had just stayed in to show everyone else men were superior and he couldn't be taken by a mere female. I drew him out — I wasn't so intent on winning chips as winning a psychological advantage over the rest of the table, aka audience. The Flop didn't help with a pair of fives and an unsuited nine. Still, I had a straight draw to his likely midlevel pair, even odds. When he didn't go for the jugular at the pair of fives on The Flop, I knew I might get lucky. The Turn brought a Queen for me. He raised, but only to scare me off. I called and a Jack fell on The River. When I called, he thought he was in. He raised. I called. He reraised. I called.

The look on his face was priceless when I flipped over my straight to his dealer-turned two pair. "I think she is cheating," he muttered.

I'd earned the respect of the audience, which I would need the next hand.

I got a ballerina (deuce pair) in my pocket. Ouch. Smiling to hide the pain, I tried to envision how I could justify a non-committed bet with 20 percent odds on a 2 of hearts, 2 of spades. It might be time to fold, but I didn't. Blackie did. She was shook. Good. It looked like she might sacrifice her blinds the rest of the night. I rode out the pair conservatively and chose to fold before The River. Right decision, since a bicycle (Ace, 2, 3, 4, 5) would have beat me in the end. I would've hated that — beat by the lowest possible straight. Ugh. Luck was with the Whiner that hand.

At the next break, I visited the registration desk. "I wanted to check on the name of a player."

"We can't give out that information. The identities of our players are protected." The brush pursed her lips disapprovingly.

Maybe I should ask the kidnappers. They seemed to know everything about everyone.

"Bee!" I turned and saw Carey waving wildly and jumping up and down behind the barrier. To save the rest of the gallery, I rushed to stop her. A six foot three inch man in a bodacious miniskirt and triple-D halter top is not necessarily something you want to bouncing around three feet from you. "I'm taking you to dinner, girlfrien'."

Women in "poker babes" shirts behind the rail waved and displayed a sign or two debunking Paul and praising me as I returned to the tournament. I gave them a thumbs up as Ben eased up beside me. "Where've you been?" I asked as I searched the crowd milling behind me for my police tail.

"Around."

"I wish you would quit sulking about bust-ing out of the tournament. Everybody has a bad game sometimes, although I don't know how you went from chip leader to nada so fast."

Ben ignored my unspoken question. "Shana's psychic wants to talk to her. I'm going to go with her."

"Why would you want to, after the character flogging she gave you earlier?"

Ben shrugged. It wasn't like him to be a martyr. This stranger in my twin's body was continuing to get on my nerves.

"What about Ingrid?"

"I'm leaving her here with you."

"Frank's not going to like that," I said.

"Frank's not here," Ben said.

I studied him as he walked off, through the casino, collecting Shana from a black-jack table. Ingrid drifted in my direction until she caught sight of me, then she freight-trained over. I was in trouble.

She shook her finger at me. "What happened to your day-two fashion?"

"I decided to wear this instead."

"You have no solitary say. You are part of a whole, like the arm of the body. The rest of the body that is Bee Cool decided you wear the hot green number, not this black sack." Oh, Ingrid of the odd analogy. Sometimes I think she was too smart for everyone's own good. She shook her head. "I am going to have to fix this."

"Whatever, as long as I don't have to wear that algae-looking outfit."

Still disgusted, but distracted by the possible fashion damage control options knocking around in her head, she handed me a money envelope. "What's this?" I asked.

"I sold your day-one fashion on eBay with PayPal."

"What?"

"Look, Bee, someone has to have some business sense around here. You are a hot property today and you might be dog meat tomorrow. You need to save for your retirement and this is the way."

"It's kind of creepy, that someone would want it."

"It's called commerce. Somebody wanted it. They paid for it. You provided it."

"No, technically, *you* provided it. Without my permission."

She glared and snatched the money out of my hand.

Arguing with Ingrid was like fighting with a brick wall. I'm hardheaded, however. "What if I wanted to wear that particular fashion again?"

She waved the money. "Buy another one."

Argh. I gave up and walked back into the

ballroom to finish up the night's play. Before I got to the table, my phone vibrated. "Honey Bee Bee," Frank purred over the wireless. "No matter whaaaat. I luuuuv you."

The line went dead.

The call had come from an unidentified number. The only thing I could identify was Frank was drunk.

Sixteen

There was no telling how long the phone had been ringing. Despite being exhausted, I'd slept only fleetingly overnight — thinking I was hearing Frank come in about twenty times, waiting for him to open the door to check on us, then going to check his bedroom when he didn't. Ben still slept in the room alone at last check. At daybreak, finally sleep hit me like a sledgehammer. It was now 10:11. The buzz I'd assumed was the alarm was coming from the living room phone.

I scrambled up, fell out the door and snatched the receiver to my ear. "Frank?"

"Your bodyguard boyfriend is busy," the voice said flatly.

"Joe?"

"Today is your day off the tournament," the voice continued. The kidnappers. I fought the chill that slid up my spine with the knowledge that these guys seemed to know everything. "After lunch, wait for the rear corner table in the Mellagio's high-stakes room. Collude with the player wearing a Redskins jersey. You two will wipe everyone else out. He will let you win the third or fourth hand after that — go all in and take it home. Wait for the cash. Don't accept a check or house credit even though they will try to squeeze you into it. You will bring the money to the corner of Feil and Rickshaw within thirty minutes of the cash-out. Do this if you want your goddaughter to have another day."

"I'm not doing this unless I know she's not hurt." I surprised myself with my boldness, but the request made me cranky. I hate it when people ask me to lie, cheat or steal. As I've said, I have guilt issues.

I heard a click, then "Aunt Bee?"

Another click then, "So, you heard her."

"Yeah, on a tape recorder."

He swore under his breath. "Ask her any question this time. Then we are hanging up, and you do as you are told."

Click. "Aunt Bee?"

"Aph, where are you?" Well, he said any question.

I could hear swearing in the background. Someone ordered her to answer. At least I knew it was the real thing, that Affie was

216

okay for now. I allowed myself a measure of relief as I held my breath for her answer. I could get a miracle — like latitude and longitude of her location. I was due a bit of luck, wasn't I? She sniffed back a tear. "God only knows," she said. Click.

Super. Maybe I could look up Reverend Paul and he could help me out with a land-line to heaven. I was being set up and blackmailed while my goddaughter was kidnapped. My boyfriend had fallen off the wagon at exactly the worst time. I had to find out who Blackie was because she might just be the closest person I could find who might have an answer.

"It's not like Aphrodite to use God's name in vain. My mother would kill her," Shana mused after I woke her up to tell her Affie was alive. "She'd have to spend the rest of her life saying Hail Marys."

"I know. It was like Aph was giving me another clue, but like the red and yellow thing, I'm not catching on as well as she probably hopes. I know it's the best she could do, with the bad guys breathing down her neck. They aren't catching on either, which is the only thing we have going for us right now. So maybe she can keep sending them until something clicks."

Shana held my hands in hers and looked into my eyes with her liquid dark ones, still not ready to let herself believe. "You're sure it was her?"

I nodded.

She sagged against the wall in relief.

"What did Moon have to say last night?"

"She keeps insisting Affie is at a camp full of teenagers." She rolled her eyes. "And, that they go to a circus tent every day. I think you might have been right, I might have wasted my money. But I had to try. At least she's nice."

"To you, she is. Any more digs at Ben?" I asked, lightheartedly.

Shana turned away from me. "Listen, Bee, Ben's been a good strong shoulder these last couple of days."

"Don't get used to it," I muttered. "He doesn't want to be counted on. I know you've had off and on stud crushes on him through the years, but he's not good for you long-term."

"I realize that. I go through periods where I think he's what I want, hot and fun and driven, but then I know he's probably impossible to live with. The older Affie gets the more I feel compelled to set a proper example for her."

I didn't want to tell Shana that all her wild

carrying on when Aph was a child had done the damage it was going to do. Fortunately Aph had been smarter and stronger than to let her mother's partying do anything but positively influence her — she was turning out to be the exact opposite. But I wasn't going to give Shana this lecture. Not now, when she was so vulnerable. Besides, I should be pleased that my wild, but good-hearted, friend was considering settling down. No matter what the reason and no matter how fleeting.

"Ben hasn't been too hot or fun this trip," I observed drily.

"No, but he has been solid as a rock." Shana batted away a tear. "And I've needed that."

"Humph. Maybe he's trying a new strategy — strong and sensitive instead of hot to trot. He is over forty now, you know. Maybe that pace is wearing on that aging body."

"Look who's talking," Ben said through a huge yawn as he came out of the bedroom in just his boxers. His black hair was tousled by the pillow more expertly than Johnny Depp's was by the movie hairstylist. His green eyes sparkled like he'd already had a pot of coffee, and his abs were tight enough to have endured a million sit-ups I knew they'd never suffered. Shana watched him, despite her lip service, a bit dreamy eyed. Well, I guess it didn't hurt a girl to fantasize. But this was a bit different. This almost looked like . . . love?

"Hey, I have a lot less miles on my speedometer," I told Ben, still watching Shana. Only other time I'd seen her look like this was when she talked about a boy she'd had a one-night stand with at a college party — Aph's dad. Shana only told me once. And from what I understood, she'd never seen him again. She didn't even know his name.

"And you're proud to be like Grandma's Buick that never gets out of the garage — faded and old but ready to be ridden by the next generation?" Ben retorted.

Shana giggled. Even at my expense, I was glad to hear it. Maybe both brother and friend were getting back to a semblance of normalcy. "Leave it to you to degrade what could only be viewed as a positive."

"Leave it to you to walk straight into the opportunity," Ben shot back with a quick grin.

There was no winning barb trading with the king of the quick tongue. I hated to give up, though, so it was fortunate for me that a knock sounded at the door.

The door opened before I could reach it. Joe walked in. "Sorry," he said when he saw our shocked faces. "Frank gave me his key so I wouldn't have to wake you to check on you."

Hmm. A plausible explanation but it didn't feel right. Joe got right down to business, accepting the cup of coffee Shana brought to him. Ben ambled over, grabbed her by the elbow and whispered in her ear. They wandered off to the far corner of the living area.

"Frank confirmed with our source yesterday that it is the Medula gang that you apparently are tangled up with. They run a myriad of criminal organizations — from drugs to prostitution to a variety of urban extortionist activities and apparently are trying to break into gambling — although we can't figure out how they intend to make money in mainstream poker tournaments or why they've targeted you. They do have history of kidnappings and murders. They are active in Vegas right now."

"Why wouldn't they target me?"

"Well, usually it's easier and safer for crooks to blackmail someone into crime with a monetary motive. Like if you were deeply in debt, your family was in financial trouble, that kind of thing. Violent personal crimes carry higher penalties, not to mention tend to be messier. Of course, from what we hear, if properly motivated by money, Medulas don't mind messy."

"Tell me about it," I muttered, remembering all too clearly the gaping wound in Tasser's neck magnified underwater.

I told Joe about the kidnappers' demand this morning. He listened intently, unhappily, tensely. I could sense him wishing for Frank. He dialed him on his cell phone and left a message when Frank didn't answer. "I don't know, Bee, it might be a trap."

"Why would they trap me? I'm the one doing their bidding. Maybe they are finally going to show why they are using me — I'm expected to make them money. I refuse to collude, but I will try to win. I will take them what they want. All that would be legal."

"What will you do if you can't win without collusion?"

To save Affie? Good question. I think I knew the answer but I hoped I wouldn't have to find out for sure. "I guess I'll have to make that call when the time comes."

"Anyway, our source has a couple pals inside of Medula who might be able to find out more. He'll let Frank know if he gets another lead."

"Joe, where is he?"

Joe swallowed. Marlboro-Man-meets-

Rambo suddenly looked much smaller, and lost. "I don't know."

"Joe, this isn't about protecting him, this is about helping him. He's drunk, isn't he?"

"Maybe." He admitted woodenly.

I waited. He didn't speak.

I waited.

Finally, Joe muttered to the floor, "He's done this before — fallen out of an investigation like this."

Joe wouldn't meet my eyes. I bit my tongue and waited. Finally, he said, "Once before."

"When?"

"When we went after Trucek."

"You knew him then?"

"Frank and I have been friends since we were kids."

Bingo. I knew it! A treasure chest of information about Frank Gilbert stood in the room with me. The problem would be opening it. I watched him pace the room. I might have to hypnotize Joe to get it but I'd vowed to find out every detail.

"He drinks, almost never now, but even before, he was careful never to compromise an investigation. He's a real pro."

"Except Trucek's. And now this one. Why did this one become so personal, then?"

"Besides the fact that you're in the middle

of it?" Joe asked softly but very pointedly.

Guilt shot through me. "Besides that," I answered, remembering a third time he'd gotten lost in the bottle since I'd known him — during our last deadly trip to Vegas. I guess Joe didn't know about that one. I'd guess no one but I knew about that one.

"I guess it was Serrano."

"But what does Serrano have to do with all this?" Frank was allergic to coincidence, so I assumed Joe was too.

"I haven't got a clue, but it seems weird for him to just show up like this, at your table out of the thousands of others."

"Does he know Serrano's murder was on the news?"

Joe nodded. "I talked to him when he was on his way to the prison."

I asked the hard question: "Does he know he's a suspect?"

Joe's head snapped up. "I didn't know that."

"Trankosky dropped a hint or two tonight. Joe, Frank didn't come back until after dawn yesterday."

"I know," was all Joe had to say.

Was that "I know, he offed the dude" or "I know, because I know what kept him out all night" or "I know, he informed me about the fact and said no more"? I opened my palms up. Joe shook his head in refusal. Joe had saved my life a couple of times, so I felt like I couldn't get too cranky with him right now. Maybe later.

"So if he doesn't show up in the next couple of hours, where can we assume he is? Caught by the kidnappers?"

"No way. Frank would be dead before he'd ever let himself get captured." He paused when he saw how his comment struck me. "Oh, sorry, Bee, I didn't mean to upset you. It should make you feel better. In other words, odds are, he's alive and free."

"Okay, so if that's the case, where do we look for him?"

"If he's bad drunk, only one person will know."

I saw the answer in his face.

"Monica," I whispered to myself.

Frank either went underground to avoid the cops or was curled up with a bottle of V.O. Wow. What a pair of options. Of course I wasn't as convinced as Joe was that Frank was immune to capture, so in my mind Frank could be three places, none of them where I needed him to be.

SEVENTEEN

I got ready for the day as Joe went off in search of information about Serrano. I'd decided that it might not have been a co-incidence that he ended up at my table at the WSOP, and if it wasn't a coincidence, what had been his purpose? Maybe it had been simply a vendetta against Frank. If so, he had terrible timing.

And he'd paid for it. But who'd made him pay — and why? In my heart I knew it couldn't be Frank.

But my heart also would've argued Frank wouldn't've tortured three men.

The bloody puzzle around me was becoming disconcerting. If I could see how I was tied to the events, it might not be acceptable but it would be at least logical — as our last disaster in Vegas had. I'd heard a death threat, my brother had been snatched up because of what he knew. We were obvious targets. I still didn't know what I was the target of here — besides Reverend Phineas Paul's moral judgment and bad karma.

Speaking of Paul, I hadn't decided what to do with Thelma's revelation. Maybe nothing. It depended on how seriously he pissed me off. Under normal circumstances I would've enjoyed challenging him to a real debate but I was distracted by more important things like kidnappings and murders.

Someone (read: tall, blonde Amazonian goddess) had invaded the bedroom while I showered and laid out my day-off outfit — a grass green and eggplant, diagonal-striped body-hugging wraparound raison minidress with some coordinated acrylic clunky jewelry. Every unintentional bulge on my body was going to be magnified by the clingy, striped fabric. Shaking my head, I went to the closet to see it completely emptied out save my shoe collection (there was a God!). My Burberry was gone.

Flinging open the door, I hollered: "Ingrid! Bring back my suitcase! Now!"

Shana, on the couch, going through more personal knickknacks to take to Moon for her psychometry, blinked at me innocently. Ben spoke into his cell phone, "I know. I'll tell her." He covered the phone with his hand. "Ma says if you were nicer to your friends, you'd have more of them." He looked down at Shana. "She says you're a saint for putting up with such a prima donna."

"Now Ma's talking about you," I shot back.

"I don't think so," he sang, going back to his conversation.

I slammed the door and looked at the outfit again. Ugh. Why me? This would be one I wouldn't mind going straight to eBay. At least I wouldn't be facing any TV reporters today. I couldn't bear to see the camera add ten pounds to me in this atrocity.

I tied myself into it and mulled over which shoes would minimize the damage. I chose the gold, pointy-toed ballerina flats, sucked in a breath, threw open the door, and Jack fell into the bedroom.

"Jack!" I watched him flail on the floor, then scramble to his oversize feet. "What were you doing there?"

Hyperventilating, he stuttered for a few moments incoherently, blushing madly, sweating profusely. Mostly his social anxiety disorder stayed in remission when he was around me, but every now and then I was reminded of what Jack was like when I first met him — under a table, hiding from the world. I put my hand on his shoulder. "Take a deep breath. Another. Another."

Finally, Jack hung his head and mumbled, "I-Ingrid w-wanted me to be sure you wore what you were s-s-supposed to."

I raised my eyebrows. "I see. You're the one doing her dirty work."

"Bee! She asked m-me."

Shaking my head, I immediately forgave him. Ingrid'd better stay true to him or she'd have me to contend with. Over time I'd come to like her and even trust her but she remained an enigma. "I won't ask how *hearing* me dress was going to help you keep me on the straight and narrow."

After I'd gotten over my mad, we decided to lunch at The Refuge — a quiet restaurant a block off The Strip where we could compare notes.

Jack spoke first: "At first I thought I was getting somewhere with the talk of collusion but that was pretty much a dead end. Every time I turned a corner I got shut down. But, by accident, I started finding out about this Paul character, like where his church is based, what version of Christianity he preaches."

My gosh, he had the Thelma disease. I shook my head. "Jack, I think you might just be wasting your time."

"Nah, Bee, don't worry about it. I already

got the go-ahead from my editor to work on a piece about the protest for the next issue, and Diane called."

"Whoo-hoo," I whistled as I high-fived him. Jack blushed again. Ingrid kissed him on the cheek.

"Anyhow, they want a spot on *GMA* to run in conjunction with the last day of the WSOP. They are planning a live broadcast from The Strip that day."

"Really? Poker's going major network. Huh. That will make Paul's week," I muttered, glad for my friend but hating that the creepy preacher was getting any attention to justify his cause. I blew out a breath. "Go for it, then, Jack. Dig up the dirt. You might become Diane's right-hand man. Watch out, Chris Cuomo."

Ingrid arched an eyebrow, looking like she might have an issue with that.

The poker room at the Mellagio is usually a full house — the managers do a good job of keeping things moving. Personally, I like the atmosphere, businesslike — productive, quiet and generally respectful. Most who sit down there want a solid game. For that reason, sometimes it is hard to win there if you aren't getting cards, because there aren't usually a lot of jackals. Even the fish tend to bail if they aren't drawing well. Each poker room on The Strip has its own unique character, drawing its own unique type of clientele. It's a chicken and the egg deal — I don't know if that is the type of client the casino seeks or whether that is the kind that has gravitated to the room and therefore the atmosphere follows. There are some poker rooms I won't play unless I'm trying to make a point, because they disrespect women. There are some poker rooms I won't play because it's a bunch of pro hard timers who live next to Moon and are out to make the rent by the end of the business day. There are some I won't play because they are full of young guns, there on Daddy's dime, dripping money. They want to win wild and big and loud and lose the same way. Some capable poker players like that kind of room, because it's an easy win for a patient Rock who likes to squish a table of cocky fish. I play poker — usually — for fun and that isn't part of the fun for me, so I avoid those situations.

Having said that, I'd never played in the high-stakes room at the Mellagio. The general poker room was set up in the corner of the casino, along an open hallway. Unlike many casino poker rooms, which were sequestered by solid or glass walls, this one had no solid barriers, so passersby could watch and hear as they walked by. It was probably a good way to draw in the crowd as well as keep players on their best behavior. I'm sure it was an intentional psychological effect that the high-stakes room was placed just off center within the main room, the floor raised five feet higher and cordoned off by half walls of frosted glass. I wasn't sure I was going to like this at all.

I knew I had to prove my ability to play with the big boys. I'd withdrawn fifty thousand dollars from my savings account on the way. I'd almost thrown up my swordfish dinner.

"Welcome to our high-stakes room, Bee Cool." The poker room manager came by as I checked in at the desk and shook my hand. "I wondered how long it would take you to get here."

Forever would have been the answer if it weren't for gangs and kidnappers and missing goddaughters. I was a natural chicken when it came to big cash games. I'd much rather invest small and win big in a tournament than the opposite, which is how I interpreted most ring games. I told him I wanted to wait for the far corner table. Rabbit's foot and all that. He nodded, apparently used to this kind of request. "It might be a few minutes. We have a Saudi Arabian prince who's about blown his wad."

"What would be the size of a prince's wad?" I whispered to Shana. Her awesome eyebrow wiggle told me she might try to find out. I was glad to see my friend showing glimmers of her hedonistic self. Because, while I might want to remake her the way I thought she should be, I still loved her for who she was.

We ambled up the far ramp and peeked behind the frosted glass at the handful of tables in the high-stakes room. There was a rail here, making us true railbirds until one of us played. I wished it would be Shana instead of me.

After watching the only table that the logistics allowed us to see for thirty minutes, I was called to play. We'd seen some big names — mostly the young geniuses who wore athletic shoes with no socks and sports jerseys, and ate their meals out of boxes at the table so as to not miss a hand — make some money. In one hand, twenty-two-year-old Jerrod Nealy had shoved in all his chips and had to grapple for forty thousand dollars in bills in the pocket of his Suns shorts to go all in. Ack. I didn't know if I could hang with these guys. That was some people's entire net worth. I think the other guy ended up winning 150 thousand dollars but I couldn't count that fast.

It was heady if you were watching. Scary if you had to play.

"Good thing you have the thirty thousand Ben passed you," Shana commented in my ear at the time.

I hadn't wanted to take the cash Ben gave me on my way to purgatory. But I had taken it. For Affie.

Now, signaled by the room manager, I sidled over to the far table. Everybody stared at the striped atrocity I had on and the lumps under it, no doubt. I had noticed the player in the Redskins jersey first, when we'd come to the rail. If he hadn't been there, trust me, I would have bailed. I sat down in the open seat across from him. The rest of the table (aside from Redskin) was — from what I could gather — a collection of middle-aged, extremely well-heeled American amateurs, a millionaire from Hong Kong, a South African diamond heir who passed me his card with his room number and another hard-nosed pro out of Rincon. There were only two women in the entire room. One of them was me. The other was Cyndy Violette. I was grateful she wasn't at my table.

The sound of the chips clinking seemed magnified here, where talk was limited to a few exchanged words spaced between long silences. A sheen of sweat filmed Redskin's face. He didn't look too mentally stable. That probably would be bad if I'd planned to collude, but since I'd decided I was going to blow him off, it meant I could psyche him out. I hoped so anyway. I was the big blind, which wasn't as terrible as it might have seemed. I might lose this thousand but I would get the next seven hands to read the table. The dealer finished the shuffle and dished out the hole cards. An unsuited Queen/8 was a perfect fold but I rode out my big blind through the calls of the first round. Redskin was tapping on his cards. He wore an MP3 player so I assumed in the back of my mind that he was jamming to his tunes. The Flop came an 8 of diamonds and blanks — an Ace and 3 of spades. Then I did fold — too cheap and unsure to go in for Hong Kong's ten-thousand raise. Hong Kong had two pair, Redskin had pocket rockets.

The next three hands I folded straight away. Redskin was still tapping. Somehow that tapping looked familiar. After a royal flush draw Flop and King on The Turn, he folded too, but accidentally flipped over his cards at the end of the hand — once more, he had a pair. Hmm. He accidentally fumbled over his cards again on hands six and nine — one a flush draw and another a straight draw. He was chastised by the dealer and made an excuse about having some sort of neurological condition that made his hands go numb.

Sure.

It had taken ten hands for me to figure out that Redskin was actually tapping out a morse code of his cards — the way we were supposed to collude.

Two hours later, I was finding it difficult to ignore his tapping, so I struck up a conversation with the South African who had the hots for me. It was going to be difficult to extricate myself from some extracurricular plans he'd have for later tonight, ones he kept alluding to, but I had to worry about one pain in the ass at a time. Right now, I just had to win a bucket full of money. This was a tough table in one sense while being an unusually cool one in another sense, because the only one at it who saw me as a woman (and therefore handicapped) was South Africa. The rest just took me as a player. I wasn't used to that.

It made playing a bit more straightforward

even though I got less gimme opportunities from being underestimated. The pots made me extremely nervous, though. I'd held my own, even was ahead a bit, but only by betting when I had the nuts. I had yet to take a single chance.

"I never pegged you for a Mouse, Bee Cool," the Chicago hotelier commented. "I always marveled in the Big Kahuna, then when they broadcast the Gambler tournament, how predictably unpredictable you play and still consistently win."

I smiled. "Maybe this room intimidates me. And the stakes. Tournaments seem so much safer — just lose chips and your entry fee, not real greenbacks."

They did play with real cash, if the chips ran out during a hand. In one I thankfully had folded, Hong Kong and the California investor went heads-up on a royal straight flush draw. Hong Kong dug in his pocket for forty thousand-dollar bills. Ack.

"It's all in the mindset. You just have to imagine this is your local brick-and-mortar with dollar bills, or your twenty buck sit and go. Then, you can judge the cards fairly, read everyone's tells with the proper perspective."

Nodding, I thanked him. It was excellent advice. I laid a bad beat, winning forty-three thousand dollars on the next hand with four of a kind — fives — I wouldn't have stayed around to play an hour before.

"Hey, what kind of secret did you tell her?" Hong Kong argued.

The hotelier smiled, despite losing a fifer to me. South Africa sulked, since twenty-five thousand of that had been his. I guess we weren't going to as nice a place for the dinner he had already invited me to.

Redskin was seriously sweating now. I wasn't responding to his signals, and it was making him crazy. If I could figure out his motivation, I might get a lead on Affie. Probably midtwenties, he was white as they come — blond, blue eyed and corn raised. He didn't talk much, but I could've sworn I heard a Midwest accent. No visible tattoos, but that didn't mean he didn't have one. I just didn't see him hanging with Dragsnashark; he looked more like a skinhead candidate, but of course so had Happy Ending. I was developing an alarming headache. I excused myself to go to the restroom and stopped to talk to Shana. "Where's Ben?"

"The tattoo creep came around, and he followed him."

My heart seized. "What? How did he know it was him?"

"That snake/dragon/shark thing on his

neck is hard to miss."

"Why didn't he call Joe and have him do it?"

"He said Joe needs to be here for you."

I looked around nervously, noticing a couple of others brave enough to skinny along the narrow ramp and belly up to the high-stakes rail. The casino didn't make it inviting, so you either had to know someone playing or have balls enough to try to look over a million-dollar player's shoulder, waiting for a pit boss to breathe down your neck. Neither railbird revealed the telltale tattoo. "Look, Shan, I'd feel better if you played a little at a table down in the poker room. At least you'd be in the middle of things and not easy to snatch up if someone wanted to."

"I'll be fine. I have a good set of lungs."

"Which I'm sure they know and know how to neutralize. What if some old gentle-looking grandma came to tell you that your daughter sent a message that she was waiting outside the hotel right now?"

Shana looked down, caught. "I'd go. I'd have to. Just in case."

"Exactly my point — they'd hand Grandma a C-note, shove you into a car and whisk you away. These guys are ruthless. I can't lose you too. Besides, I need the extra pair of legs to help find Aph."

Shana sighed. "Okay, I'll go play."

"I'll come back for you. Don't leave with anyone else. Under any circumstances."

Nodding, she wandered off to sign up for a table. I locked myself into a stall in the restroom and heard the restroom door open. The knock at my stall door sent my heart to my throat. "Bee Cool?"

When I opened my mouth, but couldn't make a sound come out, the female voice demanded: "Cool!?"

"Y-yes?"

"It's Thelma. I got some good scoop and I thought you'd never get up from that damned table."

EIGHTEEN

Thelma already had her hand out by the time I exited the stall. Sighing, I reached into my Betsey Johnson and pulled out a hundred for her. I think I'd created a monster. She cocked her head at it. "What I got is damned good. It might be worth more, I'm thinking."

It was one thing to be motivated. It was another to be greedy. I just wasn't sure how much I could trust greedy information. I'd just have to wait and see. Thelma must've been doing more nosing around for me than playing poker. I raised my eyebrows. "If it's that good, I'll pay double for the next report."

"I guess that's fair." A good sign, apparently she thought there was more where that came from.

After a long pause, I nudged, "I've got to get back, Thelma, let's have it."

"The Reverend Phineas Paul is a big creep."

I shouldn't have encouraged her the first time when she had something on the stupid pain-in-the-you-know-what minister. I wanted something on the Medula and Dragsnashark and his friends. Instead my paid informant was wasting time and money on Paul. "Thelma —"

"And the church is a cult."

"What do you mean?"

"Y'know, like the Branch Davidians, Jim Jones' People's Temple, the Uganda doomsday sect, he has a compound and everything. In southwestern Oregon, on the Idaho border. A day's drive from here. In the woods."

Woods? Idaho? Oregon? That rang a recent bell but I couldn't remember why. "Old timers" was setting in. Or maybe "overwhelmers."

"Where did you hear this?"

"Hey, I'm not stupid. I tell you and you cut me out."

The level of trust was heartwarming. "Look, Thelma, I just want to make sure your source is reliable."

"I don't think you got much room for being choosy. I don't notice no information train heading through your crib."

Now I was getting sass. I think I needed a lesson in managing informants. I sighed —

of course she was also right. I had exactly one car on my info train. "Okay, Thelma, go ahead with whatever else you've got. Even though I was kind of hoping for something on the Medula — the creeps with the dragon/shark/snake tattoos instead of crosses."

"I don't know nothing about them, but I've heard talk about snakes with the Bible thumpers."

"What about snakes?" Here was the first connection — snake head in the tattoo of the Medula, snakes in Paul's church. I prayed it wasn't a coincidence. With my luck it would be.

"That this Church of the Believers might be a sect of those snake handlers."

I shivered. I actually owned a snake. A pet. Grog had been an inheritance I didn't want. Although I'd become attached to mine, I don't like the fanged reptiles as a general rule. I especially didn't like them wielded by bloodthirsty criminals and religious zealots. "What else?"

"Whoo, Cool, you never satisfied, are you?"

I swallowed my comeback, hiding it with a smile. "Thanks, so much, Thelma."

"See that was worth more than a pissy hundred, now, right?"

I nodded, not trusting myself to speak as I pushed my way out the bathroom door and back to the high-stakes room. I was angry at Phineas Paul, not only for distracting me with his rhetoric, but every ear to the ground I had as well. I might just have to put him in his place the next time I saw him.

Back at the table, Redskin had raked in a hand or two by the looks of it. I found that difficult to believe, since he seemed only a marginally capable player, certainly not one who could hang in the ranks of a prince, diamond heir and trillionaire hotelier. Sweat beaded his upper lip as soon as he saw me. I guess I was the only one who made him nervous.

That was probably good, because I was tired of this game and ready to put everyone out of their misery, especially me.

Unfortunately the cards weren't on the same page. I was dealt a Doyle Brunson, of all things. I stared at the deuce of diamonds, 10 of diamonds, disgusted. Only one person in America could be lucky enough to win with this — Doyle had done it, twice, in the WSOP years ago.

"Ready for dinner yet, doll?" South Africa whispered.

Grr. I called the big blind and the reraise

for twenty-three thousand dollars. This is not an advisable option — betting to prove a man wrong — but sometimes Lady Luck remembers which gender pool she belongs to. The Flop came a deuce of spades, 10 of hearts and 5 of diamonds. I had two pair now, not super, but beating out anyone who might hold pocket rockets. If somebody had fives in the hole, well, I was sunk. I raised. Everyone hung in, which was disturbing. South Africa reraised, so I went along, just because. Fourth Street came another diamond, a 9 — now I had a flush draw too and still the high pair playing off the board. Goody.

With about two hundred thousand in the pot, The River brought a 10 of spades. I had the nuts. I went all in. Everyone folded but a perplexed Redskin who'd been tapping furiously to no avail and my would-be date. He went all in too.

"How many suckout hands have you gotten anyway?" South Africa whined.

"Not as many as you remember," I commented as I hauled in my chips and random cash, counting in my head as I did.

The hotelier said: "Beat out by what made you rich — diamonds. That's a helluva thing, isn't it?"

I counted my money — I'd made enough

to call it an afternoon. I thanked the boys, picked up my stack and went to cash out.

For some reason, South Africa had forgotten his invitation. Dinner wasn't mentioned in the grunted good-bye.

The kidnappers had been right. It took forever to get the cash. No less than fifteen times, someone from the casino office came out to ask me if I wouldn't rather have casino credit, a check, anything but greenbacks. The longer I sat at the three-card poker table, the more money I made.

Unfortunately for them, it was still my lucky day and I'd won another thirty-three hundred dollars by the time they finally delivered me my winnings. I'd seen the other gang member lurking and wondered if he wasn't supposed to be following me to the drop since Ben had neutralized Dragsnashark. Ingrid had passed by about thirty minutes before to inform me she was picking up Shana and would meet us at the suite after the drop. Now I hoped Joe had gotten my page and was waiting for me outside the hotel. I was tough, I was independent, but I didn't want to walk around Vegas with this much money, a cop on my tail, a bad guy in spitting distance and probably a few religious heretics behind a pillar or two without my own personal Marlboro Man in my back pocket.

The drop went off quietly, although along the way Joe had disappeared and had yet to reappear. I guessed if Frank ever showed again, the permanent loss of his right-hand man would tick him off, and since for some reason I cared about that, I retraced my steps before meeting up with the group in case Joe had sprained his ankle or something.

I was almost back to the Mellagio when a hand reached out and grabbed me, dragging me into a sex store. My heart pounded. My palms sweated.

Darn it. It was just Joe.

Having a serious conversation with my boyfriend's hot assistant between a leather and chain bustier and a whip collection was a bit disarming, although Joe didn't seem to notice where we were at all.

"Do you know that the Redskins' colors are red and yellow?"

"Okay?" I said, slowly, distracted by the odd-shaped plastic thing hanging from the ceiling. "What's that?"

Joe put his knuckle under my chin and forced my focus back to him. "And Affie sent you that note in red and yellow . . ."

I guess I had just spent six hours *not* making that connection. *Duh.*

"Do you think it means something?"

"I don't know. Maybe. I lost you because I had an opportunity to chat with your poker buddy." Joe was staring down at his hand, flexing his fingers, examining his palm.

"My supposed collusion partner? Where is he?" I looked around, why I don't know since I didn't expect him to have hung around, becoming Joe's best friend. One could hope, however.

"At the hospital, I guess."

"What?"

"Well, he wasn't as forthcoming as I'd have liked. I was nice. I threw him out on the sidewalk so someone would call an ambulance."

"Joe! You can't hurt people to get information."

"Why not? They're hurting Affie and she didn't do anything to deserve it. Look at it in terms of a business goal, Bee, and how to reach it. There are lots of paths to the same destination — it depends on how fast you want to get there. I'd like to take a Learjet instead of walking to find this girl. At FBG, we are cleared to use what it takes at the time."

I swallowed, trying not to think about

Frank telling them to kill people to meet the "goal." "It didn't really do any good this time, though, did it?" I asked a bit self-righteously, I'll admit.

"It actually might have. I'll let you know after I follow up on a couple of leads.

"Why can't you tell me now?"

"Because I don't want you going after what I'm going after. When Frank gets back, he'll kill me."

"Don't you mean 'if'?" I corrected.

Joe shot me a warning look as he grabbed my elbow and led me along like a reluctant kindergartener to the restaurant.

Despite the fact that I had grilled Joe all the way back — about the Redskin information and Frank's past — I knew nothing more than that he'd been captain of his high school baseball team and he'd lived on MoonPies and Mountain Dew as a nine-year-old. Believe me, I'd looked him up on Google enough times, but Frank Gilbert is a pretty common name and he'd never told me exactly where in California he'd grown up. I still didn't know, by the way. I wasn't finished working on Joe, but I obviously was going to have to get more creative in my investigative techniques. Maybe I'd sic Thelma on him.

"Where's Ben?" I asked when Shana and Ingrid came around the corner of the restaurant, having apparently not yet committed to a table.

"Don't tell her yet," was Ingrid's recommendation.

"He's gone to the tattoo place."

"Why? Did he forget something last night?"

"No, he is going to get the shark/snake/dragon tattooed on his neck and try to break into the gang."

I tried to maintain some semblance of sanity so I modulated my voice when I said: "WHAT?!"

"His idea. He insisted." Shana explained.

"Okay, none of this is making sense. I'm touched my brother cares about my goddaughter but this is a bit over the top. I need to know what is going on."

"Bee," Shana said, "you are always talking about his focus mode. Remember how wrapped up in Steely Stan he got and he didn't even personally know the guy . . . maybe he's using focus mode now for a better cause."

"I'm sure that's the case but why?"

I could tell she knew something but wasn't going to tell me. Shana crossed her arms over her chest and said quietly, "Whatever the reason, I'm grateful."

"I'm scared. These guys are ruthless kill-ers."

"And they have my baby."

I shut up and ran out the door, headed for the Tattoo Palace.

NINETEEN

I was too late.

Either that or Ben had spread a lot of money around to make sure folks at the Palace kept their mouths shut. Or maybe he just flirted with the walking artwork behind the desk. Sometimes that's all it took for Ben to win undying loyalty.

"I thought it took longer than an hour and a half to get an elaborate tattoo?" I argued with the Garden of Eden who wore a peeka-boo dress that looked like a collection of vines.

"Perhaps your brother changed his mind and went simple," she said, without looking up from the current issue of *Ink World*. "Perhaps you misjudged the time it was when he arrived."

I sighed. I wasn't getting a lot of sympathy here. I opened my wallet, extracted a hundred-dollar bill and waved it under Garden's nose. She finally raised her gaze and stared at me without blinking for longer than I thought humanly possible. Perhaps she was part lizard. She had the heart of one.

"Miss Cooley, this is not a craps table. I advise you return to The Strip and use that there."

I looked back in my wallet. Only one hundred remained. I should have stuffed some of that fifty thousand into my bra before I'd left the hotel. I pulled it out and waved it around.

Garden looked back down at her magazine.

Sighing, I turned like I was going to leave, then spun and sprinted down the hallway, ignoring her hollering at me to stop. At Joaquin's door, I knocked but didn't wait, flinging it open to see the tattoo artist bent over what had to be a two-hundred-pound, lily white rump that was adorned with half a tiger.

Meow.

"Sorry," I choked out.

Joaquin leaped up and came to the door. "Bee Cool, what's got you so worked up? Didn't you like what I put on your back?"

Slightly alarmed, I realized I hadn't even checked what damage he'd done to my back. I made a mental note to see that along with the website when I got back to the hotel, then I explained why I was there. He shook his head, sadly, and, dammit, I believed him. "I haven't seen Ben. But I've been busy." He waved toward his client. I gulped as the tiger undulated when the woman pushed herself up off the table to wiggle her fingers in a wave. "But that doesn't mean he didn't use another artist here."

"Do you think you could find out? The receptionist wasn't helpful."

A hand clamped onto my upper arm and dragged me back into the hall. "Hey!" I argued as another hand clamped onto the opposite arm. I was flanked by a pair of overtattooed, overgrown bullies. Bouncers at a tattoo parlor? This town had to have the highest per capita bouncer population in the world. I bet even the McDonald's had a couple.

"Chill, dudes," Joaquin said soothingly. "She's cool. She's leaving. Right, Bee?"

His eyes were both apologetic and pleading with me to leave. It looked like for my own good.

"Sure," I said. Reluctantly, they loosened their grips to mere bruise-causing clamps.

"Come on, let her go," Joaquin urged.

Even more reluctantly, they released my

arms. I shook them out with great relief and started back the way I'd come, peering into open rooms, listening for the sound of Ben's voice. The pair of goons followed so closely they were breathing on the top of my head. As we passed Garden, she didn't look up from her magazine, but as she tapped her fingers on the desk, a muscle in her upper arm jumped, making the snake's tongue look like it was moving back and forth.

It looked like I had a ride back to The Strip or to the clink. Trankosky leaned against his unmarked sedan, its engine idling, outside the front door of the Tattoo Palace. He pushed off and went around to the passenger side, opening the door for me. "Belinda, if you please . . ."

I glared, and glanced around for a moment. Full dark had descended while I was in the building. A couple of unsavories were hanging out at the far end of the parking lot, keeping a close eye on what their radar had told them was a cop. It had been difficult enough to hail a cab on The Strip, no telling how long I'd have to hang out to get one on the way out of this joint. None happened to be gliding by the Parlor at the moment. I know the Die Hard cop wasn't my favorite person but he was a known enemy at least. I slid into the seat.

"Gosh, if I'd known you were following me, you could have given me a ride over here and saved me cab fare."

"If I'd been following you, I think you would've known it."

"Not necessarily. I've been a little distracted lately." For some reason, tears welled up behind my eyelids. I forced them away. Feeling sorry for myself wasn't going to help Affie, Frank or Ben. Or me. Then, suddenly I was tempted to tell Detective Growly of all people all about the kidnappings, the disappearances, the blackmail. I bit my tongue. *Bad Bee. Bee Strong.*

"Yes, distracted by making money drops to gangbangers, being the whipping girl of the Church of the Believers and getting smack in the middle of rumors of two separate incidents of collusion?"

"What?" I blurted to the last. The cops already knew about the marked WSOP chips and Redskin's morse coding at the high-stakes table?

"That's the buzz about Bee on the street," he said with a light tone, apparently amused by his own joke.

"It almost looks like you're being set up, by someone in the inside, another player maybe . . . except I know better."

I blew out a breath. Every time he acted like he might believe my innocence he went hard on me again.

Neither of us said anything for a full minute, then he added quietly, "You know Belinda, if you tell me what you're not telling me, or even part of what you're not telling me, maybe I could help you, maybe I could help keep the brass from pushing this investigation so hard."

I shook my head. "I haven't done anything wrong."

"Except get involved with a bad ex-cop." Trankosky wasn't joking anymore. His voice was now as merciless as his face. His ironic mouth just looked disappointed.

I held my breath, hoping he would say more about Frank without my asking. Finally I said, "Joaquin is an ex-cop? Wow. Who knew."

"Who's Joaquin?"

"The tattoo artist."

His eyebrows flew up as he exclaimed, "You're involved with the tattoo guy?"

"No, not involved *that* way, he's an aquaintance."

Trankosky hit the heel of his hand to his head. "I feel like I am in a Cary Grant/Doris Day flick."

"Flattering yourself, aren't you?"

He shook his head, fighting down the corners of his mouth. At least I'd distracted him from Frank. I really wasn't ready to hear how bad Frank was. Not yet.

"One day, Miss Cooley, your cheekiness is going to get you into trouble."

"You are way too late with that warning."

Trankosky smiled. "You know, you are one of the most likable criminals I've ever encountered in twenty years on the force."

"Maybe that's because I'm not a criminal. You don't have any proof I am, or you'd have arrested me already."

"That's not always the way it works, sometimes we hope you'll lead us to a bigger jackpot."

"You might still hit a jackpot following me around, but it's not because I'm doing anything wrong."

"You're going to have to be incredibly lucky or incredibly smart to get yourself out of the mess you're in now," Trankosky said, throwing the Crown Vic into park. "You'd better hope all you lose is your freedom, and not your life." His fingers opened my fisted hand, slid in his card with a cell phone number scribbled on the face and closed my fingers back around it.

"Thank you for not dipping," I said, nodding to the snuff box in the console he'd been toying with distractedly since I'd gotten in the car.

"Oh, that." He sighed. "It's nasty, isn't it? I quit smoking last month and a friend suggested I dip tobacco to smooth the transition. Bad advice because now I've got that to quit. I'm at twelve hours and counting. Maybe you'll live to see me hit twenty-four."

Every time he said something approaching likable he ruined it. I opened my door. He got out to hold it for me, but I'd already slammed it and made it six feet down the sidewalk before he reached the passenger side of the sedan. "When you get ready to tell me what you aren't telling me, call." I could feel him watching me walk away. For some odd reason, it gave me a sense of security. Maybe he was right. Maybe jail was the safest place for me right now.

Shana and Ingrid weren't back when I let myself into our suite. They'd gone to take Moon another item for her psychometry. I didn't know how a bra of Affie's that ended up in Shana's luggage would help, but I wasn't about to tell Shana not to try it. Besides, it made her feel useful. She was nearing an emotional breakdown; I could feel it. That was one thing about people so charismatic, so electric — sometimes they faded fast. My pet name for Shana when we used to go clubbing was Firefly because that's as bright as she was, how drawn others were to her.

I didn't know if Ben going off half-cocked was going to help or hurt her ability to maintain. He'd been hovering so, it would have driven me crazy a long time ago.

The phone rang, and again, stupidly I assumed it was one of my friends.

"Miss Cooley, you didn't do as we asked. Your goddaughter's time is running out."

"Excuse me, but I *did* do as you asked. I delivered you actually *more* than you asked for. If you didn't get it, well, I'd call the cops and report it stolen."

"Very amusing. We have the cash. But you failed to collude to get it."

"Why would that matter to you?" Where was Frank when I needed him? He'd be able to make sense of this puzzle.

I could hear the receiver being covered. A muffled, unintelligible conversation taking place. "You can't always rely on luck to win. If we want you to win, you'd better or your Aphrodite is dead. You're not going to be able to keep that up every day. No one can."

I thought about Affie in the clutches of these money-hungry gangbangers, Ben off to commit suicide by joining the selfsame killers, Frank missing and/or drunk and/or a hunted murderer. I thought about mathematician Richard's theory on luck and love. Everything I loved was pretty much having bad luck right now. It was worth a gamble. "Wanna bet?"

"You shouldn't be betting with your Aphrodite's life. We'll be in touch."

I jumped at the knock at the door. That was certainly quick. The wimp in me was tempted to not answer it. The rest of me went straight to the knob and yanked it open violently without looking through the peephole.

I'd scared Ringo out of his wits. As he hesitated, I grabbed him by the arm and pulled him inside. The hallway was empty, but I wasn't taking any chances with my friends.

"What's wrong, Bee?"

Everything. "Nothing, Ringo." I couldn't tell one of the sweetest people I'd ever had the pleasure to call a friend even a tenth of what was happening. For one, I hated to mar the innocent, naive soul I so often envied. Furthermore, he was so devoted to me that I was afraid he would storm Medula gangland with a burning torch to bring Affie back. Ringo had the street smarts of a domestic rabbit.

"I've got it! You're just tired from all that winning at the Main Event." He high-fived me. "Great play. Lucky cards."

"No kidding. About the luck, that is."

"Once again, you're way too modest. There's really something bothering you." He peered at me. "Is it that crazy preacher, eh?"

"Phineas Paul is a bit distracting."

"Well, I've got something to cheer you up."

I could think of a half dozen things that would cheer me up, none of which Ringo would be privy to. "What?" I asked anyway.

"Chanel is ecstatic about your exposure on all the news stations. They want you to be their model."

"Obviously I am, every time I wear a pair of their sunglasses."

"No, Bee, they want to make it official. It's kind of sudden, but they want to do a shoot tomorrow morning at the hotel, before the next round."

"What? No!" I was used to being on the other end of ad campaigns, behind the camera not in front of it.

Ringo looked like I shot his favorite dog. He hung his head. "I thought you'd be excited."

"Excited?" I let out a breath. "I *am* excited. Thrilled in fact. It's just unexpected.

A shock."

"Just like Christmas!" Ringo rubbed his hands together. "Or a surprise birthday party!"

Look at that face, how was I going to say no?

"What time are we supposed to be there?" I asked Ringo as Joe let himself into the suite. "Where's the party?" he asked Ringo, shaking his hand.

"Not a party. An ad shoot."

Joe looked in question at me. "I didn't know you were working here."

"I'm not the agent. I'm the model for this one."

"Huh," Joe said. "Sorry Frank's not here to see this."

"Maybe he will be."

"It doesn't look like it, does it?"

When I didn't answer, he passed over a fax. "That's the report on Affie's note. Her handwriting. Common Crayola pens. Common generic copy paper, used in about three hundred million copiers, faxes and printers throughout the world. No finger-prints we could match through the database. But there was one thing . . ."

I looked at the sheet. It was gobbledygook to me. "What?" I demanded.

"There were some microscopic traces on

the paper — usually this is what we are going for when we test. We don't know what
they mean, but —"

"Joe, get on with it."

"There was pollen from a certain spring
flower indigenous to the northern Rockies
and snake skin."

Snake? Before Joe could add any more, I
picked up the landline and dialed home.

I withstood five minutes of small talk
about a scourge of white flies on her toma-
toes and before I finally broke down I asked,
"Mom, how's my snake?"

"Pookie, you know I hate that thing."

"I know, Mom. That's why I asked Dad to
take care of him."

Pause. Sound of Mom pulling weeds in
her garden. Sound of Dad starting up lawn-
mower so I couldn't even hope for him to
save me.

"So has Dad been taking care of him?" I
prayed for patience.

Sound of huge guilt-inducing sigh.

"No, I didn't want to tell you because I
was afraid you'd be upset."

Ten-nine-eight-seven . . . "Tell me what,
Mom?"

"The wretched reptile disappeared. The
same night Affie did."

Huh. I didn't know what that meant. Why

would some kidnappers have let Affie lug along a ten-foot-long pet? Joe was asking me something but my mind was too full of possibilities to listen.

"Bee?" Joe asked after a pause.

I glanced from the carpet that I wished held all the answers back up to his face. "Did you hear me?" he asked.

"No, I'm sorry."

"I asked if your pet is a rattlesnake?"

"No, Grog is a python."

"Then it's not your snake's skin traces on the note. This snake was a rattler."

TWENTY

Reverend Phineas Paul stood on a riser in the middle of a crowd of people on the sidewalk in front of the Fortune. It was pretty easy to tell his followers from the Vegas tourists by their dress. In fact, I'd looked a little like a follower yesterday. Not today, though, not in the getup Ingrid had messengered over for me to wear for the shoot.

"Do you good people know there is a bunch of sinners, many of them here in this city for this godforsaken tournament, who say they pray to the '*Church* of Texas Hold 'Em'? This is a sacrilege. This is the work of the devil. The game might seem an innocent diversion at first, for your youth, your brothers, your sisters, your wives, your husbands, but soon instead of holding a Bible, they will be holding cards. Instead of giving to a collection plate for God's work, they'll be giving to a felt table, paying for the devil to drag them straight down to the depths of hell!"

Okay. Paul was pretty worked up today. He was fascinating to watch. Even though I despised the man and disagreed with everything that came out of his mouth, I couldn't tear my gaze away. He had charisma plus.

"They tempt you by saying 'come worship' — in their altar of sin? Why would someone succumb to that, I ask."

I was rethinking my brave thought of taking him on and had decided to quietly skirt the group when he caught sight of me.

"I ask that of you, Bee Cool." He spat my name like I was Mary Magdalene before she was forgiven. Perfect day to take on the holy roller, since I looked like a modern version of what Mary had been, in the clingy silk shortie dress in a rainbow of colors. I don't know what I'd been thinking when I'd expected to sneak by when I was impossible to miss. "I ask you, oh you queen of gamblers, what you say about a secular — nay, a sinful — organization calling innocents to pray in a temple of money and greed?"

"Uh, I don't belong to the Church of Texas Hold 'Em, Mr. Paul, but if you ask me, I think it's just a bit of a light take on poker, an irony. Like, a joke?"

"God is a . . ." Gasp. Grab throat. ". . .

267

joke, Miss Cooley?"

"That's not what I said, Mr. Paul."

"That is *Reverend* Paul to you."

Okay, time to take the gloves off. Time to show some teeth. The cameras, which had been busy with the interview of the current chip leader, Rahn Vinoy, at the other end of the sidewalk, moved in on the two of us now, like sharks smelling blood in the water.

"Reverend Paul, what would you call what you do? Seducing young girls with the selfsame money you criticize?"

A gasp rose from the gathered crowd. Paul went apoplectic, his mouth opening and closing, his face glowing red.

I couldn't get away with the illusion that he was a pimp for much longer, so I continued. "Paying them to walk your picket line when they don't believe the messages they hold?"

"Who doesn't BEE-LIEVE the messages they hold?" he boomed at the teenage picketers. A couple of them looked curiously at the signs they held. I tried not to laugh out loud. No one, however, volunteered to answer his question.

"If so, you may bring me your sign. Turn it in. I will find someone else to carry on your holy work. There is no reason for you to walk down the road to salvation if you do not BEE-LIEVE."

No takers. The girls just kept walking. Bunch of zombies.

Paul had carefully not denied my claim.

Time to push. "Can you deny that you pay these girls to protest for you?"

"Not for me, for our community. For the world," he said, his voice rising in a crescendo, his hand on his heart, his eyes heavenward. "Other valuable members of my congregation are occupied with blessed duties that these girls are not yet able to perform. The means always justify the ends when the end is a holy work of the Lord. It will all make sense when we come to judgment.

"When we come to judgment, Miss Cooley, wouldn't you rather BEE-lieve than BEE Cool? Repent and live forever! Repent and save the millions you are corrupting. Repent and save the world from the evil legacy of poker."

I suppressed the shiver. And was saved by the sunglasses, as the Chanel reps surrounded me and led me into the hotel.

The shoot went relatively smoothly and painlessly, so much so that it tempted me to change careers. Modeling gigs might be the way to go. Of course, at forty-one, what was

I a potential candidate for besides poker-appropriate eyewear? Antiaging creams? Cellulite busters? Eighteen-hour support bras?

I managed to depress myself by the time I got to my table, a whole half hour early. Blackie was already there, as she always was. I wondered what time she got there.

"Do you sleep under the table or something?" I grumped.

She shook her head perhaps a centimeter back and forth, that was all, but I could tell she was making fun of me. How could someone with no sound and no facial expression mock someone else? What an art form.

What self-control.

I think she was my new hero.

"Where are you from?" I asked.

No answer.

"Are you so unfriendly because you're in your zone, or because you don't like anyone else?

"You know, I want to beat you just to see if you stand up and swear at me in Vietnamese or something."

She clearly wasn't Vietnamese but I thought that might get her talking.

"Watch out. If you cuss at me in Filipino, I'll know what you're saying because my best friend's mom is from Manila."

Nothing. No response. She could be dead.

If so, she might really be my hero, because I'd be put out of my current misery.

"Good talk," I told Blackie.

The dealer looked between the two of us and raised his eyebrows. At tournaments, the dealers are rotated every twenty minutes or so to prevent any kind of cheating. This year, the WSOP was doing random rotations, different amounts of time, unpredictable tables. We'd had this particular dealer, Ronnie, several times and he seemed to have a sense of humor. Some of them don't, and, trust me, it's a drag.

"Ladies." He nodded to us as he sat down.

"What's new?" I asked, feeling particularly punchy. I hadn't slept well two nights in a row, my mind full of clues, my body startling at every sound that could be Frank. If he didn't show by the end of tonight, I knew what I had to do and didn't want to think about it.

"The talk this morning's been that big bust of some Hold 'Em players at the Toucan."

"What bust?"

"Didn't you see the paper? It's the on front page." Ronnie took the *Las Vegas Tribune* out from under his arm and handed

271

it to me. A photo of some middle-aged men and some young-looking teens being herded into paddy wagons by police. "This was an in-house tournament of some pros that play pretty low-level games but are household names around Vegas, old-timers. They were caught with underage girls — the girls are claiming consensual sex but that's still jail time, right?"

"Hold 'Em's really getting a black eye this Main Event, isn't it?" I observed, peering closer at the photo. One of the girls was wearing an Abercrombie shirt like the little brunette who'd hit me up for an autograph and bus fare. She was standing next to a blonde with a Juicy shirt on and a side ponytail . . .

"Hey, I know these two," I blurted.

Ronnie raised his eyebrows. "What kind of crowd do you hang with?"

"These girls hit me up for bus fare home a couple of days ago." I sighed. "Guess they didn't go home, huh?"

"Where was home?"

"Oregon, they said."

Ronnie shrugged. "No good deed goes unpunished. See, now you can feel guilty."

"Too late, I already did."

I guess it was fortunate that my life was falling apart around me, because it certainly made playing cards easier. When the lives of most people I loved hung in the balance, suddenly the cards, chips and bets seemed trivial. Knowing I wouldn't be sitting there unless one of those lives depended on it made the game just another job. It's how I managed the Big Kahuna, my entrée into Hold 'Em. It was how I would manage getting through the biggest poker tournament in the history of the world.

I don't know if I've mentioned it before, but I don't play, aka do leisure time, well. I *do* work well. Or rather, more precisely, I work better than I play. So I was going to work at this Main Event. Deciding that took a huge and sudden load off my shoulders.

First order of business: read the players. We started the deal with five. Blackie I knew, or rather, was familiar with. I didn't know how well I really understood her but, so far, I'd let my intuition read her, and it was doing well enough to spare me any intellectual analysis. The other five were a veterinarian who played with his mustache anytime he didn't have the nuts, a local twenty-one dealer off The Strip who had so many facial expressions it was like seeing his cards, a Cincinnati computer expert who muttered nonsense to himself, a young man who said his wife had just given birth to quadruplets and who sighed heavily when he had a betting hand, and a woman who tortured her cuticles when she had a pair.

In my first pocket I got a Michael Jordan — those of you who know basketball *and* Hold 'Em are crying, because you know that's a two/three. All black, spade and club respectively. That was a no-brainer if I were anywhere but in the big blind. Come on, with as much as I had on the felt, I had to hang. Like Mike.

A 2 of clubs, Queen of diamonds and Jack of clubs Flop. I should have folded. But since Blackie didn't breathe, Cincinnati was sweating so much he had a swimming pool behind his shades and was muttering double time, and Twenty-one sure enough had a Big Slick straight draw, I decided to stay in. It didn't cost much because everybody left had turned into calling stations.

Fourth Street brought a 2 of hearts. Big deal. I was betting Cincinnati had a pair of Queens in his pocket. But if so, it was time for him to raise and he didn't. I didn't know if he was trying to slow play me or if I'd misread his hand as just a pair. I called because I couldn't decide. Blackie hung in too, although I wasn't sure why unless she had some Jack interest. I couldn't believe it when The River fell another deuce. What were the odds of me drawing four of a kind twice in forty-eight hours? It hadn't been masterful play, but I had been lucky. And I had so tentatively played the whole hand that I kept it up, small raising and waiting for Twenty-one to reraise. Nobody knew what anyone had, so Blackie reraised. The pot was looking more comfortable when I flipped over the nuts.

Everyone glared. I think Cincinnati said a bad word. It wasn't by artifice, but now no one was going to be able to read me for at least a couple more hands, because I wouldn't have been able to read myself on that one.

Five hands later, I'd folded two, lost one and won a big one. The latter was a gift, as most luck is. I had what Ben likes to call a "flat tire" in my pocket. Guess it yet? It's a Jack/four, as in a flat tire is what you use a jack for. Heart/diamond. Anyway, it's not much to hang a call, much less a bet, on. I was in late position, which is the only reason why I called when three others had folded. It wasn't too expensive to see The Flop. So, I succumbed to temptation:

Four of hearts, 10 of hearts, 4 of spades. No kidding.

Gotta love that.

Unless you're Phineas Paul, who would hate that I'd been rewarded for sin.

That made me even happier.

I stayed cool, calling, allowing anyone who thought they had a flush draw or straight draw to have hope. The vet, who may have had a ten pair or three of a kind, raised and the rest of us called. I don't think anyone figured I had the nuts. When The Turn came a Queen of hearts, I was thrilled. This was shaping up to make me some money. A ten could fall on The River and mess me up big time with a bigger four of a kind, but that was it. I held the Jack of hearts, preventing a royal flush even if someone had an Ace of hearts, King of hearts. I raised about a quarter of my stack. Eyebrows went up but the vet hid a smile as he reraised. Yep, he had a pair of tens in his pocket. He was a jackal for sure, since it apparently hadn't occurred to him I might already have four of a kind. I think he pegged me for the flush. I called him and only stayed in, hoping I'd imagine to see a royal flush. On The River's Ace of hearts, I went all in expecting everyone to bail. But Twenty-one went for broke too. Now I had a stack that let me play almost any way I wanted for the rest of the night.

276

■ ■ ■ ■

Again, the phone rang when I walked in the door of the suite. The last time it creeped me out. This time it irritated me.

I let it ring. And ring. And ring. As my heart pounded and pounded and pounded. My mouth went dry. What would happen if I didn't answer? What if it was Frank?

Finally, I picked up.

"Don't play with us, Miss Cooley. You won't like what happens when you do."

"Maybe I want to find out if you're bluffing while I'm betting."

"Cute card analogy. It won't be so cute when we send you your goddaughter's head in a box."

The matter-of-fact way he said it made me believe it. Unquestionably. And I had asked for it. I blinked back tears. "Is she okay?" My voice wavered. I hated myself.

"She's alive."

I breathed deeply for a few moments to regain my composure.

"This time we provide the cash, and you lose it all. It should improve your odds the next time you play."

"It's heartwarming for you to be so considerate of me, but somehow I don't think that's your motivation. Losing all your money doesn't make any sense."

"You don't understand, Miss Cooley, this doesn't have to make sense. You just have to do it. Don't go out for breakfast tomorrow, the money will be brought to your door in a room-service table. Go to the high-stakes room in Poseidon's, play at a table with a man wearing an emerald in his right ear. Lose every bit of our money, but take at least an hour and a half to do it."

"Uh-huh. And then what?"

"And then wait for us to tell you what to do."

"Where's Affie?"

"You don't need to know."

I peered at the phone in my hand. The religious slap on the wrist was weird, but even the Sopranos went to church so I guessed Dragsnashark-tattooed gangbangers could too. I buried my head in my hands. What was I supposed to do now? I thought they were just using me to *make* money, but now I was supposed to *lose* their money? This puzzle had become a riddle with no answer. I needed Frank.

At the very least, I needed to know where to look for him. After I'd hung up the phone, sat down and contemplated the carpet for what seemed like hours, I finally made the call I'd been dreading.

TWENTY-ONE

"Have you ever considered that another player might be framing you?"

"What do you mean?" I asked Joe. We sat in the suite, with our morning coffee, going through the leads he'd followed up to no avail, and my night at the table. I waited for him to expound on what seemed to be a popular theory.

"Well, it just seems strange that of the hundreds of visibly recognizable Hold 'Em players here for the Main Event, you'd be the one with a kidnapped goddaughter. You'd be the one with a knife in the felt and swimming with a dead body within twelve hours of the first deal. You are the one the good reverend decides to pick on. I mean, there are plenty of players who walk the line between right and wrong he could easily find to throw stones at. Heck, Owen Gibbs is an open devil worshipper. Why not him? Why not the guy who runs the Church of Texas Hold 'Em site — Father Ashley. He's here. No, instead it's nice but often raunchily dressed Bee Cool he chooses as his scapegoat. Why?"

"But why would another player want to do this to me?"

"You've risen in the ranks of Hold 'Em amateurs relatively quickly. Some might resent that."

"With the advent of Internet play, lots of people have come from nowhere to land on the poker map."

"Not a lot have gotten endorsements. Not a lot have a website with a million hits."

I shrugged, wondering how he got that statistic when I didn't even know it. "I can't take credit for the website, Ingrid does that. And, a couple dozen free sunglasses isn't that big a deal."

"They aren't paying you for the commercial?"

"Oh that, well yeah, but that came after all this drama at the Main Event."

"And you *are* beautiful."

I squirmed. "Not any more than many women who play Hold 'Em."

He raised his eyebrows. I squirmed harder. I cleared my throat. "Really, what kind of reason is that to frame me?"

"You'd be surprised." Joe paused for an

awkward moment. "Okay," he continued, dropping that subject, thank goodness. "Any enemies?"

I thought about the last two major tournaments I'd played. "Sure, but I think they are all either dead or in jail. Except maybe Denton Ferris, who I wouldn't call an enemy, exactly, just a weirdo."

"He doesn't like you?"

"He doesn't like anybody."

Ingrid burst through the door. "I can't find Smack anywhere."

"When is the last time you saw Jack?" I asked Ingrid, after pouring her a glass of Perrier (she refused coffee — it was bad for her complexion) and making her sit down on the couch. She finally stopped hyperventilating. It had been fascinating to watch. Ingrid was such a control freak and I realized now that for the last year, I'd always seen her in her element — bossing people around. I'd never seen her when control had been snatched away. Add in the fact that she actually seemed to be in love with Jack and I was doubly amazed. I hadn't been convinced Ingrid possessed any deep emotion until now.

"Smack didn't come back to his apartment last night. He won't answer his phone.

I've been to every poker room in town I can think of, but nobody's seen him."

"That doesn't mean much. They don't see him when he is there." I pointed out.

"I looked under the tables too."

"Maybe he's with Frank."

"I doubt it," Ingrid said drily. I guess *everybody* thought Frank was curled up with a bottle somewhere.

I sighed. "Maybe he's with Ben."

"Where's Ben?" Ingrid looked at Shana, who'd just come yawning out of the bedroom.

"He took off, determined to get that shark/snake/dragon tattoo and infiltrate the Medula."

Ingrid buried her head in her hands for a few moments. With a huge sigh, she raised her gaze. You know, when I got frazzled I looked like I'd been pulled through a knothole backward then across the desert in the peak of summer by a crazed camel. Ingrid looked tragically beautiful. Her aquamarine eyes blinked liquidly with no trace of mascara streaks. Her flushed face added the perfect touch of pink to her perfect complexion. Life wasn't fair.

"Jack couldn't do that — get tattooed and run with a gang." Ingrid breathed. "Could he?"

I shook my head to reassure her, but frankly I wasn't sure. Watching Ingrid wring her hands, completely out of character, I realized this trip had shifted us all out of our elements. No one seemed to be acting themselves. Jack, SAD sufferer, could have dyed his hair pink, joined the national Mary Kay tour and been speaking to thousands at conventions around the country for all I could guess.

"Don't panic, Ingrid," I finally said. "Aside from reporting him as a missing person, which I think is premature, we have to just wait and hope he's busy. That's what I'm doing with Frank."

Well . . . that wasn't exactly precise, but she didn't have to know what I'd done. Not yet, anyway.

"I like action," Ingrid said, a little of her bossy self returning. "I need something to do."

"Redo the website."

"Too late, already did that this morning."

"It's still morning." I pointed out. "When did you do it?"

"Four."

I watched her blank face sympathetically. "Couldn't sleep because you were worried about Jack, huh?"

Ingrid drew back with a strange look on

her face. "I always get up at four. No one needs more than four hours of sleep."

"Of course." I remembered why I hated her besides her looks, the woman made me feel like a first-class slug.

"So? What else can I do? I can't sit here thinking about not thinking about Smack."

"Okay," I said. "While I go lose the bad guys' money at Poseidon's, you and Shana could go to the sheriff's department ostensibly to look for your "sister" and really find out what those girls in the raid on the front page of the newspaper were really doing."

Ingrid frowned, obviously well versed with the entire newspaper in the six hours she'd been awake but not following my line of reasoning. "What do you mean? They were young whores looking for johns."

"I don't think so. Two of those girls hit me up for an autograph and then money to get home. They might be teenage con artists, looking to do anything to score cash, but it feels like there's more to it than that."

Shana paced next to the window, watching the carpet intently.

"Are you going to be okay doing this?" I asked, wondering if the teenage girls far away from home wouldn't tweak her heartstrings like they did mine.

"I'm not gonna lie, it'll be difficult, but,

like Ingrid, I'd rather be doing something than nothing. You know that, Bee. I thought the longer she'd been gone, the easier it would be to tolerate, but I was wrong. It's like rubbing and rubbing a raw wound."

I walked over and wrapped her in a strong hug. "You go investigate. Maybe by helping these girls, you can help ours."

An hour later, dressed in my Ingrid-ordered day-off fashion disaster number two — a folk-print cotton nightgown with a yolk neck and fringy hem, cinched in with a wraparound-three-times metallic skinny belt that brought the dress to midthigh, toe-cleavage-revealing ballerina flats in grass green, earthy red ostrich tassel bag and gypsy earrings — I was still waiting for room service, half hoping that it wouldn't show up. Surely the bad guys wouldn't hold me responsible for a letdown on their end? *Duh.* Of course they could. They were ruthless killers, kidnappers, extorters. What was a small bit of unfair blame? My mouth went dry, and my heart pounded. Should I call to make sure room service had an order for me or would that mess it up?

At the knock a few minutes later, I flew to the door and pulled it open, yanking Joe off his feet as he slid Frank's key card in the lock. As his caiman Noconas scrambled for purchase, I grabbed the belt loop of his Wranglers to steady him. Joe was six foot three inches, two hundred and twenty pounds of pure muscle. I was a hundred and something pounds (I'm not telling you!) of semifit flab. Instead of fixing the balance, I distorted it worse. I ended up toppling on top of Joe as he bounced off the couch and hit the carpet.

Joe laughed as he helped me up. "Bee, sometimes I think you could win a war by accident."

"Great compliment, thanks." Joe was a nice, straightforward guy with a good sense of humor and once again I willed myself to fall in love with him instead of complicated, skeletons-in-the-closet Frank. It wasn't working. Dammit. "At least you didn't say lose the war."

"Well, when it's by accident, it could probably go either way."

"You should have shut up while you were still ahead," I warned him.

I offered him something to drink and he opted for a hot cup of tea. As it brewed, I caught him up on everything except my recent visit with Trankosky. He didn't offer anything, but I didn't expect him to. Frank hated when I investigated and I'm sure he instructed Joe to tell me nothing if not under duress. I considered telling him about the Trankosky conversation to barter for what he had, but something about the innuendo made me hesitate.

As if Joe read my mind, he asked: "Bee, have you considered the police could be framing you?"

"What? The police? The Clark County guys?"

"Come on, Bee, there was a cop behind your last brush with crime in Vegas." Joe nudged my memory, which didn't need much of a nudge. Blood, guts and gore do that to a person, especially a peace-loving individual such as myself.

"He was a dirty cop, though."

"So? You don't think there are others? Don't tell me you're that naive."

I was actually embarrassed to admit it hadn't occurred to me that the cops might be in on the drama unfolding around me. Yes, I'd considered I wasn't number one on their hit parade, but I hadn't thought they might be stacking the deck on purpose against me. Was that why Trankosky was trying to throw suspicion at my poker colleagues — so I wouldn't look at *his* colleagues?

Or, worse, at him?

Maybe my first impression had been right.

Or maybe this was just muddying the water, as Aunt Hilda would say.

"But what would their motivation be?"

"Motivation behind most things boils down to money, power or sex."

"I suppose someone is pocketing all the money I made them last night. I suppose they could ask for all my WSOP winnings in exchange for Affie. But, what about losing all the money? What about that? If that is their motivation."

Joe shrugged.

"And as for sex," I mused, "I just can't see how that one would make sense."

"Trankosky has the hots for you," Joe observed drily.

My face flushed hot. I fought the urge to fan myself. "I don't think so."

"You don't need to *think.* You know so." He waved at my face. "Apparently."

Joe was ticked off and not hiding it well. Frank was his best friend as well as his boss. I didn't want to let him get to me. I had nothing to feel guilty about. I couldn't help that the cop flirted with me. I tried to cloak myself in my infamous cool. After a deep breath or two, I'd tamed the blush. "You've been following me when I don't know it?"

Joe looked straight at me, unapologetic.

"Someone has to. Boss' orders. Sometimes our surveillance guy has to have a break."

"Well, sex just doesn't make sense in your scenario. Unless the cops are planning on passing me around the jailhouse, how good could it be for them with me behind bars? You think I'm the type to try to trade sex for cop favors?"

"No, Bee I don't think that," Joe said quietly, bowing his head a bit remorsefully. *Good.* "A better scenario is he's setting you up so you feel vulnerable and scared and he steps in as a savior. Superman to the rescue. He makes all the smoke he created go away by putting out his own fire. Makes your world right again."

Maybe I could help you, maybe I could help keep the brass from pushing this investigation so hard. Uh-oh. What if Joe were right? Just when I thought I might have someone else to trust — was he using me to get me?

"What about power?" I changed the subject.

Joe threw me a quick look. He knew I was trying to distract him. "Maybe we should look at who the new sheriff of Clark County is. Or who wants to be sheriff."

"What will that prove?"

"The eyes of the world are on Vegas right now with the most internationally popular game's biggest tournament underway. What better time to create a crime, one that has all the best elements of a movie — sexy game, sexier woman, innocent child, religious zealot, violent murders and millions of dollars — and then solve it to get the job of your dreams."

"That's sick."

"It *would* work, though, wouldn't it?"

I didn't want to admit it, but I imagined it would. "Unless you got caught," I answered.

"And who might best catch you but another cop?"

"Frank? They did something with Frank."

"Maybe." Joe nodded thoughtfully. "And the one thing that is irrefutable with cops is, the best ones are the ones who best understand the criminal mind. The best ones walk the line between good and bad. It just takes one misstep to end up on the wrong side of that line."

"Were you a cop, Joe?"

"How else would I know this so well?"

Joe's analysis did nothing to reassure me. Every time I found a refuge, it was revealed to be a possible trap. I ached for Frank, but then told myself I shouldn't want him. Not only had Serrano painted him a coldhearted bastard killer, but he was a struggling alcoholic, had a surreptitious job that I'd hate to live with twenty-four hours a day and another family I had yet to meet. What a mess. Why desire a mess? I should be glad he disappeared and use the excuse to wash my hands of him.

If I made that a mantra, would I come to believe it?

TWENTY-TWO

Joe advised that I take the cash they gave me and send it to the FBG lab for fingerprint and extended fiber analysis. I was to use my own cash to lose at the high-stakes table instead. Goody, everyone loves spending fifty thousand of their own dollars in a game they have been bound to lose.

We decided fifty thousand was fair because they couldn't know how much money I'd lost. We still couldn't figure out why they wanted the money lost, but that was the requirement. And apparently Affie's life depended on it.

I arrived at Poseidon's with Joe in tow. He'd called in another member of FBG's surveillance team to take over once he'd gotten me there, while he took the cash to their lab. I still didn't know who from the cop shop had my tail, although I was beginning to wonder if that wasn't all just a bluff after all. The poker room was perhaps the polar opposite of the Mellagio room in that you reached it through a long corridor that kept it completely isolated from the rest of the casino, from onlookers, from everything. One you overcame the intimidation, it was a great place to focus on the game. I checked in with the desk, bought my chips, but paused when I was asked which game I'd like to sit in on. An emerald earring on a woman is one thing, on a man it is often obscure. I made a bathroom excuse to tour the room. He turned out to be near the front. I wouldn't have guessed that.

Losing money on purpose playing poker is harder than it sounds. And of course, I just kept getting cards, wishing with each nut hand that I could save it for the Main Event.

Because the house got suspicious when I kept folding, even on the big blind, I ended up only betting bad hands, and even there I ended up winning.

How do you win with a Dolly Parton (nine/five) on a table with eight players?

When the only one left at The River misses a straight draw and you squeak by with a middle pair.

"How bad are the hands you are folding, Bee Cool, if you played that one?" the Nascar driver to my right asked.

I just smiled. How bad was my luck if I just kept getting impossible-to-fight good luck when that was the last thing I needed? Karma again.

I knew I should be using this opportunity as a great tutorial for tells and the nature of the game, but Emerald Ear was glaring at me so intensely I couldn't think of anything but getting through this with no chips left. I was also running out of time. It was eleven fifteen. Play at the Fortune started at noon.

Finally, I tried a reverse strategy. I went all in on The Flop with the nuts. I had three Aces with an Ace of hearts, Jack of spades and 3 of diamonds on the board. Emerald Ear growled low in his throat. The Nascar driver was the only one left after that. Oops. I guess I might have scared everyone away. He still remembered me playing the lame Dolly Parton. He probably thought I had muck. Although I had the nuts now, a host of hands could beat me. The only thing I had beat was a kicker, a pair or smaller three of a kinds. Still, I had an intuition that Nascar was operating under the assumption I was betting on a King kicker. I kept my fingers crossed under the table that Fourth and Fifth Streets would help him win.

The dealer was playing this out, drawing players from other tables to the rail to see what was going to happen.

My phone rang, and I saw it was Joe. I had to let it go to voice mail as the dealer turned over a deuce of hearts on The Turn. I prayed Nascar had the flush draw with two hearts in his pocket, with one to come floating in on The River. Otherwise I was about to win with only another fifteen minutes to lose twice what I walked in with.

This was crazy.

A 10 of spades fell on Fifth Street.

Nascar whooped as he flipped over his straight. I nearly passed out with relief, pushing up from the table and nodding good luck to everyone.

"Why the rush?" the floor manager asked.

"Gotta get to the Main Event."

"Oh, right, it's about that time, isn't it?" He commented, glancing at his watch. "Good thing you used up your bad luck here, huh?"

I tried not to smile as I nodded and waved over my shoulder. As I walked down the corridor, I realized how backward my life had become when I'd lost fifty thousand dollars and felt like I'd won the million-dollar lottery.

I didn't remember Joe's call until I'd reached the end of the corridor. I paused to check his message. "Bee, get out of there now, it's an ambush. I got a wild hair to check that cash before I took it to the lab and it's counterfeit —"

"Excuse me, ma'am." I spun at the hand on my shoulder. Behind me were a phalanx of casino security, flanked by what looked like the Blues Brothers and were likely the FBI. "Y-yes?"

"You're blocking the corridor. We need to get by."

"Oh, I apologize." I stepped out of the way and they jogged to the poker room. I turned and hustled to the casino floor, hopefully blending in as I raced to the nearest exit. Why had they wanted me to get caught with counterfeit money? That almost made less sense than losing money. Unless the cops were trying to frame me. Or a competitor was. But who?

Apparently when well motivated, I can lose a tail. Joe called as I was slipping out onto The Strip to say their man had lost me outside the sports room. I imagine that is precisely when I realized that everyone in the poker room had recognized me and the authorities would come after me for questioning no matter how fast I ran. I sat down in front of the horse race for a moment to compose myself. I guess the tail kept going.

I made a mental note of that. I suppose up to now, I'd been terribly predictable to follow.

"Joe, what is going on?"

"I wish I knew, Bee. But it was a good call not to use what you'd been given."

"No kidding," I breathed as I walked straight into a picket line.

Phineas Paul stood not far from his followers, because his voice boomed through the crowd. "There she is, the infamous Bee Cool, on her way to lay more than most hardworking people make in a lifetime down on a single bet. A half million dollars at a time, can you believe that? Where've you been, Miss Cooley, fleecing more senior citizens out of their life savings under the pretense of 'entertainment'?"

"Actually, Reverend, the senior citizens just finished fleecing *me.*"

"Hallelujah, proof there is a God."

There were more adults with him this time. They chorused on his second "hallelujah!" clasped hands and raised them in the air next to their signs. I hated to tell him but they made a better accompaniment than the brooding teens.

"Do you good people know how much money Miss Cooley will make if she wins the World Series of Poker? Fourteen million dollars!"

They murmured disapprovingly "devil's work" and "hell money" among other things I didn't strain to hear.

"Shall we challenge Miss Cooley to donate her winnings to a charity to make the world a better place?"

I very well might donate my winnings but it wouldn't be to the Church of the Believers. "But Reverend, your church certainly wouldn't accept 'hell money,' now would it?"

"Of course we would, Miss Cooley, the means justify the end. Our ends are always holy. It is a way to wash clean the money you garnered in a less-than-devout way. It might allow you to repent as well."

Without answering, I turned and walked toward the Fortune.

If I took a page off Frank's book and didn't believe in coincidences, I would say that had almost been scripted. If so, I'd walked straight into a trap. There again, why? So that he could guilt me into turning over my winnings? It was the wrong tactic to use on me, since bullies made me obstinate.

How did Paul know I'd been in Poseidon's? Was he having me followed too? If so, pretty soon I was going to start looking like some kind of bizarre Pied Piper.

Jack caught me by the arm. "Sam Hyun's here."

"What?" I demanded. "I thought he was in jail."

"Out on bail, apparently, and playing in the Main Event. He's shaved his head, and is being real low-key. No one knew he was here until now, when one of the reporters saw his name on the registration list."

"Is that legal — to be under indictment for kidnapping and still able to play in the tournament?"

"Yes, Bee, this isn't like joining the Secret Service, they don't do criminal checks on the players. I don't have any hard evidence yet, but it looks like he might be the one behind the talk of using you as a scapegoat for bad poker player behavior."

"Darn." Sam didn't like me. Worse, actually. He had a weird vendetta against me for being a woman and a visibly successful poker player. There were hundreds of others who fit that bill, certainly, but apparently I'd been the lucky one singled out for Sam to hate. Sam had been a legend in his time playing the game, but he hadn't made the transition from a smoky backroom game to the media-blitzed glitz game that it was now. The only time I'd ever seen him he'd vowed to kill my game and did his best to carry through with that promise. This was a player that might have enough angst to set me up with counterfeit bills and call the cops, but I couldn't see him kidnapping my goddaughter. That part didn't make sense.

"You're thinking too hard," Jack said, watching me closely. Sirens sounded somewhere outside The Strip. It wasn't uncommon to hear them here in Vegas, although I was pretty sure they only used them when they had to for PR's sake, so I only made a note in the back of my mind.

"Smoke's coming out your ears," Jack joked.

I smiled at him distractedly, then remembered Ingrid. "Hey, hey! Your girlfriend is beside herself with worry over you. You'd better call her right now."

Jack lit up. "Really? Ingrid's worried?"

"Jack, you ought to be ashamed of yourself. She is almost sick with it."

He sighed and sucked on his front teeth for a second. "I'm sorry, Bee. Ingrid is rather hard to read."

I nodded. The phrase "emotional mummy" came to mind but I kept it there.

"And I just wonder sometimes why an absolute knockout and one of the world's smartest women would want anything to do with me."

Jack was no Ben, but he wasn't ugly. Five nine and one hundred thirty pounds, he was awkward, but at the same time, endearingly cute with his big dark puppy dog eyes, long arms, long legs and wide-open smile. He was good through and through. No artifice here. And talk about uncomplicated. "Don't sell yourself short, Jack. I'd love to fall in love with you."

"Aw, Bee." Jack nudged me with his shoulder. "That's the nicest thing anyone's ever said to me."

"It's true." Unfortunately. Wouldn't it be better if I weren't trying to fall in love with every appealing bachelor I knew instead of just accepting who I was in love with? "Now call your gal pal. It's not nice to torture her, even though she probably deserved it."

"I will call her, but first, let me tell you where I'm going next."

Running late by now, I jogged to the Fortune. As I turned the last corner, I paused at the commotion on the street in front of the hotel. Now I knew where the sirens had been headed. Sheriff's department cruisers were parked at odd angles. Officers were jumping out of their vehicles to block off traffic. A body lay in the middle of the street, facedown, arms askew, legs at unreal angles, bloody. And eerily still.

"Do you know anything about this?" One of the officers demanded of me as an ambulance screeched up to the curb.

"No, of course not. I just got here," I said, self-righteously. Despite telling myself not to, I looked down as the paramedics turned the poor woman over. I gasped, "But I know her!"

"Of course you do," Trankosky moaned behind me.

"Detective Dale," I said.

"That makes me sound like some kind of cartoon character," he muttered.

"If the shoe fits," I began.

He held up his hand, murmured in the officer's ear, cupped my elbow and led me toward the hotel.

Like an apparition, Phineas Paul had materialized amidst his picketers. "Is he a ghost or something? I just saw him in front of Poseidon's," I told Trankosky.

Paul's voice carried even without his ever-present megaphone. "Look at God's judgment. That poor woman succumbed to the work of the devil — she played poker, she was a gambler — and this is her judgment day. Who do you think she stands in front of right now? God is sending her to where she belongs!" — he pointed dramatically straight down — "with him."

"How does he know she was a poker player?"

"Easy guess, wouldn't you say, since about 101 percent of the people entering the Fortune right now are going to play or watch in the Main Event? And she damned sure wasn't dressed like a whore."

I shrugged, conceding the point. Poor Thelma wore the same thing she had on the last time I'd seen her.

"What do you think happened?"

"She got hit by a car."

"But why?"

"That's what you are going to tell me," he said, turning me to face him.

"I have to get in and make my table." I didn't think the kidnappers would take some random hit-and-run as an acceptable excuse not to make the cut.

"I'll escort you there, and, on the way, tell me this woman's name and how you know her. I'll make sure you'll be able to play."

Gosh, thanks. This was all playing into Joe's supposition. "You think I had something to do with her death?" I asked, accusingly.

Trankosky nodded with his cop's face I recognized from my time with Frank. "Indirectly, yes, I do."

TWENTY-THREE

Distracted as I was by Thelma's death, Trankosky's possible frame job and Hyun in town determined to make me look bad, I didn't start a pivotal day in the right frame of mind. Not to mention, I hadn't heard from the person I'd called to come in to help me find Frank. By the first break, after two hours of play, I'd lost at least a quarter of my stack. That's really the only way I had come to be able to think of my chip load in this tournament, because the thought of millions made me unable to concentrate. Really, if life were a true balance, the cards I got in the first level of the day were fair. The ones I'd been dealt at Poseidon's had been good enough to blow out half my WSOP table. Of course, at this point, those kind of cards had run dry. I just had to withstand whatever I was dealt and shore up for a long haul of bad cards.

The Jordan, deuce/three suited spades was

a horror as a first pocket for the next level. I was in early position, small blind, which was sizable. Hanging around for The Flop was worth it, though, as it fell Ace of spades, 5 of spades and Queen of hearts. I wouldn't have stayed in had it not been for my blind investment. Good thing. With my luck, though, I had to be prepared for nothing more than a straight flush draw.

What to do, since everyone was betting on this one. I guess a few might have had flush draws, maybe someone had a pair, three of a kind. Everyone could hold a low straight draw for all I knew.

Four of spades fell on The Turn, squelching my suspense, thank goodness. I had the nuts for sure, the second-highest possible hand with no one able to make the highest hand — a royal flush. I needed to slow play this one or I would scare everyone off. I moderately raised, as if I'd landed a pair or perhaps a low trips. When The River came a Jack of spades, I could swear I heard a swallowed gasp from the one who'd landed a flush. I couldn't be more pleased since that meant more chips for me. I bet then waited as the flush pushed. I called and simply cleaned up.

The tournament broke for a meal at eight. Trankosky had threatened to take me to dinner to quiz me about Thelma in detail. I wished I had an excuse, but Shana and Ingrid were off to visit Moon again, Ben and Frank were MIA, Jack was undercover, Joe wasn't answering his phone, and Carey was dancing as a Wall Street Woman.

I'd just have to get busy making more friends in Vegas, I guess.

Trankosky was waiting for me as I exited the ballroom — by some stroke of luck — having guessed which of the multitude of doors I would use. Humph. Sometimes I wondered if he hadn't fitted me with a homing device.

He fell into step with me, going, where? I wasn't at all sure. "Can I take you to dinner?" he asked.

How gallant. *What if I said no?*

"Then I would have to take you to jail."

"Excuse me, did I *say* something?" I asked, shocked.

"No, I was reading your mind."

Huh. "I guess you're accustomed to rejection."

"I'll take you to your favorite Egyptian restaurant."

"How would you know where that is?"

He looked at me and smiled.

"Oh, sorry, I forgot. You read minds."

"Or know the right people."

It couldn't be Frank. He disliked Frank. Suddenly it occurred to me, "Chief Patterson. You talked to him, didn't you?"

"It's not what you know, it's who you know."

"Let's go eat." If Patterson spoke to him, he wasn't all bad.

Trankosky was a rather charming dinner date, for a cop, only intermittently pumping me for information and moderately satisfied when I gave him tidbits. I still withheld the whole Affie kidnapping — for two reasons. Either he knew all about it because he was behind it all, as Joe suspected, or if he hadn't known, I was afraid he'd try to fix it and get Aph killed in the process. He sensed I was hiding something but didn't press so hard that he threatened to pull my toenails out or anything. Good thing too, because I think I would roll over on the toenail torture. I can't even stand a hangnail.

What's more, he only growled twice (surely a record), when he asked where Frank was and I told him it was none of his business. And then I asked what he knew about the Medula.

"Why do you need to know about them?"

"Well, the person who tried to kidnap me at the Image that first night is one of their

309

members. I just thought I ought to know more about them," I said, trying to sound conversational, hoping he wouldn't read the "and my brother has gone to join them" that kept flashing through my mind.

"How do you know that's who it was?"

I gave him a raised-eyebrow look because I wasn't mentioning Frank's name again.

"Oh," he said, getting it. "I'm sure then I don't know more than you do. They run a variety of criminal syndicates throughout the West and Southwest. We know who the leaders are but only ever catch the underlings, all of whom have either killed themselves or been killed in jail before they talk. Not a good group to hang with," he said pointedly, pinning me with a hard look. "You're lucky you got away."

I couldn't swallow. Suddenly I wanted to tell him everything, just to save Ben. I wished I trusted him more. I wished he were Frank. My life was such a pretzel.

After a few moments in which he ate and I scooted the kofta around on my plate, he observed wryly: "Here this was my idea and I think you are the one doing the interrogating, instead of me."

I leaped at the opportunity. "Since you don't mind, I have another question: Do you know anything about a psychic named

Moon? Lives in the Happy Homes trailer park off Hibiscus?"

"Why?" he answered, his eyes narrowing.

Uh-oh. He knew her. "My best friend, Shana, seems to have stumbled upon her and is paying her to tell her future," I said casually. "Shana is impressionable so I just wanted to make sure it was harmless diversion."

"It's a waste of money if she wants to know the future," he began.

"Oh well," I said.

"But Moon is pretty decent at pointing you in the right direction if you have a missing person."

I choked on a sip of pinot grigio. Trankosky smoothed his hand across my shoulders as I waved off his help and dabbed at my lips. He continued. "The department has used her a few times over the years depending on who the head honcho is at the time. Some aren't as open-minded about that kind of thing."

"Speaking of sheriff, who wants to be head honcho now? Has Patterson been replaced?"

Bingo. He studied my face again. I forced myself to look the picture of innocence. "Now I think you're the one who is reading minds. Actually, Mickey Juarez is acting sheriff, but the Republican party is trying to talk me into running. Why do you ask?"

I shrugged. "Curious. Patterson was a good guy."

"Still is. Now it's my turn," he said between bites of mombar mahshy. "Do you know anything about the rumor that players in the Poseidon's poker room were using counterfeit money?"

"Is that where all those FBI guys were going when I left there this morning?"

Trankosky smiled tightly. "I wondered if you'd admit to being there."

I blinked. "I didn't do anything wrong except play poorly. Why wouldn't I admit to that?"

He studied me for a moment, not believing me but not having any proof otherwise. "How do you know what FBI guys look like?"

"I watch TV along with the rest of America."

He let it go. "So go back to the beginning and tell me how you knew Thelma."

"Only in passing. She often played tournaments, but lately was more of a railbird. I think she was making more money sponging off flush players, hitting up the new ones who are feeling generous and don't know they are opening up a bottomless pit of begging if they shell out even a ten-dollar bill."

"The underbelly of poker. Sounds like you have some experience."

"Isn't that how we learn best?"

"I like to think so." His blue eyes twinkled. I squirmed in my seat. That didn't help the direction my thoughts had taken with his simple statement.

"Is it illegal to pay someone for information?"

Trankosky shook his head. "But ignorance is not protection from the law, so the next time you do something questionable, you probably should check it out first so I don't have to drag you to the clink."

"Hmm. Okay, Thelma got sidetracked and instead of finding out why people were using my name in a cheating context, she dug up some dirt on the big-mouth preacher."

"And what was that?" Trankosky asked, more politely than interested.

"That Paul pays those girls to walk the pickets."

"He's probably not the only one in history who's done that. Again, unless they are under sixteen, not against the law, but not very morally or ethically correct either."

"Oh," I said, deflated.

"Then I sent her off yesterday to find out more about the rumors circulating about me being a dirty player."

"Really? And what did she discover?"

"I don't know. I never talked to her again." I felt the tears welling and willed them back where they came from. I might have succeeded had Trankosky not leaned over and drawn my hand into his.

"I'm sorry. I didn't mean to make you feel bad about the accident, which I don't think was an accident at all. You didn't intentionally send her off to her death."

"That doesn't help much." I sniffled. He handed me his handkerchief. I blew my nose, wiped at the mascara tracks on my cheeks and dreaded looking in the mirror. "Why don't you think it's an accident?"

"Because witnesses saw the van swerve and speed up to hit Thelma, the tire marks support that. The vehicle had no license plates."

"What kind of van?"

"Unfortunately, the kind every rental outfit in Vegas got a package deal on — there are thousands in town."

"Smart killer," I mused.

"Exactly, which gets you off the hook for this one too."

"Very funny," more insulted than relieved, evidence of my truly perverse nature. "Do you have any more leads on who killed

Tasser?"

"No, but you are the common denominator. A popular theory at the station house is that locking you up will reduce the body count more than catching the real killer."

"But you'll stave off those theorists?" I asked, holding my breath, thinking of Joe's suspicions.

"If you share the bourtaka muhallabieh with me," he said, and I let out the breath with a smile. Orange custard? Suddenly I didn't mind if he were using me. Food extortion I could definitely deal with.

Two levels and four hours later, the tournament was down to twenty-seven. I eliminated Blackie. What a sense of accomplishment, although, suddenly and inexplicably, I felt lonely, a bit bereft. The enemy was leaving the building. I wondered if I would ever really know who she was. I expected her to grunt, perhaps, if she were feeling generous and wander off under the shelter of her cloak, gloves and glasses. Instead, she reached across the table and shook my hand.

"Congratulations, Bee," she said clearly, with her other hand pulling back the hood she wore to reveal her face, sliding her sunglasses off and placing them on the felt.

She was lovely — midthirties, with a round face, flawless skin, an easy smile and warm brown eyes that drew you in like a comforting blanket. Her blond hair, sun streaked, was smooth and shiny. I almost fainted in shock. How could the woman I'd envisioned beneath her strange dress alternately as Cruella De Vil and Morticia from *The Addams Family* be so normal? No, better than normal. She was someone I'd want as a friend. Gosh, she was someone I would want to be. Her soul shone through bright and clear. She glowed with goodness. With psychic balance.

"Th-thank you," I stuttered as I took her hand.

She was a little taken aback by my shock. Her face shuttered a bit. "You've seen photos, then, I suppose."

Was she someone famous I was supposed to know? Oops. I racked my knowledge, but sadly I didn't have the time nor the inclination to haunt poker sites in a celebrity search. Maybe that was it, she was a Hollywood star. She was lovely enough, somehow reminding me of Grace Kelly in her elegant composure. "I'm sorry, no, I haven't seen photos . . ."

Suddenly, her face relaxed in relief and a trace of sadness. "Yes, I guess I was silly to think so. I am Monica Gilbert."

If she had told me she was an alien from Pluto, I wouldn't have been more stunned. "B-but," I stammered, again, begging myself for the composure she commanded effortlessly, "When I called you, I thought you were in L.A.?"

"I'm sorry for all this." She waved at her cloak, her sunglasses and her gloves that she now pulled finger-by-finger off her hands. Still, she hadn't risen from the chair. Because she couldn't. I felt sick suddenly as she continued, "But, I beg you to understand. I know Frank was getting serious about you. I just wanted to be sure when the kids spent time with you two that it was going to be okay for them. I had to meet you without meeting you." She paused and sighed heavily, dropping her pleading gaze for a moment to gather her thoughts. "You don't have children. I don't know that you will understand. But I can only beg —"

Emotions that I had no idea I possessed were welling in me. As I sat back down, I spoke without thinking. "But I do understand. I don't know how, or why, but I understand. Although I don't think you have to worry about Frank exposing me to the kids, because he protects all of you on the other side of a great wall that I am not

317

allowed to broach verbally, and certainly not physically."

Monica shook her head, smiling bitter-sweetly. "He's ready. I can see it in him. I can *feel* it in him."

A flash of jealousy ripped through me. His ex-wife knew Frank better than I did. The head in me said: Well of course she does, she's known him longer, they have children together. The heart in me said: To hell with this, let her have him back.

"Well, I'm glad someone can, because he can't."

"Don't worry, he will."

I was glad she was so confident. "If he ever surfaces," I put in.

"We'll work on that," she said, revealing herself as an investigator's wife, well versed in unexpected absences. Turning over her palm, she wiggled her fingers barely and a woman came through the side doors of the ballroom with a wheelchair.

As she eased into the chair, I said: "You certainly did have your disguise well planned. I wondered why you always beat me to the table."

She smiled, with a touch of sadness. "You have to understand, I thought this was the best way to see you unguarded. As you are. I couldn't exactly hire you for an ad campaign for a company I don't own, or encounter you at a health club, obviously." She paused to wave at her useless legs without rancor and with total acceptance of reality. "Neither of those would be ideal, regardless. I thought, since poker is rather new to you, that I would see you a little in control sometimes and a little vulnerable sometimes. That is the best way to glimpse a person's real character."

"I guess you've played a long time. You are quite good."

She nodded. "I've played for twenty years. Not big-time tournaments, but steady local games. Lately, some Internet dabbling."

I envisioned her and Frank playing together as newlyweds. I ached. Swallowing the pain, ready to snatch opportunity when I saw it, I asked: "So tell me why Frank quit playing."

Monica shook her head. "You have to ask him."

Did I invite people to shut doors in my face? Here I thought we were getting along great. "I have asked. He didn't tell."

Smiling like a beautiful, self-possessed Buddha, she said: "He will. In time." It must be a Gilbert family theme song.

"That's the problem. I'm not very patient."

"With Frank, you need to learn to be."

Suddenly, I was tired of her Frank lessons. They were accurate, and dammit, why couldn't *I* give them? I forced a smile. "Where are the kids?"

"They're here," answered the wheelchair-wielding senior citizen who flashed Monica's smile. "Off with Grandpa right now to watch the Mellagio fountains dance at midnight."

Frank's children were perfect. Well-behaved, well-adjusted and gorgeous little things. They made me sick.

How could Frank live away from them? How could I keep him away from them? How could she let him ever leave such precious packages?

"I think you need to come stay in our hotel," Katie told me with an endearing lisp. "I can do your hair. It looks like fire, don't you think, Mamma?"

Monica smiled. "Yes, I do, vibrant description, sweetie. Good job."

"I bet your friend would play bull rider with me, wouldn't she?" Matthew asked his mom.

"Bull rider?" I asked.

"He rides you like a bull, hands and knees, lots of bucking, that kind of thing." She looked skeptically at my stilettos and miniskirt. "I would never ask you to —"

I nodded. "I would love that."

"Cool!" he shouted, starting a bout of wrestling with his grandfather, Randolph.

"I'm sorry you busted out of the tournament, dear," her mother, Wilma, told her.

Monica looked at me and said: "That's okay, Mom. I think I ended up richer in the end anyway."

I don't think she knew how true her words were. I had decided something seeing them, meeting them. When her mother turned away to help Katie with her bow, I asked Monica, "Do you have any ideas on where I can look for Frank?"

"I called him, after you called me," she said. "He is on his way back. He got a little distracted in L.A. after he visited the prison. With what happened here to Rudy Serrano, he had some things he said he had to deal with."

And couldn't answer his phone and couldn't tell me but he could tell his ex-wife. I tried to swallow my jealousy. After all I'd asked her to help, hadn't I? "Thank you."

We watched the kids play for a few minutes, so carefree and real, that I felt rejuvenated until she added: "He *had* been drinking. I don't know what to tell you other than, I'd hoped he'd gotten a handle on that."

I turned and smiled at her, genuinely, because I was stone-cold clear about the future. "That's okay. I think I know what he needs to keep him out of all that."

Her big emotive eyes softened. "I hope so. God bless you if you find the answer."

It was looking me in the face.

Twenty-Four

Ingrid nearly attacked me when I let myself into the suite. "Where have you been? Why aren't you answering your phone?"

"My phone hasn't rung."

Reaching into my tassel bag, I handed it to Ingrid, who pressed some buttons and then shook it in my face. "It's silenced!"

"I didn't do that," I mused, trying to remember when I had last checked my phone. Then I remembered, I'd left it on the table when I went to the restroom at the restaurant. Trankosky? I checked my voice mail and had twelve messages: ten from Shana and Ingrid, one from Mom and one from Frank.

"Is it Affie?" I asked, frantically searching their faces.

Shana shook her head. Ingrid waved her hand in the air. "Of course not, do you think we'd hang around for you if we'd found the girl?"

"Is it Ben?"

Shana shook her head again. Ingrid snorted, "That fool is on his own, probably sashimi by now."

Shana and I winced. Ingrid, the epitome of sensitivity and tact, didn't notice. I listened to Frank's message. "Honey Bee, we'll talk when I get back tonight."

Weak. He was mad at me for calling his ex and too proud to apologize for disappearing. And, I hated myself for the intense relief flooding through me at the sound of his voice.

Mom's message was typical and guilt inducing. She wanted to know where Ben was because he wasn't answering his phone. That's because he'd left his phone on his dresser to reduce the chance of being found out by the gang. Good thing, because Mom calling would have been a certain death sentence. She spoke into the phone at thirty-eight thousand decibels so that everyone within a mile radius could hear her clearly.

"Are you finished yet?" Ingrid demanded, shoving her hands on her hips.

I slipped the phone back into my purse. "Did Jack find you?"

She arched an eyebrow at me. "Yes, although I don't know why he found you first."

"Oh, get over yourself, Ingrid. He needed to tell me something." I looked at Shana. "Why were you calling?"

"Moon thinks she's finally got a good feel on where Affie is."

I paused. If they'd told me this earlier today I would've scoffed. Now, I wasn't sure. Unless Moon was a setup too, but how could that be? "How did you find Moon?" I asked Shana.

"In the phone book. Why does that matter?"

"Go on with what she said."

"You're being a bossy bitch," Ingrid pouted.

"Takes one to know one," I shot back.

She glared.

"I'm a little stressed, Ingrid," I said, backing off just a bit.

"Freaking out isn't going to help."

Well, she was right, but I wasn't going to give her the satisfaction. She displayed the self-possession of a rock and it rubbed me the wrong way when she told me I was a basket case, even when I was.

"Moon says Affie is north of California, but west of Nevada."

"She's talking about a lot of land," I said distractedly.

"Hey, what did those girls say when you went to the jail?"

"That's the weird thing," Shana said. "They didn't say much, but we went straight over to Moon and that's when she said she could get a good feel, when she touched my hand, the hand I'd used to grab the blonde's arm when she'd tried to turn away from me."

"Those girls said they were going home to Oregon."

Ingrid turned away from the mirror where she'd been plucking her eyebrow. "I think I need to go see those chicks. Alone."

We didn't exactly know what Ingrid hoped to accomplish going to the jail after visiting hours, but I wouldn't put it past her to work a miracle. She was getting on my nerves, but she also had the ability to pull off the impossible in ways I couldn't possibly imagine. And probably shouldn't. I don't know if she'd break into the jail and hold the girls' heads in the toilet 'til they talked, sleep her way into the facility with a guard she'd later hog-tie or spread enough money around to get her in then torture the girls for information. Maybe she was a shape-shifter and turned herself into a mouse, then whispered in their ears and got them to fess up. Maybe she did voodoo and scared them into a confession. None of it would surprise me, frankly, but no matter how, I certainly expected her to come back with something that would lead us straight to Aph.

The landline rang about ten minutes after she'd left. Shana was dressing for bed. I was contemplating the nonsensical series of events and evidence scattered through the last couple of days. The emotions surrounding Frank and his ex-wife kept trying to elbow their way into my thoughts, but I shoved them out. I'd decided how to deal with all that, and that decision was supposed to make the messiness go away. It wasn't working.

So I was a bit cranky when I picked up the phone. "You didn't lose our money," the voice said.

"I lost fifty thousand, your guy won fifty thousand, that's all I was asked to do."

"You were asked to use *our* money."

"How do you know I didn't?"

There was a long pause. The receiver was covered. After a few moments, he said, "You'd better not get smart on us."

"You'd better not get me to do something illegal because I know I can't help my god-daughter behind bars. The cops sniff around me any more and I'll just have to tell them what you've done."

"You do that, and Aphrodite will die."

"She might die anyway, isn't that right?"

They hung up. Shana stood in the door-way, gripping the molding like it was a lifeline, paling so quickly I thought she'd faint.

I went into the bathroom and threw up.

Frank arrived in the middle of the night. I heard him whisper my name at the bedroom door, but didn't get up. I was too exhausted, too conflicted to try to face him yet.

I heard Ingrid and him talking as I woke, showered and dressed. I felt too vulnerable for him to see me in my robe. I needed some armor and what better armor than my day-six fashion. It was double retro, as if single retro wasn't bad enough — sixties mod pattern in bright orange, green and yellow in an eighties body-hugging style that made me look like a walking roller coaster, coupled with some of those open-toed Lo-Presti boots I'd been coveting. It was sure to repel most normal people on sight. Perhaps it would keep him at arm's length until I was ready to have him closer.

Just the sight of him made my traitorous knees go weak. Clearly I had a battle ahead of me. Ingrid had just left. He walked over, handed me a steaming cup of coffee and kissed the top of my head, slipping a hank of hair I'd missed into my braid behind my ear. *Damn him.*

"I missed you," he said. "I'm sorry I didn't call and had you worried."

"What did you expect?"

He shrugged as he turned away. "I don't know why you had to call Monica, though, Honey Bee. It's just going to complicate matters."

"I'm not the one who complicated matters," I returned softly. "You knew I had an ex-fiancé, a crazy twin, certifiable parents. With me what you see is what you get."

"Not exactly." He smiled wryly. "And, the body count that follows you in poker tournaments wasn't an advertised part of the bargain."

Frank had me there. "Those aren't my fault."

"And I can't escape my past."

"I'm not asking you to. I'm asking you to be honest about it, and how it affects the present and the future."

"I told you I wasn't good for you, Honey Bee." He actually had, sort of, in his own way, warned me. I'm hardheaded. I didn't listen. And I didn't now. He looked sad, suddenly vulnerable. I went to him and gathered him in my arms.

"Frank, why did you drink again?"

"Serrano and I shared a lot of history, a lot of memories I didn't want to relive. When I heard about what happened, I should have come right back to you instead of having that one drink I thought might make it easier to deal with. He was here to follow you, although I don't know why. He arranged to be at your table."

"You didn't kill him, did you?"

"How can you ask that?"

"I think I know you, Frank, and then you go off like you did and I realize I don't know parts of you at all. I don't know what to think about the story Serrano told me about the murders of the men who hurt Monica in L.A. I don't know what you are capable of."

"Loving you."

"That part I know. A lot of the rest is still in shadow."

"Why didn't you ask Monica when you talked to her on the phone?" he asked defensively.

"Because I don't think it's fair to ask her to relive something that must be painful to her when it's your place to tell me. I asked Joe, but he won't tell me." I held my palms up. "Ball's back in your court."

"We need to call Monica and let her know I made it back to Vegas safely. I think your call might have stirred up some bad memories."

"No need to call. Go see her. She's here."

"Here? In Vegas?"

"She's been playing at my table in the tournament the whole time. I knocked her out last night and that's when she introduced herself. We had a nice visit. Met the kids, her parents."

Frank blinked, shell-shocked. "You met Katie? Matthew? Monica's never played in a big poker tournament before . . ."

"She came just to check me out."

"That's . . ." He offered a small smile. "Just like her actually. Or like she was before . . ."

"Go find her. Spend the day with the kids. They're adorable."

"I can't." He regained his closed-cop face. "I have to fly to Oregon and find Affie."

"Why do you think she's in Oregon?"

"Ingrid got the two snots in jail to talk. We're guessing they're girls from the Medula, even though they don't have the tattoo. They said they live in a compound in Oregon and a fifteen-year-old girl with a python arrived there just before they were sent off to do this job."

"What job was that?"

"We don't know any more than that because Ingrid got interrupted."

A sharp knock sounded at the door. I expected Joe to be there when I opened it, but instead, Trankosky surprised me, by tipping his head. "Belinda, I'm sorry to bother you, but I was hoping to have a word with Mr. Gilbert at headquarters. We need a signed statement from him."

Frank rose, and walked away from me. "If you can't go, I will," I said.

He shook his head. "No, you won't. You don't know where to start."

"Tell me."

"See you soon, Honey Bee."

Trankosky turned to pull the door shut behind them and met my gaze. His was full of questions. I looked away. He wouldn't like the answers.

Neither did I.

"Welcome to the second to the last day of the largest poker tournament in history!" The anchorman paused in the middle of his stand-up, flashing his fake teeth. Ick. I tried not to grimace as I snuck by as far away as possible from the bad reverend who was shepherding his band of followers into the view of the cameras. "The 2008 World

Series of Poker starring some of the most talented, lucky and scrappy players braving the game of Texas Hold 'Em is upping the ante today. Just a week ago, ten thousand people from all over the world began with high hopes of winning the millions at stake, each with an even chance to win the grand prize of fourteen million dollars. Today, the field has been whittled to just twenty-seven players. Tomorrow only nine will remain." He paused and sucked in a dramatic breath. "This year, however they play under a cloud of controversy. The Reverend Phineas Paul of the Church of the Believers has been staging protests against the morality of this particular gambling game — currently the most popular in the world. Picketers carry signs denouncing the poker tournament as the devil's work. Paul has even challenged a player to give her winnings to charity, most specifically, his church."

I suppose they were now showing my sound bite. I was glad I couldn't hear or see it a second time. Once was one time too many.

"Now, the World Series of Poker has made a historical decision. They are issuing an invitation. Here to explain it is President of the Main Event, Walker Whitting."

"Mr. Paul, in the interest of free speech,

we would like to provide a forum for you to have your say," the WSOP president announced. "A debate of sorts. With a member of our final table to support our position that Texas Hold 'Em is a valid, healthy form of entertainment."

I almost groaned out loud. I didn't need an advertising degree to know that the WSOP was making a PR play — trying to boost their already out-of-sight ratings with a Rosie/Donald knock-down, drag-out. How popular was too popular, I wondered, as I reached the door.

"On behalf of the church and the holy interest of society in general, we accept, only if we can choose the player I will spar with."

"Fair enough, Reverend," Whitting hollered.

"There," I heard Paul boom behind me. "We want her."

The bouncer at the door put his hand on my shoulder to stop me. Oh no. No way. I couldn't be unlucky enough to be in the wrong place at the wrong time again, could I?

"Belinda Cooley, Bee Cool, the epitome of the seductive evil of the game — glamorous on the outside and rotten inside — a microcosm of what greed and gambling do to beauty."

"How do you know Miss Cooley will make the final table? Do you have an alternate choice?"

"She'll make it."

"But how do you know?"

"I want no one else."

"Okay. It's a deal, Reverend."

The PR director was rubbing her hands together in excitement. Reporters, photographers, cameramen began running around like fire ants whose bed had been disturbed. I looked at the bouncer. "Please, please if you have an ounce of decency, let me in so I can hide."

"Come on, face the cameras, think of the fame, think of the endorsements. Think of the money."

"I don't want any of that. I just want to be left alone."

"You came to the wrong place for that, lady."

TWENTY-FIVE

As I entered the ballroom, I sensed the still electricity of an impending thunderstorm. When a thousand tables had been reduced to three, it changed the atmosphere. When what was effectively at stake went from losing a ten-thousand-dollar seat to winning fourteen million dollars, it changed the universe.

We'd all win something of course. But perhaps Paul was right about one thing. Greed did play a factor. Who wanted to settle for the twenty-seventh-place winnings when you could smell enough to buy you a medium-size island in the Caribbean?

Having said all that, I was truly the aberration. I didn't want to win. I just wanted my brother and my goddaughter back. I wanted a minute to myself to think about Frank. I wanted to never know of a gang that tattooed parts of snakes, dragons and sharks on their necks. I wanted to never hear of a Phineas Paul and the Church of the Believers. I wanted to rewind life and *not* do all this again.

My dad has always told me that life is all journey. There is no destination. Relish each step along your trip. But, couldn't I wish I'd taken a different fork in the road?

We redrew for tables. One of the players at my table introduced himself as Drew Terry. Clean-cut, well dressed and ordinary as your next-door neighbor, he made my skin crawl. Thank goodness he drew the seat across from me. I couldn't bear footsies with him.

The chemistry of our table was slightly off. A handful of players had gotten this far by chipping away slowly and patiently at other's stacks — the most often recommended tournament strategy — and the rest had lucked into it, both in cards and in timing of their bluffs. It made for a rather bipolar group. And then there was me, who alternately played both ways, depending on the tells around me and environmental factors like how many bodies had been slashed to death around me in the last twenty-four hours. I had a suspicion that affected the quality of my strategy.

I heard one of the commentators call me "patient and methodical" while the other argued I was a loose cannon. I guess it depended on which hand they watched me play. The third commentator settled on comparing my play to the behavior of his manic-depressive aunt who was completely unpredictable off her medication — sane one minute and crazed the next. "But throughout, she's got alligator blood. You never see her rattled."

I had to smile at that. That's exactly the way I wanted to play because no one would be able to beat me with anything but better cards.

The first level of the night was a bust for me. I didn't get one decent pocket, failed one bluff and sat back and let everyone steal my blinds for the rest of the two-hour block. I could see myself doomed to twenty-seventh place and was almost welcoming it when, the last deal before the break, I got cowboys.

A pair of Kings in the pocket guarantees nothing except a beatable hand, but for some reason, I love this deal. It makes me warm and hopeful. Go figure. Sometimes feeling good is all you have in life. I called in late position to see The Flop.

Another King, and two spades fell — a seven and a deuce. I forced myself to check-raise so I wouldn't scare off the conserva-

338

tives at the table. There were two guys at our table — one a major pro — who were carefully plotting their ways to a win, never making a mistake, surely checking their poker manual under the table, and I was pretty sure check-raising a three-of-a-kind nuts with two blanks on the board wasn't in there.

I had been full-house poor the whole tournament so when another seven fell on The Turn, I tried not to even breathe harder. Nobody but someone holding pocket rockets or double sevens could best me right now. I reconfigured the odds and liked them. Still, I check-raised again, drawing the mice in, hoping I could salvage this level well enough to stay in. When blinds are nearing a half million, you had to pay attention.

Drew Terry, the skin crawler, had been tapping the table oddly off and on during the night. He was a bit of a Nervous Nelly. It reminded me of something but I couldn't place it offhand. Besides, I was busy now trying to negotiate a win and didn't have time to rack my brain.

I had to push when we got to the 3 of diamonds on The River. I know a couple of players were tempted to force me to show my hand but none of them felt rich enough.

They all folded — no one would see my nuts. And that was okay, because they also wouldn't be able to say whether or not I'd been bluffing. My play had not been linear. The pro to my right gave me a sidelong look that I knew said, "Can you even count? And how lucky are you?"

Those were the kind of guys I was dying to show my hand to, but also the kind I was dying to bust out of the game. Patience was not my strong suit, but poker was a great game to teach me that quality. I knew I could bust this know-it-all pro out, but I had to watch and wait.

I giggled, winked at him and gathered my chips, just solidifying his impression of me as a lucky airhead. I'd use that later.

I was on the way to the restroom at the break when Drew Terry walked up next to me, leaned in and whispered: "I can help you win."

I drew back, shocked. "I don't need help, thanks."

"Everybody needs help. Watch my fingers. I'll tell you when we can squeeze the table."

Watch my fingers. That was it! That was what had been bothering me. His weird tapping was similar to what Emerald Ear had done at Neptune's. Poker players did all sorts of things with their hands and I guess their appearances had been so dissimilar I hadn't easily made the connection. Was he a member of the Medula? It seemed unlikely, but then the Happy Ending guy running around Neptune's with Dragsnashark had been a surprisingly a clean-cut preppy type too. Maybe it was part of their cover.

I narrowed my eyes at the choir boy. "Where is my goddaughter?"

He blinked innocently. "What are you talking about?"

"I know your people have Affie. I want her released."

"You're crazy, lady. I just want to do some back scratching so we can both profit."

Uh-huh. "If you don't help me save a life, I won't help you, you jerk."

His eyes narrowed to scary slits. He didn't look so much like a choir boy any more. "You'll be sorry, Bee Cool."

"We'll see who's sorry," I said, hustling into the ladies' room as soon as I could. Only as the door was easing shut did I see the TV cameras passing by in the hallway. Dammit, were eyes everywhere? I wasn't doing anything wrong and somehow it might look like it. I had to get Terry out of the game and thus reduce the chances he'd drag me into trouble.

I snatched the sunglasses off the top of my head and set them on the counter, suddenly remembering Ringo. Where had he been? I felt a shot of guilt that I hadn't missed him with his usual sunglass check when I'd started the game. Fortunately, I'd had about five pair in my purse and had plucked one out without any thought. I looked in the mirror — I'd put on the Stylists, now on the top of my head. Since I'd started playing tournament poker, I hadn't had to do without Ringo at the start of a game. It was a bad sign.

I dialed Ringo now and got no answer. Maybe he was off enjoying Vegas and not obsessing about my game. I hoped so. "Hey, Ringo, I just wanted to let you know without your expert opinion today, I went with the Stylists. I hope that's okay. See you soon!"

On the way back to the table, I prayed Terry would jump out from behind a potted plant and agree to give me information on Affie. Of course I was dreaming. He was seated and started tapping the moment he saw me as a creepy reminder. It didn't take long to eliminate him, though. The first deal was a pair of eights, which made me pause, and frankly, with now seven at our table, I would have folded had it not been for my fury. Terry was tapping furiously. I was ignoring him. I had the small blind, which gave me good enough reason to see The Flop. The pair of Aces on the board should have only convinced me to bail. But I checked and rode out the hand to Fourth Street where a four fell. The muck made everyone fold but Terry, the man who held the Ace in his pocket — three of a kind — and me with my dead man's hand.

Two pair — eights and Aces — were what Wild Bill Hickok held when he was shot dead at the table. What a portentous sign.

The eight on The River saved me. I had regained what I'd lost in the span of the last couple of hours and knocked another out. Terry held only enough chips for the next blind and he'd have to get lucky to last. He didn't, and faded away when he caught the next small blind. "Damn you. You should have taken my offer because now you won't be the only one who's sorry."

The rest of the table looked at me and shared bemused glances, before watching Terry as he slammed his chair back and stalked out of the room.

The WSOP officials announced the dinner break before I could even consider who I might want to share dinner with. As I strode out the ballroom door and into the hallway,

Trankosky sidled up next to me. "Your boyfriend spent the day in the cop shop."

"You did that on purpose," I said more vehemently than I'd meant, worried about the lost time finding Affie.

He ground his jaw. "Yes, it was on purpose. Because of a murder investigation. I'm insulted you'd suggest otherwise."

"I'm insulted you're letting a man get in the way of the job you have to do."

"We let him go and I see he didn't come running back to you."

"He has a job to do."

"What *exactly* do you know about his job?"

"Why do you care?"

"That's a loaded question. Do you really want to hear the answer right now?"

I held his gaze. Oops. "No."

"I didn't think so." He slid his hand across my shoulder as he walked on. "You let me know when you want to hear the answer."

"Bee!" I turned to the sound of the voice and saw Ringo and Carey hurrying up to me.

Beyond the facts that Carey was dressed in breast-to-thigh gold spandex, Ringo wore rainbow plaid Bermudas and it was Vegas, this was certainly an odd pair — Carey nearly a foot taller than Ringo in her five-

344

inch light-up platforms. They were jostling, giggling and generally being goofy. Uh-oh. "What are you two doing?"

"Girlfrien'! Ringo was stressing because he didn't get here in time to make sure your sunglass attire was squared away," Carey said.

"Good choice." He approved the Stylists.

"What have you been up to?"

They exchanged a look, then burst out laughing. "I've been showing Ringo *my* Vegas."

I grabbed Carey's arm and told her, "Be gentle, he's very sweet."

Carey hooted. "She thinks you're sweet, dude."

Ringo blushed. I rolled my eyes; clearly this relationship was beyond my control. "Okay, I have a job for you two. Listen up."

Because I'd had to share a rather morbid dinner at Rotoo's — one of my favorites — with Joe, who not only was ticked at me for speaking to Trankosky, but was probably more ticked Frank had given him babysitting duty, I hadn't eaten much. The lack of appetite was completely unlike me, but as it turned out, it was a good thing, because the last couple of levels tested my stomach.

I was fortunate that none of the big-time

pros was at my table, but I was less fortunate in that some real wild cards were. They were all totally unpredictable. It was justice, I suppose, that I was playing a half dozen of me. What the hell kind of strategy was I supposed to adopt?

In the first hand, one guy who called himself an Internet pro and who was chip poor coming into the deal, pushed before The Flop with a deuce/five unsuited and won a boatload on the bluff. That kind of pissed people off, so on the next hand the guy to his right, who was a dealer from New Orleans, went all in on the Jack of hearts, King of hearts, 3 of hearts Flop with only a pair of sixes in his pocket that he rode all the way to Fifth Street. I had folded both those hands, losing a small blind when I thought the water was a bit too turbulent to try to navigate safely. By the time I was ready to bet, the Internet pro had busted, and everyone at the table was reeling from shell shock.

I had to drag my mind from Frank on his way to rescue Affie from the Medula and play my way back into the game.

Four grueling hours later, having fought my way into the final table, I dragged myself back to the Mellagio, slid my key card and opened the door to the suite. Exhausted, I pitched my Kate Spade bag over the back of the maroon couch and swore when it slid off onto the floor. But when I turned back to get it, I saw I had much bigger problems. The floor was wet with blood.

TWENTY-SIX

In my shock and rush to get around the couch to see if the source of the blood was Shana or Ingrid or Ben, I tripped on the carpet and almost landed right on top of the corpse of the Skincrawler, aka Drew Terry, his throat slashed as Tasser's had been. I fought the urge to run to the bathroom to vomit and kicked off my shoes instead, carefully reaching around the blood and into my purse for my canister of pepper spray, which I'd learned the hard way was a handy and effective weapon. Armed, I tiptoed through the suite to check for the murderer or more bodies.

I found neither.

I returned to stare at Drew Terry, wishing I could ask him what the hell he was doing in my suite.

Then I went to throw up.

As I came back into the living area, I heard a noise behind me, spun and sprayed.

And got Ingrid square in the face. I dropped the spray and tried to grab her as she went down. Shana, who'd been behind her, started coughing from the fumes. Ingrid was gagging, gasping, writhing on the floor. I hurt for her. Pepper spray was the worst experience I'd ever had, and lately I'd had some bad experiences. It worse than burned your sinuses, lungs, mouth — I'm sure acid did more damage but it couldn't hurt more than pepper spray.

"Ingrid, I am so so so sorry."

She was hacking now, her corneas blood-red, eyes streaming with tears. The destruction of her perfection was almost as upsetting as hurting her.

"I thought you were the killer," I explained.

Shana had run to the bathroom, and I could hear water running. She returned, still sniffling, with a washcloth which Ingrid took and breathed into deeply.

"What killer?" Shana asked me.

I cocked my head at the couch as I covered Shana's mouth with my hand just in time to muffle the scream. "What happened?" she said behind my fingers.

Ingrid struggled to her feet and stumbled over to the couch. She shook her head, gagged out a nasty swearword and lurched into the bathroom, battling a new fit of coughing.

"Who *is* this guy?" Shana asked as we heard the shower running.

"He was a jerk at my tournament table. He tried to get me to collude, but I knocked him out instead. He made a scene in front of everyone and told me he'd get even," I recalled. "It was very disconcerting. I kept thinking he might be connected to the gang who has Affie, but all the pieces don't fit. Especially now."

"What are we going to do?" Shana asked.

An obvious question with no obvious answer. I didn't want to call Frank right now in case the cops had the phone tapped. It would be nice to call Trankosky to take care of things, if I wouldn't be the immediate first suspect. I doubted he could get me out of this one if he wanted to. Joe had disappeared some time after dinner, leaving me either with a Frank-ordered tail I didn't know about or alone to walk back to the Mellagio.

I'd disabled Ingrid, so I looked at Shana and said: "I guess we'll have to take care of him."

" 'We'?" she wiped her nose with a tissue. "Are you kidding?"

"Do you have a better idea?"

The phone rang and we both jumped. We stared at the phone. Ring. We stared at each other. Ring. Ring.

I reached over and picked it up without answering. "I guess you've found our little message."

"Your message?"

"Don't be coy, Bee Cool, it doesn't become you. What you found will be the way you will find your goddaughter if you don't cooperate."

Hurry, Frank. "I have been cooperating."

"Not entirely. You were lucky to win tonight. You should have let our friends in the right places help."

"I'm not doing anything illegal," I said bravely, as I stared at the gaping bloody smile on Terry's neck. Except harbor a murdered body in my suite.

"You'll do what you have to, I imagine," he said rather sagely. "And, by the way, you might want to get rid of our little message before the police catch you because if you can't play tomorrow, Aphrodite dies."

"But, I don't know how to get rid of, um, it." I spared a glance at Terry and grimaced. "I know the police can trace hairs and fibers from our clothes, our fingerprints."

He laughed. I shivered. "I don't care if they catch you two days or two weeks from

351

now after they do their tests on the body, you stupid woman. I just care if they catch you in the next twenty-four hours. So get rid of it now!"

I fought the wave of nausea filling the back of my throat. He continued, "Tomorrow, you'll have to find a way to win on your own because, as you can see, your help is no longer available. During the game, order a vodka gimlet from the waitress and the location of the drop will come with the drink. When they cash you out, you bring the money directly to the drop."

"Where do you expect me to end up?"

"This mission had a particular earning ratio and that should be met if you end up in the top half of the final table. Just don't win first."

"Don't win first," I repeated, trying to calculate his mixed language that sounded like it was coming from both a general and a CEO.

"First drags in too much attention; you won't be left alone for weeks."

"I won't win first. And what about Affie?"

"We get our money and you'll get her back. In that order."

"But —"

"I think you're not in any position to try to bargain. Just hope your luck holds beyond the tournament."

The base of my throat closed with tears. "Why are you doing this?"

"Because we can."

I could tell Shana had been holding her breath as she listened, because she began to weave. I forced myself to be strong for her. I hung up the phone and put my arm around her shoulders, easing her down onto a barstool. "This is about to be over. Frank's on his way to her now."

Nodding, she said: "We called him with more information about her location that Moon gave us tonight. Now what are we going to do about that guy?"

I followed her gaze to the corpse. I'd been knocking around possibilities in my mind but nothing that I could even seriously consider. They all revolved around the fact that Terry had threatened me, so I would have some sort of self-defense option. I looked closely at him, trying to figure out if he'd been killed on the couch or somewhere else. It was hard to tell how much blood was in the couch since it was essentially the same color. There were no splatter marks, though, which would seem to be a requirement if you sliced a jugular vein. I didn't know what the security cameras in the hallway had recorded — when he'd arrived and with whom, so claiming he'd broken in and tried to kill me probably wouldn't fly since the wound was older than the twenty minutes I'd been in the room.

"Let's throw him out the window," Shana said. "You've done that before."

"I have *not* done that before!"

"Well, sort of. Someone fell out your hotel window. Same difference."

"Not really, Shana. Besides, what about the people you'd hit with the body? Wouldn't you feel bad if you squished a half dozen tourists in the process?"

"Oh. Won't they get out of the way?"

"Do you regularly look up when you're on the sidewalk to make sure bodies aren't raining from the sky?"

She stuck out her lower lip. "It was an idea. It's more than you have."

Maybe not. If the killers were smart, wouldn't they have dismantled the security cameras so they couldn't record the killers' presence?

Hmm. Ingrid came, still sniffling, coughing and gagging, out of the bedroom, wearing my robe. "I can't see."

"That happened to me too," I told her. "Get some Visine out of my makeup bag, lie down on the bed and close your eyes for about thirty minutes and your vision will get better."

"But, we need to take care of the body," Ingrid argued.

"We'll do it," I said.

Her bloodshot eyes gave me a totally skeptical look. "Just . . ." She paused for a coughing fit. ". . . wait for me. You don't know what you're doing."

"Okay, Shana and I will have a drink with him while you get better." I smiled, guiding her into the bedroom and shutting the door. Putting my finger to my lips to make sure Shana didn't say anything, I let myself out into the hallway. Bingo. There was a maintenance man on a ladder examining a light fixture that I know had been operating when I'd walked down the hallway minutes ago. "Good evening," I said cheerily. "What's up?"

"Ur, bulb's out," he grunted.

"Too bad," I commiserated as I kept walking toward the elevators.

The third one from the left opened and another maintenance man hollered at his colleague, "This one's down too, Hector. We gotta go get the camera equipment."

Hector cocked his head at me and I smiled largely at the man coming out of the elevator as I got in. "Good evening."

I pressed the button to go three floors

down. As soon as I got there, I pressed the elevator to go back to my floor. When the doors opened, the maintenance men were both waiting by the freight elevator.

"I am so stupid," I giggled. "I forgot my purse!"

They nodded, rolling their eyes only after they thought I wasn't looking. I ambled back down the hallway, making sure I didn't reach my room until they'd disappeared.

"Shana, go get one of Ben's shirts out of the dry-cleaning bag in his room," I whispered as I rummaged through Frank's briefcase for the evidence gloves he kept in a side pocket. I donned a pair, then snatched a pair of scissors out of my purse and began cutting the bloody shirt off Terry.

Shana returned with a red button-down. "Good thinking," I said as I handed her some gloves.

We struggled and got him into the shirt. A two-hundred-pound rag doll is not easy to dress. "Now, sneak into my bedroom and get one of my scarves. Preferably a dark color."

I heard Shana say something to Ingrid as she slipped in, returning an instant later with a floral-print scarf. "That doesn't match the button-down," I commented.

Shana gave me an exasperated look. "Just

joking," I said.

She shook her head. "Why are we re-dressing him?"

"Because we have to hold him between us as we walk down the hallway in case anyone comes out. He'll just look drunk. Hurry."

I opened the doorway and peeked both ways. The coast was clear for now, so we panted, struggling to keep him upright between us, on our way toward the eleva-tors, which seemed marathon miles away instead of mere meters. Our luck held and the hallway stayed empty. I reached over to press the button for the elevator. "Press both," Shana recommended.

The problem here was we had to stand here until the right elevator came along — third from the left. I kept an eye on the freight elevator, praying the maintenance men would take a few more minutes. The first elevator dinged, going up. I held my breath. It was empty. I pressed the up arrow again. The second elevator dinged, going down. It opened and I cringed as a man poked his head out. We were angled away, so all he could see was our backs. "Hey man, got two for the night, huh? Menais je tois. Want a fourth?"

"Sorry, buddy." Shana used her best fake

Jersey accent. "Three's our lucky number."

As the doors slid shut on that elevator, ours arrived. Now we just had to hope it would be empty.

It wasn't empty. Of course. But the couple who was in it was rather busy. Shana gasped. I tried to figure out what that position would be called as I held the up button to keep the elevator in place. "I gotta go, I gotta go, this is our floor," he was saying as she chanted, "Yes. Yes. Yes!"

"Be quiet. What if my wife hears you?" he whispered. Perfect. Even if he saw something suspicious, I had something on him.

Leaning Terry against the wall, I stepped in front of him and Shana, so the coupling pair couldn't see them clearly. "Are you two going to get out of there tonight?" I demanded.

His head spun around. They hadn't known we were there. He jumped away from her and out the door. "Wait, you bastard," she yelled. "You owe me!"

He ran, she ran. We shoved Terry into the elevator, pushed the up button and ran too, reaching our room behind them before they reached his.

As we doubled over to catch our breath I was disturbed by how easy it had been to dispose of a dead body, but resolved not to analyze that until after this nightmare was over.

We'd cut up Terry's shirt into tiny little pieces and flushed them down the toilet. The couch was another story. Fortunately, upon closer inspection, the blood in the cushion was almost invisible because of the color match. Though, even if we rented a steam cleaner, it wouldn't fool any crime-scene team. I blotted up the worst of it with a wet towel, then sent that in pieces to join the shirt. Shana was running a hairdryer on the couch when the phone rang.

"Belinda," said a familiar voice. "You wouldn't know anything about a dead body in the elevator of your hotel, would you?"

"What?" I exclaimed, willing my voice to sound sleepy yet stunned. "Who died?"

"We don't know yet. But it is such a co-incidence to have found another body under a roof you share, also coincidentally in an elevator with a disabled security camera. And by the way, of all the floors in the hotel, the only one with a nonworking security camera is yours."

"You're making me feel very unsafe, Detective."

"Belinda," he said, "I don't think you killed this guy. Just tell me what is going on so I can help before *you* end up dead some-where."

I thought about Joe's theory. This fell right in with it. *Yeah, right, Trankosky.* Although, another part of me was tempted to spill the story by the invitation in his voice.

"Where is your boyfriend, Belinda?"

"Good question," I answered, relieved I could finally be honest.

A red-eyed, red-nosed Ingrid opened the door and looked at the couch in shock. "Where did it go?"

By morning, Terry's murder was all over the news, although they had yet to identify him. Although police didn't speculate on the similarity of the MO's of this murder and the one at the Image, reporters glee-fully did. They did man-on-the-street inter-views asking tourists if they were worried there was a Jack the Ripper on the loose in Vegas, which most hadn't considered until it was suggested. By midmorning the mayor had to call a press conference to reassure The Strip that these were likely targeted gangland killings and not random acts of a psychotic serial murderer.

It just managed to up the ante. Between the World Series of Poker, the religious zealot pickets and now a bloodthirsty gang on the loose on The Strip, Vegas couldn't get more exciting.

Or so I thought.

With each step I took on the way to my debate with Paul, I prayed Frank would call to say he'd saved Affie and I wouldn't have to play in the final game of the WSOP after all. I had absolutely nothing but dread in the pit of my stomach — what if I busted out at number nine? Would they slash her throat as they did Terry's?

Jack had gone MIA again — no one had seen him since he'd last caught me on the sidewalk — so Ingrid and Shana had left earlier to try to hunt him down. Joe, I sent to hunt down the two girls who'd waylaid me for money and then had shown up trapping johns in the newspaper. I had a plan for them. And, Ben, well, I almost couldn't think about him, because when I did, I imagined him being tortured by the Medula who'd found him out. I really had no faith in Ben's ability to pull off a gang infiltration. After all, look what happened the last time he tried to play at being an investigator.

I didn't know if Joe had left one of Frank's men on my tail or not, and frankly at this point, didn't care.

So, of course, this was when I would be accosted. I felt the tug on my sleeve before the hand actually closed around my forearm and pulled me into the alley between two hotels.

I kicked out, pointy heels first, and made contact. He swore and I recognized the voice before I recognized anything else. "Sam? Sam Hyun?"

"Belinda Cooley." He nodded, still holding me, now with vise grips on either arm. This man had dangled me ten stories above the Gulf of Mexico once, but somehow I found it hard to work up the energy to be afraid of him now. Go figure.

"What are you doing here, Sam? I thought you were in jail."

He shrugged. "My attorney is working on a deal. I'm out on bond."

"Good for you, and now you're going for your second offense?"

His eyebrows drew together below his cueball head. Boy, he was one guy who shouldn't go bald on purpose. "What do you mean?"

"Sam." I stared at his hands. "You're holding me against my will. I think that is considered kidnapping, or at the very least, assault."

"Oh." He said, "But I want you to listen

to what I have to say."

"I won't go anywhere, Sam." For now. Until I see a weapon. Like a serrated knife.

He let go and stuck his hands in the pockets of his slacks. "I wanted you to know that that Paul guy is out for you."

"No kidding."

"No, Belinda, I really mean it. One of his henchmen, a guy named Drew Terry, approached me before the Main Event even started and first pumped me for info on you, then tried to talk me into drawing you into collusion. When I refused, they wanted to pay me to at least talk about you being a dirty player."

So, Terry was a Paul man. Somehow I wasn't as surprised as I should have been, perhaps because it confirmed a niggling suspicion that had been building in the back of my mind. "Well, Sam, did you do it? After all, you do that for free anyway."

"Hey, I never said you were dirty. I said you were stupid."

"Oh, right. I guess they didn't pay for that."

"No," he sulked.

"Why are you telling me this, Sam?"

"Because playing in the Main Event this year, I've come to accept how much poker has changed. I realized, more than ever you deserve to win as much as I do. Maybe."

Whoa. Now's where he pulls out the knife.

He moved his left hand, yanking it out of his pocket and extending it, empty and open, waiting for mine. "Good luck, Bee Cool."

So much for that theory. And I guess I wasn't being tailed at all because no one had come to my rescue in the alleyway, even if I didn't need to be rescued. Humph.

I guess it wasn't my day to die. Yet.

Even before I turned toward the Fortune, I could feel the electricity. The media was out in force, the fans revved up, players hopped up. And I could barely force myself to walk up to the casino. Ugh, not to mention this debate I'd been invited — forced — to join. That was the icing on my cake of misery.

I'm certain I was a fly in the World Series of Poker executive committee's ointment, if I was noticed at all. That Paul had asked me to appear as the spokeswoman for the game must have been hard to swallow, but to their credit, they didn't tell me what to say. I assumed so they could best distance themselves from what I *would* say. I knew I could be easily sacrificed — as a woman, as an amateur, as a perceived fluffhead —

much easier than the handful of household names at the final table.

As I entered the poker room, I saw they had set up a poker table with only two chairs in front of the WSOP's final table. The TV-friendly one was rife with all the props of the game, even real cash scattered about the chips and cards. True infotainment. The pretty boy network announcer who'd probably never played a hand of Hold 'Em in his life stepped in front of the scene. "This year's World Series of Poker is setting all kinds of records, for attendance at 11,202, for the winner's purse of fourteen million dollars and for the first organized protest against the game. The Reverend Phineas Paul and members of his Church of the Believers have been picketing from the first day of the tournament. On this, the final day, with the field whittled to nine players, and the world watching, the Main Event organizers have invited Paul to make his case in a three-minute debate on live television prior to the first deal."

The president of the 2008 WSOP took the mic. "To celebrate the free speech we value in America we invite Mr. Paul to have his say." He paused as he motioned Paul out from the sidelines and into the chair on the left before continuing, "Paul asked that

Miss Belinda Cooley, a relative, but extremely successful, newcomer to Texas Hold 'Em, speak for poker. We thank her for being such a lovely ambassador for the game."

I resisted the impulse to gag as I nodded and followed his sweeping arm to my own chair. He made it clear I was window dressing. I took a deep breath and focused on getting through this so I could get on with freeing Affie.

Paul's hate across the table was palpable as I eased into my seat. I marveled at the energy it took to abhor something this much; it had to be exhausting. I steeled myself to remain as calm as possible, for as irritating as he had been during this week from hell, he wasn't what I needed to focus my energies on.

"I have the easy job," he began. "God is on my side. The Bible is on my side. The devil is on yours. There is no divine defense for gambling. It is a sin, pure and simple."

"I certainly wouldn't pretend to know the Bible as well as you do, Mr. Paul."

"REVEREND Paul," he interrupted.

I nodded without verbally acknowledging his interruption, as I continued. "But I believe the good book allows for diversion and recreation alongside hard work. The interesting thing about life is, it is all about perspective. Someone's blue sky will seem purple to another. One person's job might seem like nothing but fun to another. Some people might consider your job as a preacher to be nothing but getting paid to talk —"

"Blasphemy!" Speaking of purple, that was now the color of his face. I was glad he didn't have a weapon other than his tongue.

"— but others would consider yours the most difficult job, carrying such responsibility as it does for maintaining the faith of your followers."

That mollified him for an instant. Throwing him off balance was the only way I could retain any kind of purchase in this debate. "Exactly. That faith is fragile. It is under attack daily with the crime and wanton secularity of the world today. Poker — built as it is on greed — erodes the foundation of faith that we, in the Church of the Believers, have taken on in order to rebuild the moral fiber of our people."

"How does hypocrisy fit in to rebuilding the moral fiber? How do you justify paying your young picketers to hold signs they don't believe in?"

"You are the tongue of the devil."

Whoops, he was almost frothing at the mouth. I motioned to Joe, who brought the pair of girls forward. They were both shuddering in fear, looking at me in desperate question. I'd promised I'd keep them safe, now I wasn't sure I'd been right to use them. "Did Mr. Paul pay you girls to hold these signs?"

They nodded. "And other things . . ." one of them said in a small voice.

"We are warriors!" Paul cut in. "We must make sacrifices to save the world. If these girls must sacrifice, then so be it. The means justify the right end. They were on the path to destruction anyway. I saved them, they are working toward heaven now, instead of hell."

I supressed my own shiver. "So if every poker player in the world donated her winnings to your cause, would the means justify the end, then? Would the poker devils become your warriors as well?"

He stood violently.

Something struck me as he shoved his chair back and turned away from the camera: Paul's tie was red and yellow. A coincidence? The WSOP president shook my hand, beaming as the camera swung back to the anchorman. I grabbed the sleeve of the WLVS cameraman who was following Paul's departure from the ballroom. He switched off the camera and turned to me as I asked, "Do you have file footage of Paul

368

relatively easy to access?"

"Of course, he's the big newsmaker right now. We carry all the file footage we might need in the live truck outside."

"Can I see it?" I had to temper my adrenaline. He told me he'd have to ask the producer and disappeared. I had exactly an hour before the tournament began. I hoped they were organized enough for us to find it in that time.

After a moment, the producer was produced. She considered my request, calculating, not ready to give something for nothing. "You can see the tape, if you grant us an exclusive interview after you're finished playing today."

"Deal," I said. It was okay with me, because I hated owing anyone. This would make us even.

And I'd see proof of whether this was who Affie had been warning me about days and days ago. Proof that I'd been blind.

The film editor and I were reviewing the last piece of file footage when the door to the live truck opened and Jack stumbled in. "There you are!" he said.

"Look who's talking," I murmured over my shoulder as the editor named Gary and I nodded to each other. Paul's tie was red and yellow on the first day of the World Series too. I spun in the chair to face Jack and my mouth dropped open. "What in the world happened to you?"

He hadn't shaved, was pale and shaky, wearing the clothes he'd had on the day before, except they were filthy, and black half moons underscored his eyes. I asked the editor for water, and Jack gulped it gratefully when it was produced. Finally, he began, "I m-m-m-managed . . ."

He sucked in a breath. I willed myself to patience. Rushing him would only make matters worse. Once he got going it would be fine. ". . . to sneak into the Church of the Believers office in that building Carey found when he followed D-D-Dragsnashark. Problem was, while I was poking around, some people came in and I was stuck behind a bunch of boxes. It turned out to be great in the end, though, because I heard everything. He's b-behind it *all*, Bee."

"What are you talking about?"

He took another swallow of water and I felt guilty for pushing him so hard. I put my hand on his shoulder. "Sit down and relax."

"We don't have t-time for that. I have a lot of it recorded, enough to put Paul away for g-good, I think. Enough to get Affie freed, even without Frank and his men in b-black. Enough to bring in the authorities."

I didn't have the faith in authorities that Jack had, but I wouldn't burst his bubble right now. "Jack, what does Affie have to do with Paul?"

"It's not the Medula who kidnapped Affie — it's Paul."

"What? But —"

"Let me f-finish, and it will all make s-sense." Jack paused. "S-sick sense, but sense nonetheless."

I nodded. He continued. "The Medula are extorting money from you that they get to keep, as their part of the arrangement with Paul. His goal is to put poker down across the world, run it back to the backrooms where he thinks it belongs. It's his mission. He's smart, though. He knew he couldn't attack the nameless, faceless game in this media-driven age. He had to chose a scapegoat and no better one than you. To reveal a woman who seems to be the antithesis of rotten as truly bad would be doing the same to a game that seems like harmless entertainment. And, what's more, it would be dramatic. He and his chief deacon likened it to a child opening a beautifully wrapped Christmas gift to find a rotting, dead puppy inside."

"That man is not right," I said, pulling a face.

"He started long ago, sending church members into play in poker rooms, planting seeds of rumors of collusion and your dirty play, trying to bribe other players to spread the word too. But the deeper his spies got into it, the more they came to realize simple bad talking would not be enough to scare you into doing something wrong. That's when he joined up with the Medula, who were to use whatever means they could to squeeze you. They killed Tasser in order to frame you for the crime eventually — after the WSOP — after you'd made them the money. They kidnapped Affie, but didn't want to have the hassle of keeping her, so they sent her to Paul's compound."

"Like David Koresh's," I murmured, so sorry now I hadn't listened more seriously to Thelma. Then finally, realization dawned. "In southeastern Oregon. With a circus tent where they have services, with lots of other teenage girls like the ones picketing . . ."

Jack nodded.

"It's been right in front of us."

"C-come on, Bee. Don't be so hard on yourself. If you t-told me what I'm telling you I still might not b-believe it. But I heard them."

"I just don't understand about this Terry guy . . ."

"Some guy named D-drew came in last night, furious, frustrated, s-spouting off that he was going to b-bring you down no matter what. Paul told him the best soldiers were the bravest, told a story about the samurai's hari-kiri, and it was major creepy. It was almost like he was talking him into committing suicide."

"Suicide?" I whispered with a shudder. "I found his body, throat slashed with a serrated knife in our suite last night." I didn't look very hard for the knife, though, did I?

"Whoa. Who could actually do that? S-s-scary. Is Ingrid okay?"

"What about Serrano?" I mused, as I nodded in answer.

"Wrong place, wrong time. He apparently was killed by Dragsnashark because Serrano hassled him when he was following you."

That made me sad.

Jack wrapped my shoulders in a hug. "I already called Frank and left him a message with the address for the compound. We need to tell him the rest."

Jack and I left the live truck to get a cell

phone signal to call Frank, when we saw Trankosky leaning against his Crown Victoria. He pushed off when he saw us, nodding to Jack as I introduced him. They shook hands. "I follow your work. You're a good poker dick," he said. Jack blushed. Pushover.

"Belinda, you're in big trouble and I can't do anything to help you now."

Uh-oh, they'd found out about Terry. I guess it was bound to happen. I wondered what the punishment was for corrupting a crime scene and improperly disposing of a dead body.

"Aren't you going to ask what you did?"

"I don't know how he died."

Jack shot me a warning look to shut up. Even though he didn't know about Terry, apparently he could sense me putting foot in mouth. "C-cut to the chase, Detective."

Trankosky's eyebrows had drawn together as he considered what I'd said, but then he turned to Jack and answered his question. "The FBI has apparently authenticated Belinda's signature on documents that prove she attempted to bribe casino officials."

"What?!" I blurted.

He looked at me and I saw he was disappointed. "They have phone records from your cell phone that you placed calls to known criminals and they found fifty thousand dollars in bills they can link to a crime scene here in Vegas. Serrano was working undercover for the FBI when he was murdered. They are at court right now waiting for the judge to sign the warrant for your arrest."

"I don't understand. I didn't do any of those things." My mind was flashing like a strobe light, hitting me with thoughts, images and memories too brief to make sense. I saw myself turning my cell phone over to Trankosky, then forgetting to cut off service until two days later. I saw myself signing that thick sheaf of papers as an autograph. I saw myself leaving that stash of money in the trash can.

"You're the one who had my phone," I said accusingly.

"I just checked the evidence room. It's gone. Why didn't you cut off your service if you didn't make these calls?"

"Because I forgot and don't regularly expect to have to guard against being framed for crimes I don't commit. This is all new territory for me." I sucked in a breath while Trankosky watched me carefully. "Where was the money found?"

"When they raided that poker game off The Strip and found those underage girls.

I'm telling you more than I should." Those girls. Those damned girls. They worked for Paul, who was determined to set me up.

"Belinda, you've been keeping something or things from me."

"Yes, but this isn't it. This isn't even close."

"So tell me what it is," Trankosky said. "Does it have to do with your mercenary boyfriend?"

Eyes widening, I shook my head. Mercenary? I suspected he was on the scary end of the security business, but hearing him called that was a shock.

"Let me help, Belinda," Trankosky said. "You need some."

Jack said: "You're being blackmailed, Bee. If they throw you in jail, you can't do anything for Affie. You know who's behind it now. If Frank fails, let the detective pick up the lead and run with it. Do it for Aph."

I felt like I couldn't breathe.

"My goddaughter is being held hostage," I whispered roughly.

"By the gang that tried to kidnap you at the Image?"

"No, by Reverend Phineas Paul."

Twenty-Seven

After Trankosky gave Jack a threatening lecture about never leaving me alone again, he zoomed off in his unmarked sedan and we trooped back to the casino. On the way, we tried to call Frank again to make sure he knew he was storming a cult compound instead of a gangland headquarters, but he had his phone turned off. Jack left an urgent message detailing what he'd discovered. I refused to let him tell Frank about the new mess I was in with the feds and the dead body, a fact that I was pretty sure Trankosky and the rest of the CCSD was going to catch eventually. I was determined to keep Frank and his merry band of mercenaries focused on Affie. We'd get the rest sorted out later.

Reporters shouted, flashes exploded and cameramen scrambled when we turned the corner. I wanted to run and hide but there was no place for that anymore. I had to hide in plain sight like I'd done before. Now I had to play on the final table even if Affie was rescued. The longer I sat and bet, the longer I could wait for the truth to rise to the surface, the longer I could stave off handcuffs and federal prison.

The mass of media outnumbered Paul's followers for the first time, but I did notice that it was an all-teenage girl group today. They saw me and started whispering. Probably didn't approve of my braided hair or the retro outfit Ingrid had forced me into. I didn't see the bad reverend anywhere. I'd already planned to jump him and choke him to death until he agreed to let Affie go so this was a big disappointment.

"Where's Phineas Paul?" I asked one of the girls.

She shrugged, but looked like the cat that caught the mouse. "I dunno." She was obviously lying.

Good. Maybe they'd killed him for me. And chopped him up in little pieces and flushed him down the toilet.

I paused, ashamed of myself. This was warping me to an extreme. I thought I was going to need counseling after this. They probably provided that behind bars.

Once inside the casino, I was flanked by security. A legion of poker babes jumped up and down, waved, whooped and hollered when I walked by the rail. Some of the women I'd played against during the week waved and wished me luck. Gun-shy now, I pretended not to see the autograph seekers. Then I saw Frank's family gathered near the ballroom door. I veered over to them, shaking off a security guard's protective arm. I shook Randolph's hand, kissed Wilma on the cheek and took the rabbit's foot Matthew offered.

"I can't get ahold of Frank," Monica admitted, searching the crowd behind me.

"He's gone to do a job," I told her, guilty for having to talk around exactly what he was doing, but not willing to make her worry. Of course, since she knew he was a mercenary any time he was on a job would be cause for concern, wouldn't it?

I stopped my train of thought. I was getting bitter.

"I'm sorry, Bee," she said, her big eyes reflecting her sorrow. "It's not right he'll miss your big day. For work. You'd think he'd learned his lesson."

"It's okay," I told her, wishing everything really was. "Or it will be okay, soon."

She smiled bravely and patted my arm. "Go make history."

I thanked her. Security escorted me to the

ballroom door as I looked back to see Jack and Trankosky turning away, deep in conversation. The detective turned to give me a look that I couldn't say was anything other than a promise.

Having to dispose of a dead body, finding out my goddaughter had been kidnapped by a lunatic and that I was wanted for crimes I didn't commit had managed to diminish the intense atmosphere of the final table. Playing against the toughest of the pros for fourteen million dollars now was just not that big a deal anymore.

We shook hands all around. The tournament and the network had planned a long, dramatic introduction that we had to withstand. I had no idea who'd made the cut with me. It was the ultimate irony. How many times in a person's life would they beat million-to-one odds and how many times would they have a loved one kidnapped and how many times would they find a dead man in their hotel room . . . I could go on, but suffice it to say I was the only player who had no clue. And that was probably a good thing in the long run.

I had to outlast at least four of these players. I tried to concentrate on their tells from the moment we sat down. My strength was my ability to read players on a given day in a given game, not letting my imagination spin truths that weren't there. The one time I'd actually researched my final table in a tournament I'd busted the second hand, because I hadn't trusted what I saw but what I'd read.

So while five of the men at the final table probably had volumes written on what they did when they held an Ace/Jack, I was going with what my gut told me.

Ron, the player sitting to my left, leaned in. "I hear you are the worst kind of alligator blood."

I smiled at his attempt to make conversation. "You hear wrong."

"No, no, you got it all wrong, she's a Maniac," said a pro who had played against me once before.

I raised my eyebrows.

"Pot calling the kettle, Oscar," another player chimed in. "She's the dog." Poker slang for underdog. "But a damned cute one."

"I'd call her a chameleon, but I hear the females can't change colors. Does that mean they are genetically unable to play with our skill? No wonder. It won't be your fault when you bust out, Bee Cool."

That garnered a testosterone-induced

chuckle all around. The dealer, a woman named Sandy, looked askance at me for not arguing. I didn't care. In fact, I loved it. The more they underestimated me, the better.

"She's nothing but a donkey," muttered the grump across from me, who was introduced as a European champion who won a seat having never played in a U.S. tournament. His disdain for women was palpable.

"Exactly! Someone nailed the right animal on the head," I said, gladly accepting the rarely used term for a fish — novice player — and ready to end this conversation. "Thank you."

That shut the male hot doggers up and the play began. The cards didn't make life easy for me at first. An Ace of diamonds, 3 of clubs in my pocket, when I'd drawn the seat at the big blind, was not a gift but it was enough to make me stick around to see The Flop. Deuce of hearts and 4 of spades were enough to give me hope but the King of clubs was easily a counterfeit — enough for someone to land trips or at least a pair over my Ace kicker at this point. I hated to even think about a straight draw, even though I had one.

Only two on the table folded although there were checks all around. I raised small to make a statement. The Maniac man nodded to the chameleon commenter. I don't know what they thought I had but apparently everyone was into my agenda. Wouldn't they be surprised.

Another folded and the rest hung around for The Turn which was another King. Ack. I watched the table. Everyone was very stiff. Ah-ha. No one was giving me any yahoo signals. I tempered my own and when the European creep went all in I knew I had the nuts, even with only the Ace kicker. I met his push and everyone else folded. My stack had him by maybe a million, so when the five came on The River, I showed my straight, collected the pot and my statement was made. The European whiz slammed his chair back and left in a huff.

As the dealer passed out our next hand, I ordered the vodka gimlet to get the whole information-about-the-location-of-the-drop exchange over with. I had enough suspense in my life without that adding to it.

The next three pockets dealt to me were a hammer (two/seven off-suit), a Heinz (five/seven off-suit) and San Francisco busboy (Queen/three), so it was a good thing I'd stockpiled some chips and some clout. The waitress still had not produced my drink.

My next pocket deal was a Kojack (King/

Jack suited hearts) and, while not ideal, it was pretty promising. I met the reraise Pre-flop. Five of us rode into The Flop for a King, King, Jack. I wanted to faint but didn't. This never happens. I likely had the nuts and didn't know how to play it, so I remained conservative, trying to read the lip twitcher for a sign he was bluffing and the hangnail worrier to see if he had a gut-shot straight. I think the man to my right had an over card and nothing else, but that was just his bouncing leg talking.

At The Turn, I called again. I was waiting for Fifth Street to make a big move, hoping I could milk the pot as far as it would go. I was helped by another piece of paint on the board, a Queen of hearts. There were so far no flush draws with an unsuited board, but it was still a worry. A royal flush would send me packing. I raised then reraised before Fifth Street. Then the twitcher went all in. Three of us held our breaths as the dealer threw the burn card. A six of hearts fell on The River. A total blank. I'd won, the draw hopefuls held nada, and I was probably the most unpopular player at the table with six of us left.

Another hour rolled by with small gains and small losses for me. I remained rela-tively even. I won two with only King high and Queen high kickers, respectively. I'd never played in a tournament game where that would have flown but it was a strangely suited set of players where tells told the story for me. They still couldn't figure me out. I got the sense that I might be able to win the whole thing and it was slightly tempting, but only for a hand. I lost the next one to the tune of twenty million in chips.

The decent alligator blood labeler sitting next to me got knocked out on what I would have considered a pat hand — pocket rockets met with twin Aces on the board at The Flop. Poor guy, head-to-head with the pro who called me a Maniac, he lost to a royal flush when jack/ten fell on Fourth and Fifth Streets. That was just a bad beat.

It was down to four players now, and thankfully time for me to bow out. The suspense of not knowing what was happening with Affie was about to kill me. It took me five hands from that point to do it, however, as Murphy's Law kicked in and I was dealt a full house, a gutshot straight and a Jack quads. I was one off being chip leader when I finally got dealt walking sticks in my pocket (pair of sevens). Since the Maniac man had American Airlines and had started his happy sweat on his upper lip, I thought this was a good time to push. I was too eager, however, pushing on The Flop and he folded, thinking, I suppose, I had the royal flush with the royal board. Argh. Everyone else bailed too. I collected the pot without even having to show I'd won with an unintentional bluff.

Finally, Murphy hiccupped and I got ducks in a family pot. Perfect time to bow out. This time I patiently waited until someone else — Mr. Fast — pushed. Good thing he was chip leader. I pushed back.

"She's down to the felt," the dealer said.

Holding my breath and crossing my fingers under the table that another couple of deuces wouldn't land back door, I watched as my opponent made his ladies trips on The River. I blew out my breath and shook his hand as my fans moaned behind me. The rest of the table were shaking their heads, still not figuring why I would have gone all in with deuces.

"You did that on purpose, losing," the dealer whispered to me. "Why?"

I shook my head, blinking innocently. "Gosh, I thought I had the nuts."

He shook his head too, not believing me in the slightest.

I turned in my seat card, collecting the two million dollars which they most definitely did not want to give me in cash. I had to sign a form promising to report it on my taxes. (I'd be in federal prison so they'd know where to find me if I didn't.) Since I still hadn't gotten any news about Affie, I couldn't take a chance at not turning the money over to the gang. The small size of the envelope they handed me surprised me — how compressed two million could be. I shoved it into my Kate Spade. The crowd gathered at the rail cheered as I exited the office. A WSOP official tried to shush them, which frankly I never understood. It's not a library, or a chess match, it was a poker tournament. I certainly didn't need absolute silence to concentrate on counting fifty-two cards and crossing my fingers.

I waved, smiled, shook hands. The producer I'd made the deal with asked me for my interview. My heart clutched in my chest. "I plan on it. But, this money is making me nervous. Can I get it to my bank, first?"

"Just make sure you're back before nine o'clock. We've got to make the news at ten. And don't you dare talk to any other broadcast reporters!"

"No problem."

As I walked out of the casino, I was suddenly flanked by two bodies who both grabbed my arms. "Hey!" I looked to my right. Paul's right-hand man. And, on my left was Paul himself.

"Miss Cooley," he said as loudly as if he'd had a megaphone. My ears rang. "My followers and I highly recommend that you donate your winnings right now to the Church of the Believers, to repent and save your soul."

"I can't and you know it," I whispered. "I have to save my goddaughter and the animals you sicced on me are expecting it."

"Don't you understand, you stupid fool," he flashed his megawatt fake smile as he looked at me with cold snake eyes. "If she's not already dead, she will be soon. We couldn't let a witness like that walk."

I hadn't noticed, but somehow Paul's girls had surrounded us, and I expected to be mobbed and robbed. Instead, on a word from the girl in the center, they all ripped the top layer off their signs to reveal the depths of Paul's horrors — there were blown-up photos of him taunting young children with fang-bearing snakes. Photos of him applying leeches to a baby. "Church of the Torturers, led by Phineas Paul" read another. "Paul paid me three thousand dollars to walk the picket line this week," read another. "I got crack to seduce a sixty-year-old poker player so he could get caught by the cops."

The most sickening of all was this sign: "All these means justify his ends."

The right-hand man barked orders to someone into his two-way radio.

"Blasphemy!" Paul shouted. "You all have been possessed by the devil. The moral corruption in Las Vegas is too much for your young souls to fight. Get in the buses, now, you all must be exorcized immediately."

As the buses pulled up and men who looked like soldiers of fortune jumped out, the girls squeezed in on us. They began whacking their reverend with their signs. With one arm up to stave them off, Paul tried to reach into my purse. The right-hand man twisted my arm so hard I thought it was breaking. With tears rolling down my face from the pain and frustration, I knew what I had to do. With one hand I reached into my purse, found the envelope, pulled out the money and threw it straight up into the air. Two million dollars rained down on The Las Vegas Strip and chaos erupted. Then I ran as fast as I could.

A couple of hours later, back at our suite, the phone rang as we watched the Church of the Believers compound burst into flames on national TV. The compound had been stormed by law enforcement, according to the reporter. Dozens had been freed, but there was expected to be a death toll. I felt sick, imagining all my loved ones roasting in the fire. The CNN reporter on the scene couldn't tell us who'd escaped and who hadn't, just that authorities on the scene had reported seeing Paul set fire to his own creation.

As the phone rang for the seventh time, I hesitated to answer, forgetting that the bad guys wouldn't be calling me for orders anymore, not remembering that my mother didn't know that Ben might be in the inferno and not believing that I'd be lucky enough to have anyone I loved survive.

"Hello?"

"Bee Bee," he murmured. Ben sounded tired.

"Where are you, how are you, how's Aph, how's Frank?"

"Breathe, Bee Bee, breathe."

"Talk, Ben. Talk."

"Affie is okay. She's with Frank and his guys. We're going to be debriefed by the badges, then head to the airport and catch the first flight back."

The relief I felt couldn't have been measured in a universe as small as ours. I swallowed hard before I asked, "She wasn't hurt, abused, tortured?"

"No, apparently she was put in with the rest of the teenage brainwash victims in the cult. With Paul in Vegas, it operated more like summer camp with some creepy activities. They did have to do something with rattlesnakes, but she had Grog and faked out the instructor apparently. Somehow she managed to avoid being indoctrinated. Imagine that, considering who her mother is," he added drily.

I was afraid to ask the next question. "And you? Are you okay?"

"Yeah, just so happened that it was easier than I expected. When I went to the tattoo parlor, the Garden of Eden lady overheard me ask for the dragsnashark tattoo and when I was leaving she cornered me and asked if I was in the gang. Her brother is a Medula. She got me an interview with one of the lieutenants and he liked me."

"Wait a minute, Ben. You got one of those godawful tattoos."

"Yep. I'm going to have to get it removed, I guess. Unless . . ."

"Ben," I warned.

"Really, Bee Bee. The Medula gave me a new perspective on free enterprise, that's for sure," Ben said. "The guy I worked

391

under for two days, he had an MBA from Harvard."

"You're kidding?"

"Nope, the whole gang is run like a Fortune 500 company. The only difference is they don't even pretend to have scruples, morals or ethics. It makes things a lot more definite, easier, actually. They made a boatload of money in their partnership with Paul's church, I can tell you that."

"You *are* coming home, aren't you?"

"Yeah, when Paul got in trouble there, the whole gang went underground, advising their lieutenants to scatter for six months. Pretty good vacation package, don't you think?"

"Ben!"

"I was tempted, but, nah, I think I like pretending to have scruples. Speaking of which, can I talk to Shana?"

I handed the phone to my friend, thinking I'd give him a pass on the whole opportunistic moment thing. I guess he deserved to hear from a grateful, beautiful woman who'd be awed by his bravery. He'd be put in his place when he got home.

We heard on TV a while later that Grog was the true hero.

Here and I would've sworn snakes

couldn't be any good.

However, Grog defied expectations. The anchorwoman's tone was serious as she said, "Paul snuck out of Las Vegas in the midst of the chaos on The Strip, was picked up by his helicopter in a parking lot, seen clutching handfuls of the bills Bee Cooley threw up in the air. He made it to the compound hours later, determined to destroy it. Grog the boa apparently slithered up Paul's leg as he was flinging the matches onto the gasoline tracks he'd poured out and constricted him until authorities arrived. Then, apparently, it took ten men to pull him off Paul, who had fallen unconscious. It is suspected Paul may have permanent brain damage if he ever wakes from his coma."

"I've got news for them," Jack put in. "Paul had permanent brain damage *before* Grog ever got ahold of him."

I was still watching CNN — watching my snake ham it up for the camera, held by a teenage girl who'd obviously gotten friendly with him in his time at the compound. Huh. I was attached to Grog but I never expected this from him. From a dog, maybe. I'd even heard of a rare cat attacking a robber, but never a python. I suppose he was a better judge of character than I ever gave him credit for. I should have let him loose for all those stinker dates I had over the years.

Ingrid called before the story was over to inform me she'd already set Grog up with his own website. I was betting my snake was already more famous than I was. Somehow that didn't upset me.

I thought Frank had been a hero too, but that was one story we wouldn't hear on CNN or probably even from Frank. Maybe Joe would tell me one day. I'd seen my reluctant bodyguard toting an Uzi in the background of one of the live shots. Maybe he wouldn't be mad at me anymore since he got in on some action.

I refused to ask to talk to Frank. And Ben didn't offer.

The next morning I still hadn't been arrested. It was a bad feeling, like waiting for the next aftershock of an earthquake, so when Trankosky called, I was braced for the worst.

After he asked about my mental state, he got on with business. "You owe your friend, Jack. He risked his life to get you off the hook."

"I'm off the hook?"

"With the feds anyway. His tape recordings have sent them full blast after Paul. You are small potatoes, sure to be interviewed but not arrested. The sheriff's department, however, has some questions about the body we've identified as Drew Terry, deacon of the Church of the Believers, slashed to death with the same sort of weapon, a serrated knife, ten inches long, that killed Keith Tasser."

Oops, I'd forgotten to look for the knife. I peered under the couch. Nothing. I parted the cushions. Sure enough, bloody knife, serrated, about ten inches long. I coughed, turned it into a throat clearing. "Popular opinion is, I killed them?"

"Popular opinion is Terry was in your suite at some point, dead or alive. He expired, and his body left not of its own volition. And there is the matter of the scarf, too. How did he come to be wearing your scarf?"

"How did you know it was mine?" I blurted, then clamped my hand on my mouth. Too late, obviously.

"It was a little tricky. We thought it was some kind of ascot. But then someone recognized it as an original Sheila Trudeau. She only made ten. You got the prototype for doing her ad campaign."

"Oops." I paused. "What kind of cop would recognize a Trudeau accessory?"

"Krane did. You apparently inspired her

to improve her fashion sense. Ironically, it came back to bite you." He was trying hard not to laugh. I was insulted. "Belinda, a word of advice, you need to get a less distinctive wardrobe if you are going to regularly use it to dress dead bodies."

"I guess I'm nailed. Since you *are* the CCSD, what can I expect?"

"I am not the whole department. I just want to run it," he added jokingly.

"Well, pretend like you already do. What is going to happen to me?"

"Considering the evidence we have, and the remainder you will provide by *cooperating,* I'd say you might have to plea bargain for a couple hundred hours of community service, which will bring you back to Vegas for a few months later this year."

After the week I'd had, I thought that should sound worse than purgatory, but somehow it didn't sound that bad after all.

TWENTY-EIGHT

"Ben, what made you think you could pull off a miracle? That was foolhardy, dangerous grandstanding. Besides which, you mutilated yourself." I pulled a face at the tattoo. It did make him look tough, but it was ugly as all get out.

"I already called Joaquin, he's removing it tomorrow," Ben said. "Although it's growing on me."

Shana cocked her head, shooting him a warning glare. He put up his hands. "I promise. It's out of here."

"Ben, don't avoid my question," I said. "You were lucky to get out alive, and now that you have I might kill you. Didn't you learn your lesson when you pulled this James Bond business the last time we were in Vegas? Mother is beside herself with worry over you."

He shocked me by saying, "I understand."

"You *understand* Mom? Did they do a

lobotomy on you while you were in Medu-laville?"

"Not only do I understand Ma, but she will understand why I took a chance too. You do these kinds of things when you're a parent, Bee Bee."

"Okay, but . . ." I paused. "*What* did you say? And how would you know?"

Ben and Shana shared a look, like the dozens of mystery gazes they'd been throwing back and forth since the first night we'd arrived in Vegas. Shana shook her head. "Ben, until we can confirm —"

"I'm confirming it. That's all we need. We don't need blood, we don't need DNA. I'm Aph's dad, whether you want me to be or not. We'll tell her as soon as she gets here."

My mouth dropped open. My limbs went weak, and I dropped onto the couch. Wordlessly, my mouth opened and closed. I shook my head.

"This doesn't make any sense," I finally choked out.

Shana sat down on the couch next to me and patted my knee. "It's still all supposition. See, when Affie went missing, Ben asked me about her dad — whether we should contact him — and I told him I really didn't know Aph's father's name. So I told the story of how she was conceived at that masquerade party in college . . ."

I'd heard the story, of course, never guessing I might know the man in the peacock-feathered mask, much less be related to him.

Ben picked up where she trailed off ". . . I'd been in Dallas on a sales trip, when I ran into some SMU coeds at a bar and they invited me to the masquerade ball."

"Kind of old, weren't you, twenty-six and crashing a college party?" I asked.

Ben raised his eyebrows. Since when did he have any scruples?

"Never mind, stupid question."

". . . well," Shana continued, "once we realized we'd been at the same party, we got into some things about what happened that night only the two of us could know."

Shana blushed. I stared. My boisterous friend never blushed, never got embarrassed; she, proud of her intemperance, would normally be telling me the details, drawing me a picture. Not that I wanted that when my *brother* was involved. Ick. Super ick.

I shook my head. "I don't believe it. Aphrodite is way too responsible to have been spawned from the two of you, the most impulsive, hedonistic pair on the face of the earth."

And then Aphrodite walked in through

the door with Frank, Joe and Jack, and I saw it. I saw Ben in her. In the green of her eyes, in the dimple on her right cheek. In the way she strutted when she walked. Wow. How could I have not seen it before, after all these years?

Ben saw the recognition and the wonder on my face and nudged me with his shoulder, as he whispered, "Good thing she got my looks because I guess she inherited her Aunt Bee Bee's serious-as-a-heart-attack character. Poor kid." Ben grinned and ran to his two girls, grabbing them in a bear hug.

The secret was out. My brother was back. My best friend had finally grown up.

And, I had a brand-new niece.

I waited, patiently for once, for my own hug, because I wanted it to last the rest of her life.

Dale Trankosky was leaning against a white Porsche convertible in the valet area as I left the Mellagio a few hours later. *Vavoom.* "Hello, Belinda."

A silver stiletto, size eight, dangled from his index finger.

"Are you trying to be Prince Charming?"

"Is it working, Cinderella?"

"You've got a little more work to do, but

thanks," I said plucking my beloved Angel from his fingertip. "This is a good start, although I don't want you to get in trouble for swiping evidence."

"Considering they picked up your Drag-snashark, whose name is Pablo Nunez, and he's singing, they decided they didn't need it anymore."

I nodded, pleased. "How long have you been there?"

He shrugged. I guessed he was off duty, since he wore a blue and yellow striped polo, khaki shorts and deck shoes. It was a little disconcerting to see him in street clothes, because it made him seem more like a person and less like a cop. Somehow it balanced out his shaved head, softened his ironic mouth.

"You know, you could have come up to the suite, if you needed to talk to me," I told him as I approached. "And not loiter down her and scare the natives." The valets were all eyeballing him, having pegged him for a cop immediately. He had the power aura. I doubted he'd ever be able to work undercover and get away with it. Unless he went under as a crime boss.

"I didn't trust myself to behave in a private venue."

I raised my eyebrows.

"You know, Belinda," he said, "we are in the most romantic city in the world."

I perceived Vegas a lot of ways — sexy, dangerous, thrilling, bizarre, otherworldly, recently quite deadly — but never romantic. "How do you figure?"

"More people get married here than anywhere else."

"For reasons other than romance," I put in.

"I never pegged you for a cynic," Trankosky said.

"I guess you don't know me that well then, do you?"

"I'd like to . . . get to know you. Every inch of you. Inside and out."

"That's kind of suggestive, Detective."

"Only for people with dirty minds," he returned with a lopsided grin. "Those of us who see a city of neon, gamblers, pimps and prostitutes as romantic find that kind of comment . . . touching."

I belly laughed. I couldn't help it. He was actually cute — in a dog-begging-for-a-bone way, albeit an oversize trained-to-kill dog, like a mastiff. "Well, consider me touched then."

"Not yet," he murmured, wrapping his arm around my waist and pulling me just close enough to kiss.

I hesitated. He waited. Then I remembered that I'd made a decision days ago that I had to move on with my life. "You *did* quit dipping, didn't you?" I asked, surprised to feel comfortable in his arms when I had become so accustomed to another's.

He laughed and nodded. "I had a good incentive."

I relaxed, and Dale Trankosky kissed me. It wasn't a Frank kiss. It wasn't toe curling, flame inducing or wanton, but it felt soothing and nice. Maybe the cop *was* a romantic after all. I sighed. "I think I needed that after the week I've had."

He murmured, "You don't want to get married today, do you? I'm tight with an Elvis preacher who could work us in."

Smiling at his joke, I eased away. "Not today."

"Okay, Bee Cool, when you feel hot!" — he grinned at my raised eyebrows, and backed off — "or just like talking, give me a call, I can be a friendly ear. My lips are pretty friendly too, not to mention my hands . . ."

Laughing again, I put up my hand to stop him. "I get the picture, and I have your number. Now, how about giving me a ride to the airport?"

■ ■ ■ ■

Frank had slipped out during the big reunion earlier to take his kids to breakfast at the Black Bear. Monica had told me what time their flight was departing and that she and her parents were meeting Frank at the security checkpoint. I'd gotten there first because I wanted to read his face when he saw Monica for the first time in years as her mother confirmed they, not Monica, transferred the kids for Frank's visits. When I did see Frank's face, from behind the cover of a rent-a-car kiosk, I knew in my heart my decision was right. The hardness life's unfairnesses had laid around his eyes and mouth softened away. His brown eyes begged forgiveness and hungered for what had been lost. It only lasted an instant but that was all I needed to confirm what I suspected. As he gave her a small peck on the cheek, then turned his attention to the children, I approached as if I'd just arrived. After a shot of guilty surprise, he drew me into his arms and kissed me. I broke away, whispering, "Don't confuse the children, Frank."

Then I drew the kids into a circle with Monica and Frank and stepped back out of their way to chat with Monica's parents, mostly about my home renovation since Randolph was a retired contractor and had plenty of useful input. I was aching to talk to Frank about Ben and Shana and my god-daughter who was my niece, but didn't. Instead, as I listened to Randolph, I watched Frank tousle Matthew's hair and tickle Katie until she giggled. He seemed so natural with them — something I didn't expect after all their time apart. The call came for preboarding and the kids' faces fell. Wilma gathered their things. Randolph manned Monica's chair. I leaned down to kiss her cheek. "Thank you for your help."

"Thank you for making him happy," she said softly, with a smile.

I couldn't answer, so I turned away to see Katie crying quietly as she wrapped her arms around her daddy's neck and Matthew, with especially shiny eyes, high-fiving Frank over his sister's head. Smiling, I shook Randolph's hand and waved at the kids as they grabbed their grandmother's hands and bounced down the concourse behind their mother's wheelchair.

Once they'd disappeared, Frank turned to me, his face softening but nothing like it did for Monica. "She likes you," he said.

"I like her," I answered. "Who wouldn't?"

"Honey Bee," Frank slipped his arm around me. "This week was full of too many close calls. I know I sound like a broken record, but give up poker. It's your curse. You know it's not good for you."

"I'm not going to give up poker, Frank. I'm going to give up . . . you." I handed him the plane ticket I'd bought for him on my way in.

His breath caught, and he turned away. I held fast, willing myself not to touch him, not to reassure him, to be as composed and strong as Monica Gilbert was, as I let my love go.

"Frank, you have a terrific family. Other men should envy you — a lovely wife, two great kids. Go back to that. That, not me, is what can keep you stable, looking for tomorrow, not drinking. That, not me, is what you can wake up each morning to with hope and happiness. That, not me, will make life worth living."

"Honey Bee, this is about that Clark County cop, isn't it? Joe told me —"

I refused to feel guilty about the kiss, whether he knew about it or not. This wasn't about that. This was about him. About the "us" that obviously wasn't working for him. I steeled myself. "Go back to them, Frank. It's the right thing. It's the good thing. It's the only thing that will heal your soul. Good-bye."

I turned and walked away. Frank Gilbert didn't come after me. When I turned around, he was gone.

BEE'S BUZZ

BEE COOL'S TOP TIP FOR SURVIVING HIGH-PRESSURE TOURNAMENT HOLD 'EM

The question I am asked more than any (except maybe "Where do you get such awesome shoes?") is "How can I win playing a big game of Texas Hold 'Em?" Try coming up with a one-sentence answer for that one as you rush to your table, or if you're me, to the ladies' room or away from a knife-wielding murderer.

Even the most seasoned of pros will be stumped by this, really the simplest of poker questions, for a moment or two, mostly because the answer that rises to the tip of the tongue may depend on the chip stack the player is sitting behind, what's in her pocket or the memory of the last four tournaments she busted out of.

If this experience in Vegas has taught me anything, it's taught me the best one WORD answer to that question.

OPI.

Okay, so maybe it's not in the dictionary.

Yet.

Yeah, yeah, so it leads to a second question, which is "What the &%@# does OPI mean anyway?"

In an effort to make OPI a household word, or at least a true poker-room word, I will explain:

O - OBSERVE. Probably the most under-rated of all poker skills, this also could be the most difficult for many. Observing requires one to keep one's eyes and ears open and mouth shut. Make your next goal to only use the words *fold, check, raise, all in* and *call* (Okay, Mom) and *thank you* at your next Hold 'Em tournament. See how far it gets you. If you are listening and watching everyone else, you will be amazed at how much you will learn and how much you can use against your opponents later. Many times it isn't even what is said, but how it is said that you can internalize and judge. The fantasic bonus to this is that you unconsciously eliminate most of your own tells. This is where many women (men too, don't misunderstand me) make their mistakes. Part of our makeup is the desire to make others comfortable and conversation is one of the ways we are taught to do that. Unlearn that little social skill when at the felt. Act like Frank's ex did when she played.

Act mute.

P - PATIENCE. The true dinosaur of our instant-gratification society. Their ability to simply *wait* is why so many of the old-time poker players will continue to prosper in this game through their lifetimes. The new generation is handicapped because they are trained that they gotta have it *now.* Try to live in the old days when it took the Pony Express a couple of *months* to deliver the mail instead of a couple of *moments.* This kind of mindset allows you to survive throughout bad runs, until your luck turns, also through great runs, when (if you are patient) you know your luck is bound to turn back the other direction. Now you might see some impatient cardplayer win a handful of tournaments in a row, but if he's not willing to ride through being outside the payout for a string of tournaments somewhere along the way, he won't keep playing. I daresay this is the most important of all poker tips. The rewards a player reaps from mastering patience is what will keep the game of Texas Hold 'Em from being too changed by its massive popularity.

Because the turtle still wins in the long run (even if sometimes he has to act like a hare).

I - INTUITION. The flipside of the women's

difficulty in being able to simply observe is the ease in which we are able to trust what we feel. So use it, ladies! There's never a better time than when on the felt. Don't get me wrong, though. I didn't say men weren't intuitive, just they don't as easily tap into their intuition. The most intuitive group of men in the world, I believe, will be the ones seated around the final table at the WSOP. Never underestimate the boxer wearer across The Flop from you. He may be reading your surge of adrenaline at your pocket rockets better than you are.

Now I am bound to get reamed by those who misunderstand the difference between observing and intuiting. Men usually observe the gal in seat two biting her lower lip every time a ball buster falls but might not guess it's because it's made her hand. Women might sense she bites her lower lip every time she has the nuts but not notice it's when she gets the card she needs. If you are aware of both — what you've observed and what you "know" — just think how powerful you will be at the table, especially with that healthy dose of patience to wait to act on what you've observed and intuited until it is the right time!

Okay, folks, armed with OPI, now all you need is a little luck and you're in the chips.